ENIGMATA

ENIGMATA

THE WATCHER FROM WITHIN

S. ALESSANDRO MARTINEZ

For Kat, Michelle, and Dave. Thank you.

The Diary of Edith Goodner (age 15) — 4 March, 1917 (Excerpt)

I watched for Grandad from sunup to sundown all of to-day. I took a walk around the garden, but he did not come home. I played many games of marbles with Barnabas, and Grandad still did not come home. Momma asked me to go get some flour and eggs from Mister Edward, the grocer, but when I returned from my errand, Grandad was still away.

Where could he have gone? He was supposed to have come home already from the business he had gone to three days ago! [TEXT FADED] *want Grandad to come back. Momma says to me that any number of things could have delayed Grandad for a few days. Maybe the weather is bad on the road, and he has to wait out a storm. Perhaps a new business opportunity came up that he had to immediately attend to. I do not know. I have a bad feeling; a feeling that creeps into my head every day. If only Papa was still alive, we wouldn't have to only rely on Grandad for food and money. And I wouldn't feel so frightened. I only pray to God that the stories Grandad has told me all my life are untrue. Are they just "foolish old tales" like Momma said? Well, I* [TEXT FADED}

We had a pleasant supper to-gether, Momma, Barnabas and me. It was quiet in the kitchen while we ate. I could hear the wind all moaning outside, making the trees rustle and creak. Whenever I looked up at Momma, I saw deep lines creasing her face. I could tell that she was starting to worry just the same as I am.

Please come home soon, Grandad.

Diary of Edith Goodner (age 15) — 5 March, 1917 (Excerpt)

I am afraid. So very, very sc[WATER STAIN]

Lord, I do not think I will be able to sleep ever again after what I saw in the darkness of last night. I so wish I could make myself believe it had all been just a horrid nightmare caused by a stomachache or something just as mundane. But it was no dream, and I have been awake for almost two days now. No, it was all real. All too terribly real. Surely such things cannot be?

God help us. [WATER STAIN]

Last evening, after I wished Momma and Barnabas a good night, I went to bed. I was unable to sleep, though, for I kept hearing a sound: a light, peculiar tapping. At first, I believed it to be the wind playing with some tree branches outside or [TEXT ILLEGIBLE] *noticed the tapping had a steady rhythm to it. I began to shiver violently when I realized it, and any drowsiness that had taken hold of me instantly vanished. Lying quite still, I realized the tapping was* [WATER STAIN]*ing from the window. As slowly and silently as I could, I sat up to look. Dear Lord in Heaven!*

I saw Grandad's face outside my window, smiling. But it couldn't have been him. I swear it was not him! I have known my Grandad since I was born. The person I saw outside was wrong *in some way that I cannot explain.*

It was as if something was wearing his face.

CHAPTER ONE

October

Pulling her dull gray—what she preferred to think of as "dead marsh under a waning moon gray"—Ford Taurus into one of the many empty parking spaces of the Shady Tree Motel, October killed the engine and let out a deep groan. She stared at the single-story, L-shaped building with its faded creamed corn-colored paint and red, slanted roofs. It reminded her of so many other motels she'd stayed at growing up, going on road trips with her parents.

October had been driving for hours, and her butt ached, due as much to the worn-out state of the Taurus's ancient seats as to the mileage of the car ride. It had taken her two days to drive from the scorching dry climate of West Covina, California to the beautifully lush forests that cradled the town of Cinter, Washington. She was grateful to have finally arrived at her destination.

"It'll be worth it," October mumbled to herself before stepping out of the car. After stretching her back and feeling all the satisfying pops of her vertebrae, she strode into the motel's front office.

Behind the front desk sat a living skeleton; the dark graying hair above the man's cadaverous face fell to his thin shoulders in greasy strings. When he finished writing something down in a ledger, he turned watery eyes to October, looking her up and down without hurry. October wondered if anyone in this town had seen a goth before, then realized that was a stupid thought. She put on a polite smile and swallowed unconsciously while she waited for the man to finish his appraisal of her all-black clothing, bulky boots, tattoos, piercings, and dark makeup.

"Uh, hello," October said, the words catching in her throat.

The man's gaunt, stubbly face broke out into a sincere grin that spoke of a lifetime of kindness. "Good evening there. How can I help you today? Looking for a room, I bet." He chuckled.

"Oh, definitely," October said, relief flooding through her. "Two nights would be great. If you have anything available. I didn't make a reservation."

The man—Charlie, according to the name tag pinned to his t-shirt—waved away her concern. "No reservations required." He typed something into a prehistoric computer. "I'll just need your info and a credit card, and you'll be all set."

October dug out a wallet from her coffin-shaped purse and extracted her driver's license and credit card for him, then set about filling out the paper Charlie slid toward her with her information.

"October Night," Charlie read off the credit card. "What an unusual name." He took in her appearance again, still with that friendly smile that radiated curiosity, not judgement. Tilting his head to the side, he said, "It suits you. I like it. So, what brings you to Cinter, Miss October? Vacation?"

"Oh, I guess I'm seeing if I want to move here," October said. When the man raised his eyebrows, she went on. "I work for Valravn, and they're opening an office here. They offered me a transfer. If I take it, they said they'll let me work from home three days a week which would be awesome." She realized she'd been babbling. "Uh, so yeah."

"Valravn? Like the big-ass company that makes all the phones and electronics?" Charlie asked. "Don't know why they'd want to open an office around here." He tapped his chin. "Anyway, I hope you enjoy our little town. And if you're looking to check out things Cinter has to offer..." He leaned over to the corner of the counter to reach for a stack of what looked like homemade flyers printed on pink paper. He grabbed the top one. "My friend Henry Kinsey's got a niece, Adrianna. She started doing these guided nature walks this summer. She's trying to save up money for college. She's a good kid. Smart. Knows a lot about these parts. It's been real popular with visitors. The trails are nothing too strenuous. Does them every Saturday."

"So there's one tomorrow?" October said.

"Mmhm."

October took the proffered flyer. NATURE WALKS WITH ADRI-ANNA!, it announced at the top, followed by black and white photos of forests, streams, a deer, and a teenage girl wearing a large back-pack, waving at the camera with a toothy smile. There were a couple of paragraphs detailing the guided walk. She could read that later.

Might be interesting, she thought. Checking out the area was what she was here for after all. An hour stretching her legs might limber her up after two days in the car as well.

"Here's your key. Room 7." Charlie slid an actual metal key over the counter, along with her ID and credit card. "Just around the corner to your left. If you decide to do the nature walk, just come on by any time tonight before 10:00, and I'll put you on Adrianna's list for tomorrow. The group'll leave from the parking lot here just after lunch time. As for tonight, if you're looking for some dinner, I recommend Melba's. Best meatloaf you've ever had, I promise you!"

"Sounds good, I'll check it out." October picked up the key and her ID and credit card. "Thanks!"

Back outside at her car, October took in a deep breath of astonishingly clean air before retrieving her duffle bag from the backseat and heading to her motel room around the corner. The lock on the door needed a little finagling but eventually opened. Stepping inside, October shut the door behind her and dropped her things on the floor. The room's décor hadn't been updated since the 70s, it seemed. Still, it was warm, clean, and looked cozy. She moved over to the bed, threw off the comforter (those were never washed), then flumped herself down on the mattress face-first. It was oh so comfy.

The strident sound of her phone alarm snapped October awake. Groggy, she took the phone out of her purse to silence the blaring ringer. Apparently, she had dozed off for almost half an hour.

October groaned as she got off the bed and swallowed. It tasted like something had died in her mouth. She set about unpacking her toiletries and put her pill organizer case on the nightstand. The alarm indicated it was time for her meds. Opening the little cubby labeled FRI-EVE, she took out the four tablets and downed them with a bottle of warm soda from her duffle bag.

She was incredibly grateful that she and her current psychiatrist had finally found the right balance of medications to let her function at normal levels. Well, "normal" by other people's standards. Still, October felt fortunate that the meds dealt with the monster that had lived in her head since she was a kid, bringing with it major depression and all other sorts of mental crap.

The worst symptom by far was *the voice*.

The foster families that passed her around like a loaned book always reported the same thing: "October is unusually silent and doesn't seem like she wants to interact with the world." It was at age four that the voice started speaking inside her head, whispering dark, cruel, and morbid things to her on a constant basis. Her foster family at the time (she remembered very little about them) simply thought she had an imaginary friend until they learned just exactly what this voice had been saying to October when she began complying with its demands in order to get it to shut up. That was when she ended up in a group home, no other families wanting to foster her.

The group home's psychologist treated her until age eight when she finally found her forever family and went home with her new parents, Tom and Rachel Night. The doctor never did explicitly diagnose her with any one condition. At least, not that October ever learned.

Life had been a series of countless appointments with numerous different doctors and an endless parade of therapy and drugs until just last year, when October and her most recent psychiatrist, Dr. Lauren Iddrisu, had finally found the perfect combination of antidepressants, anxiolytics, and antipsychotics that had put the voice into a slumber from which it had so far not awoken.

It had been uncomfortable and weird at first, hearing only her own voice in her head. However, she soon felt so much better physically and mentally. October's life was getting back on track.

Picking up her phone, October tapped the screen and unlocked it. She stared at her background, a photo of herself, Mom, Dad, and Uncle Shane dressed as the Addams Family for Halloween almost twenty-two years ago. Going to her contacts, her thumb hovered over her mom's number. It had been two years since October had spoken with her family.

Press it.

Her thumb started to tremble.

Just press it!

With a shake of her head, October tucked the phone in her purse.

Maybe soon, she thought. *For now, food.*

Slinging her purse strap over her shoulder, October left the motel room. Walking to her car, her feet suddenly veered her toward the front office. When she neared, she could see Charlie through the window, watching something on the TV mounted on the wall, a large smile on his face. October pulled the NATURE WALKS WITH ADRIANNA! flyer out of her purse and looked it over again. The girl in the photo—presumably Adrianna—looked absolutely enthusiastic about the prospect of taking a stroll through the forest.

October *was* here to check out the area. If she was going to consider uprooting herself to this place, shouldn't she see everything it had to offer? She hadn't driven a thousand miles through two and a half states just to nap in a motel room. Besides, she loved forests. Or at least the idea of them.

"Screw it," October muttered, and went into the office to sign up for the walk.

CHAPTER TWO

Wendig

Lucas Wendig sat at the desk in his darkened home office, staring at the blinking cursor in the blank document open on his laptop. Something needed to be left behind for Jordan, a guide of some sort, in case he never returned from one of his investigations. He'd already put it off for too long. He began to type.

Enigmata: objects (Relics), living creatures (Entities), or places (Domains) that possess aspects and abilities beyond the laws of nature. Over the years, I have

Pressing the delete key, Wendig erased what he had typed. Jordan already knew this stuff.

Sleep hadn't yet graced him with its presence tonight—as was often the case. Maybe a midnight jog would help? The night's quiet darkness usually relaxed him. It was why he often stayed up late, worked late, and jogged late, all after the world had gone to sleep.

Wendig's house was nestled among the hills of Altadena, California. Unlike the roaring, overcrowded streets of nearby Los Angeles, Altadena never buzzed with much activity. The neighborhoods were mostly peaceful, filled with beautiful homes, friendly people who always greeted each other, kids, pets, and the occasional coyote that came down from the hills to skulk about.

There had been one incident in the neighborhood when a couple had moved onto Wendig's street, three houses down from him. Of course, they hadn't been aware of his late-night runs. Soon after, the newcomers had posted a warning in the local Facebook group to be on the lookout for a suspicious-looking African-American male "prowling" the streets late at night. Wendig fondly remembered many of his neighborhood friends coming vehemently to his defense.

Other than that one little incident, he found it was a good place to live. And at night, the city was more than quiet. It was empty. A welcome antithesis to his work. His search for Enigmata often took him to hell and back. A sanctuary to return to after each job was essential to his sanity.

Swiveling around in his office chair, Wendig gazed out the large window that faced the street. He noticed a good-sized opossum scuttle out from behind his neighbor's trash bin and into the driveway across the street. The opossum stopped inside the cone of light from one of the street lights and looked back, as if it somehow sensed him watching it. As it turned toward him, the sodium light reflected in the animal's beady eyes. The opossum remained immobile for a long time, looking in his direction, and Wendig could just make out three tiny babies clinging to their mother's back. Children could be so vulner-able sometimes, he thought. After a long moment, something caught the creature's attention and she scurried away, disappearing into the darkness of a nearby shrubbery, hurrying her offspring back into the safety of the shadows.

A notification beeped from his laptop. Wendig swiveled back around to face his desk.

After having stared into the night outside, the harsh light from the screen briefly overwhelmed his eyes. He moved the cursor over to the video call button flashing below the name "Jordan Valentina Ortega-Escarra," and clicked on it. After a brief delay, the face of a young woman appeared. Early twenties, tousled bleached-blonde hair, with some faded pink woven in here and there, all tied back in a loose ponytail. Multiple rings and studs pierced her lips, ears, and eyebrows, and a small tattoo—some key-shaped sword she'd tried telling him about before—marked her collarbone. Wendig's own face appeared in a small window in the lower right-hand corner of the monitor, his dark brown eyes staring at himself for a moment before returning his gaze to the caller.

"Hi, Jordan." Wendig scooted his chair closer to the laptop.

"Hey, dude," the woman replied in her naturally raspy voice. She took a quick sip of some diet soda. "I knew you'd be up late working again." She chuckled.

Wendig glanced at the computer clock. "Isn't it two in the morning in Nebraska? I think it's past your bedtime." He put a hint of teasing in his voice. Faint music came through his speakers from Jordan's end that she hummed along with.

"What? I can't stay up too?" Jordan took another swig of her soda. "I'm doing late-night work for you. And speaking of that, I found several potential leads that I think you'll find interesting." Her eyes flicked back and forth. Wendig could tell that she was searching through folders and files on her side of the computer, her blue nails tapping furiously on her keyboard for a moment.

"Good to hear." Wendig perked up and sat straighter in his chair.

"Not now, Nathan," Jordan said as a bearded dragon ambled over her keyboard. "Mommy's working."

Wendig cleared his throat loudly, amusement warring with irritation. "So, what did you find?" he asked, hoping to reclaim Jordan's focus before it wandered off track.

Jordan picked up Nathan and set him beside the keyboard. "Potential leads, as I said. Listen, are you sure you don't want a short break? We just finished the last job not too long ago, and I know it took a lot out of you. There's no need to work yourself to death."

"Come on, what do I pay you for? To be my sidekick or to be my mother?"

"Sidekick!" Jordan gasped with mock indignation. She then flipped him off. "I ain't nobody's sidekick. You'd be lost without me. Seriously, no one else would do all this secrety secret stuff while having to put up with your antics, your shenanigans, your tomfoolery."

"Did you just buy a thesaurus?" He fought back the smile that pulled at the corners of his mouth. "At any rate, I believe you came to me in the beginning there."

"Yeah, yeah," Jordan said. "Well, whatever, back to what I was saying. Let's see what we have here." She clicked something on her screen. "I have three leads at the moment. First is over in Durne, Massachusetts. A house there just up and vanished overnight. Poof. Neighbors never noticed anything until the next morning. Townspeople describe the family living in the now-disappeared house as 'strange.' Sounds cool." She clicked on something else. "The second lead is in Pennsylvania. Some nowhere town called East Marwood is home to an old prison. The thing's been abandoned since the 70s, but people have allegedly gone missing inside it while exploring."

"Intriguing," Wendig said, considering both stories. "And the third lead?"

"Have you ever heard of Shadow's Path? It's up in the Fulgent County area of Washington state that has towns like Black Ashes, Pharaoh, Marsh Chapel, and Cinter. Oh, and Devil's Eyes Lake."

"Shadow's Path, Cinter, Fulgent County," Wendig repeated.

A sense of déjà vu pulsed in his mind, as if something important was waiting for him in Cinter. Why did he get such a sense of familiarity from hearing that name? Taking a granola bar out from a desk drawer, he sifted through his memories. Had he ever been to any of those towns in Fulgent County before? Perhaps in a life lived long ago? No, that wasn't it. Had he seen something about the town on TV? Read about it in a book? Dreamt about it? Unwrapping the bar, he took a bite and pondered. He couldn't pinpoint the reason why he felt such a sense of recognition. Nothing in recent memory suggested he had any connection with a town up in the Pacific Northwest.

"Tell me more about that one," he said, picking granola crumbs off his shirt. "What happened in Shadow's Path?"

"Before we get into that." Jordan stared directly into her webcam. "When are you going to fly me out to L.A.? Nathan and I want to see

SoCal! Come on, Lucas." She held the yellow lizard up to the camera, its small dark eyes blinking slowly. Jordan adopted the gravelly, cutesy voice she always did when Nathan "spoke." "Come on, Mr. Wendig, sir. Please fly my mommy and me out to Los Angeles. I want to go to Disneyland."

"You can't take Nathan to Disneyland," The smile pulled at his lips once more. "Back to the report. I want to hear about Fulgent County." He took another bite of the granola bar.

"Fine," Jordan mumbled, setting Nathan back down on her desktop. Focusing back on her computer, she typed something on her keyboard. "Fulgent County seems like a nice place. Isolated small towns, mountains, forests. A good place for a vacation." All cheerfulness in Jordan's voice evaporated just then. "Two months ago in June, there was a nasty murder in Shadow's Path. A thirteen-year-old boy named Evan Brooks was killed in his own home one night. Not just killed. More like slaughtered. Butchered. It's really awful. The poor kid's body had been pinned to the wall of his bedroom, tortured, and mutilated." She shivered. "And his…well, I'll let you look at the crime scene photos yourself."

Wendig nodded and moved his mouse to click the OKAY button when prompted with a file transfer. Moments later, his eyes were assaulted by high-definition forensic photographs of a grisly tableau of gore from every conceivable angle. Jordan hadn't been exaggerating. The body of Evan Brooks had been staked to a wall with strange-looking metal rods and hooks, almost like some sort of crucifixion.

Goddamn, he thought, forcing himself to study the photos. Who could do something like this to a kid? There were a lot of fucking sickos out there, but this…

Zooming in on each of the pictures in turn, Wendig examined every detail. He wished he had access to those metal objects pinning the body to the wall in front of him so he could physically study them in greater detail. Some sort of language was etched into the metal, though he couldn't make anything of it. He moved on, examining photos that showed closeups of various areas of Evan's body in complete explicit detail. Gorge rising, Wendig realized that what he had first identified as copious amounts of blood covering the boy's face and body was something far worse.

"His skin is gone," he said in a quiet voice devoid of emotion, although he felt a tightness in his stomach. He clicked through more photographs.

"I know," Jordan said with another shiver. She removed her ponytail and ran a hand through her hair. "That poor kid. The police reports say that his mom found him like that when she went to wake him up for breakfast. Apparently neither she nor her husband had heard anything the night before that would have alerted them to something happening. And as if the parents' trauma wasn't enough, Evan's best friend saw all the police ruckus and ran over from next door. He somehow got past the cops and bolted into the house, only to get a good look at Evans's remains hanging up there on the wall. The two were best friends, Lucas. God, can you imagine what those people went through? What kind of therapy they probably all needed?"

"Unfortunately, I can." Wendig could imagine it too well.

"Here, I'll send over the police report." Jordan scanned through the document on her side of the computer. "The cops spent a fair amount of time questioning Evan's friend, Caleb Rivas. That's the boy who ran into the house and saw Evan on the wall." She swallowed audibly. "Let's see." Her eyes flicked back and forth while she read the text and summarized it for Wendig.

"Caleb told them that he and Evan had found some object in a cave out in the woods close to where they live. Doesn't say exactly what they found. After bringing the thing back home, Evan began to act 'weird,' according to Caleb. He said that Evan had been scared of someone, or something, he called it the 'watcher through the window,' and it had apparently visited him every night since they found the object." Jordan scrolled through the report. "It doesn't say anywhere in the report whether Caleb actually saw this 'watcher' for himself or not. The police and his parents couldn't get much more out of him, although there have been ongoing efforts."

"Can you find out Caleb's current status?" Wendig asked, making several notes on a small pad of paper while finishing his granola bar. He swallowed, grimacing when the granola momentarily stuck in his dry throat. "I'll definitely want to talk with him about all this if it's at all possible."

"So, you do think all this has something to do with an Enigmata?" Jordan said, sounding hopeful. Despite the tragedy of what she had just reported, her voice sounded more spirited than it had only moments before. He wondered if it was merely the promise of an interesting case to pursue, or hope they'd be able to do some good to balance out the evil so prominent in the world.

"We can never be one hundred percent sure without investigating," Wendig replied. "Though a 'mysterious object' found just prior to something abnormally horrific happening? I'm fairly confident." He pulled up a map on his computer to chart the drive he would have to make. "Are the police still investigating?"

"The case hasn't been officially closed," Jordan said. "But it doesn't look like any more progress has been made."

Wendig nodded. "Well, you did great work, Jordan. Send me whatever else you have on this so far. I'll look over everything. I'm going to head out tomorrow. Let me know about Caleb."

"Already located him. I'll send it all over right now. Talk to you later." With an exaggerated salute, Jordan signed off.

CALL ENDED appeared on the screen.

Wendig felt suddenly alone.

CHAPTER THREE

October

The warm parking lot of the motel felt more alive than it had the previous night. Several guests stood around chatting with each other. October sat at one of the outdoor picnic tables close by, idly fiddling with her nose ring, tuning in and out of the various conversations. She assumed everyone here was going on the nature walk, though she didn't see anyone that looked like the girl from the photo on the flyer. It was a decent-sized group of eight people.

Even though October wore her sunglasses, the day wasn't overly bright. Some cloud cover dimmed the sunlight, and the weather felt to be around a comfortable 75 degrees. She inhaled deeply. The faint smell of clean air and pine filled her nose. Much different than the smog-infused atmosphere of Los Angeles. With another deep breath, she felt her lungs being scrubbed clean of all the pollution they had inhaled over the years.

Her phone vibrated with a work email notification. She'd look at it later. The clock on the screen said it was 12:24. She put her phone back in her pouch, next to a box of Nerds and a small, plastic green pill box that contained her meds for the afternoon. Taking a swig from the water bottle she'd gotten from the vending machine next to her room, October hoped it was enough to last her the whole time. The flyer didn't say exactly how long the walk would take.

Before she could decide whether to run and get a second bottle, someone right next to her said, "Hey there. Nice piercings and tats."

October stopped herself from jumping at the sudden voice and its proximity. She looked over to see a tall kid, about sixteen or seventeen, easing himself into the spot next to her on the picnic table's bench seat. He was dressed in a pastel blue polo shirt with cargo shorts, and a pair of expensive-looking headphones hung around his neck. A faint mustache struggled to be noticed on his upper lip.

"Oh, uh, thanks," October sputtered. Strangers almost never came up to her to give compliments, and she was at a momentary loss at how to respond properly. Rather than seem unfriendly or standoffish, she offered him a quick smile before reaching to get her phone out again.

"Name's Bryan." The kid scooted closer to her and pointed to a bat tattooed on October's neck. "I really like this one. Reminds me of vampires and stuff."

Oh, he still wanted to talk.

"And this one..." He lightly touched the tattoo on her right forearm.

"Thank you." October drew her arm away. This guy sure was interested in her tattoos. Maybe he was thinking about getting one himself and was looking for inspiration? Instead of giving in to her initial discomfort, October went on. "This tattoo's inspired by H.P. Lovecraft's *The Shadow Ov—*"

"You know," Bryan interrupted her. "I've always liked the whole dark makeup, black hair, black clothes goth look."

"I—uh," October said, fumbling her words. "I like it, too. Well, obviously." She gestured at herself while scooting away.

"Me and my family are staying here in Cinter for a few days," he went on in a casual voice. "It's a small town, you know? Maybe you and I could meet up again after this dumb walk. I just got my license. I could take you out. Drive us anywhere around town."

"Oh. Ohhhhh." October let out another, more awkward chuckle. God, she could be so oblivious. She almost never realized when someone was flirting. Mainly because why would anyone ever want to flirt with her?

"What do you say?" Bryan asked, attempting to give her a smoldering smile.

"Uh, let me ask you this," October said. "How old are you? And how old do you think I am?"

"I'm seventeen since last month," he answered. "And you're, like what…twenty-one? Twenty-two?"

"That's flattering," October said. In truth, it was. Looking past Bryan, she saw the two people the teen had arrived with. "Are those your parents over there?" She nodded in the direction of the pair who wore large backpacks and were dressed as if they were ready to go on a safari. The positively cheery man was balding and wore thick glasses. A blue nylon fanny pack stretched over his wide belly. The wife wore a hat big enough to double as an umbrella, socks pulled up high, almost touching her knobby knees, and a matching fanny pack strapped to her waist.

"Yeah, I guess so." Bryan's face flushed as he stared at his mom and dad. He turned back to her. "Why?"

"You just looked too young to be on your own." October noted Bryan's offended expression at the statement. "I'm probably closer to your mom's age. I'm thirty-four. You're still in high school. And that would be gross."

"Thirty-four, oh, uh… Well, I didn't realize—I don't think it's that big of a—" Bryan stuttered for a moment, his cheeks reddening, before his mother called his name loud enough for it to echo around the parking lot.

"Bryan, come here!" His mom smiled and waved at him with unbridled enthusiasm. "You're going to need some of this!" She held up a tube of sunblock.

Bryan hung his head with a sigh, stood up, and scurried back to his parents. He gave October an ashamed glance when his mom began to apply sunblock to his face.

Relief flooded through October as the situation ended. She hoped she had handled that in a cool manner.

As she stared off into space, contemplating the weirdness that had just happened, a medium-sized bus rumbled into the motel's parking lot in a cloud of sputtering exhaust. The bus had certainly seen better days, as it was covered in dents and what used to be blue paint. It came to a stop in front of the group with a whine of the brakes. The doors hissed open, and a young woman, short and twig-thin, jumped out.

"Hello, party people!" she announced in an exuberant voice. The girl wore dirty hiking boots, a well-worn backpack, lightweight hiking shorts, and a shirt that read: *"Get Lost In The Forest And Find Yourself."* Her brown hair was plaited into two tight braids, which she flipped over her shoulders before flashing a pearlescent smile at the assembled group. "My name is Adrianna Reyes, and I want to thank all of you for signing up for my hike today! I really appreciate the support and your interest in all the wonderful nature we have around here. I'm proud to be your guide for this beautiful day! Now I have people's names here on my sheet, and I need to check you off so I know we have everybody. When I call you, if you could just let me know that you're here, and then we'll all get on the bus. Sound good?"

The group answered in unison with grunts and murmurs of acknowledgement.

She really seems to love life, October thought. She wondered what it would have been like to grow up with that sort of real happiness bubbling inside of her.

"Great!" With a flourish of her pen, Adrianna began reading and marking names off her list. "Arthur, Bernadette, and Bryan Williamson?"

"We're here!" The apparent Mrs. Williamson said. October watched as Bryan's parents waved their hands like schoolkids eager to be called on. It was as if a tomato had replaced Bryan's head. His face had gotten even redder in response to his parents' behavior. October found it amusing but felt a little sorry for him as well. Still, a faint smile tugged at the corners of her mouth.

"Fantastic! How about Noel Moss?" Adrianna called out next, looking around.

"Over here," a tall, muscular man with a short afro answered. A bulky, professional-looking camera bag was slung over his shoulder.

"Good!" Adrianna went on, marking Noel off her list. "How about Dara and Samira Nazari?"

A middle-aged man and woman—both short enough to look like hobbits standing next to Noel—stepped forward and nodded politely at the girl.

Adrianna smiled back, then stared at her list. "And…oh boy. Vee-o-ri-ca Mar-coo-less-coo? Viorica Mărculescu. Did I pronounce that right? If I didn't, please let me know."

A woman with a jawline sharp enough to double as a weapon stepped forward with cat-like litheness. "Da, you pronounced it well," she said to Adrianna in a thick accent that October identified as something Eastern European. "Very well. Mulțumesc. Thank you."

"Oh good! Alright then," Adrianna said to herself, writing something on her list. "Nice to have you along."

"I'm on vacation," the woman said without prompt, then stepped back.

"Yes, okay," Adrianna had a bemused smile on her face. "Let's get going, shall we? Everyone ready for an awesome hike through nature's beauty today?"

She didn't call me, October realized. *Dammit.* She was going to have to go up and say something. *Just go tell her. I can't. Stop being a little wimp. Everyone's going to look at me. Who cares? I'll just go back to my room and forget about it.*

Before Adrianna could turn to leave, however, October muttered "hell" under her breath and stood up, striding over to the young woman.

"Hey, hi." October noticed the entire group stop to watch the exchange. She could feel all eyes on her. Adrianna looked up with that blinding smile, and October felt her face become much too warm.

"It's just that, uh, you didn't call me." The words came out in a whisper.

"I'm sorry?" Adrianna said.

Clearing her throat, October tried again. "You didn't call my name."

"Oh? I apologize for that!" Adrianna scanned her list. "I don't have anyone else listed here. What's your name?"

"October Night," October answered, then quickly added, "I signed up last evening."

"Oh, right," Adrianna tapped her clipboard with her pen. "I saw your name this morning on the computer. It looks like it wasn't added to my printout. Who could forget such an awesome name? Anyway, sorry about that. Hey, no worries, you're on the list now!" She giggled while writing October's name down, then gestured the whole group forward. "Come on, let's get on board, everyone!"

That wasn't too hard.

This Adrianna seemed like a good person who genuinely enjoyed being around people. Maybe October could ask her for some pointers in that department.

Aha... pathetic.

Following the group, October climbed up the steps and into the idling bus, nodding to the driver, an older man with thinning blond hair and a bored expression. After everyone had boarded and settled, the doors closed with mechanical hiss.

"Good morning, peeps," Adrianna said, standing up front and getting on the bus's PA system, which seemed very unnecessary given her natural volume and the small space. "Let's all say hi to our driver, Phil."

"Hi, Phil," the group—except Bryan, October noticed—said in unison.

October could see Phil's wrinkled face look back at them in the review mirror. He gave a grunt and a half-hearted wave in response.

"Always good to have you with us, Phil," Adrianna said. "As I said before, my name is Adrianna, and I'll be your nature guide for our hike today. This is my first summer doing this. But don't worry, I've lived in Cinter all my life. I've explored every inch of forest around this town. So, you can all trust me to…"

October stared out of the window as Adrianna continued to talk. The bus pulled out of the Shady Tree Motel's parking lot and wound its way through the town, driving down the quiet streets, and passing a few people here and there. October wondered just how small the population of Cinter was. Quaint store fronts crawled by outside the bus's windows: Old Town Grocery, Pacific-Stone Hardware, Starlight Cinema, Harrington's Pharmacy, K&L Electronics, The Raven and Crow, The Magic Mirror Bookstore, Salon Red, and there was Melba's 24-Hour, where October had eaten yesterday. That meatloaf had given her some serious heartburn last night, but she had to admit it had still been worth eating the whole thing. Most of the shops and businesses looked as if they had once been Rustic-, English cottage-, and Bavarian-style homes. None of them boasted any neon. Instead, they all had hand-crafted signs carved out of wood. If she hadn't seen the bulbs glowing the night before, October could have been convinced the lamps lining the streets were all old-timey gaslights. The sidewalks, bus stops, and public benches all looked well taken care of. She couldn't spot graffiti or litter anywhere.

Cinter seemed like a town one could settle comfortably in and be at peace, although an odd place for a tech company like Valravn to open an office. Well, what did she know? She was only an administrative assistant. It was weird, but she wasn't going to question it.

Valravn had offered her the transfer just two days ago, and October had spent her lunch break that day looking up information on Cinter, Washington on her phone. One website she came across had a plethora of photos of the town. Stunning mountains. October remembered being startled at what she was seeing. She was positive she had dreamt of the exact places shown in many of the pictures not too long ago. Or was her mind playing some déjà vu trick on her? No, the feeling of familiarity had been too strong. Yet she had never heard of these places before, which was weird. The more she tried to remember what had happened in her supposed dream, the more its details had all dissolved back into the ether, save for the distinct impression it had left.

Dream or not, she was eager to see the area, somewhere that smelled fresh and had lots of trees. She wanted to be around woods, wilderness. While October wasn't the most outdoorsy person, she had always been fascinated with forests. She had always daydreamed about sprawling oceans of trees where one could get lost and delve deep into the dark, green magic that lived within the sunless bowers of an ancient primeval grove.

Cinter. The more she dwelled on that unusual name, the more it felt familiar. Not just the dream. It was as if she'd heard about Cinter…a Cinter…a long time ago. In another life.

And now here she was.

The bus hit a pothole, rocking October out of her rumination. More buildings passed by as they meandered through town.

Yeah, I guess I wouldn't mind living here, she thought. *Seems like a nice enough place so far. Phone signal's shit, though. I wonder if the houses here get fiber optic. The residents here probably won't be too happy if Valravn decides to install more cell towers.*

"Hey, would you guys like to hear about the history of our town?" Adrianna asked over the bus's speaker.

"Oh, yes please!" Bryan's father, Arthur, said with excitement. He leaned over to Dara and Samira Nazari who sat in the row across from him. "I love history, you know."

"Mmhm…" Dara replied, a polite smile on his face. "Me too."

"Then let me tell you!" Adrianna said with eagerness. "Well, Cinter was officially founded in 1891 way up here in the beautiful, isolated Fulgent Mountains. It was the first town in what would be the Fulgent County we know today. However, that's not what makes Cinter so special. Before Cinter was officially a town, a small community of people of unknown European origin settled in this area. It's said that the people who lived here were involved in occult activities and practices."

Bernadette wiggled in her seat. "Ooh, I would have loved to see that!"

Even Bryan perked up a smidgen.

"What kinds of occult activities and practices?" Adrianna went on. "Well, many different things, local scholars say. They practiced witchcraft for all sorts of reasons such as helping with the harvest, fertility, and even divination. There's evidence they worshipped deities from different cultures, Norse, Egyptian, Sumerian, and so on. These people even supposedly communed with the dead to learn secret knowledge. Spooky stuff.

"We know this because of old records and journals that a few of the more learned of these people kept. These records also show that this community never really interacted with outsiders, except for the occasional traveler who would wander into their territory. There's no indication this community ever hurt anyone who stumbled upon them. Though there are a few recorded oral statements of travelers reporting that they came into contact with this unnamed group of people and left the area feeling extremely unnerved."

Noel turned from looking out the window. "Yeah, I probably would too."

The bus passed walls of greenery on its way out of town. Endless rows of trees loomed on either side of the road like thousands of ancient, emerald sentinels noting any motorist who passed underneath their protective and watchful gaze.

"Anyway, if you're at all interested in learning even more about that, then I highly recommend you visit our little museum when we get back to town, the Cinter Museum of Local History, Folklore, and the Occult. There's some pretty fascinating stuff in there."

"We will!" Arthur said.

October could practically hear Bryan rolling his eyes at his dad. She had seen the museum mentioned on a website when first looking up Cinter. It did sound rather interesting. She considered making a trip there herself. Maybe tomorrow. She tried to look up the museum's operating hours on her phone. Of course, she had no service. She'd check when she got back to the motel.

"In 1890," Adrianna continued with her history lesson, "traveling merchants decided to visit, hoping to set up trade. When they arrived, everyone was gone. Sorta like Roanoke. Weird! It was like the entire community had simply vanished into thin air one day, leaving all their stuff behind. Among the deserted shacks and abandoned items, the merchants found an unusual stone: a deep blue lazurite, carved into an octahedral shape, about two feet high."

The lone woman whose name October couldn't remember (Vi-something) looked up from her phone at the mention of this stone.

"Inscribed on each of its eight surfaces was a phrase." Adrianna put a more dramatic tone into her voice. "Each side had that phrase in a different language, which were later identified as Aramaic, Farsi, Greek, Sanskrit, Arabic, Egyptian, and Akkadian. Various symbols of unknown origin are carved on its eighth side and still haven't been identified or decoded to this day. Translated into English, the phrase inscribed on the stone goes like this: 'Cloaked in ashes of utmost black, thy path lies in shadow. For only the Cinter shall protect flesh and soul.' Creepy, am I right?"

A hand shot up.

"And yes, Mr. Williamson, this 'Cinter Stone' is on display at the museum."

Arthur gave Adrianna a grin followed by a thumbs-up.

"As you can probably tell," Adrianna gave Arthur a wink, "when this area became more settled, three of the towns that popped up here in what eventually became Fulgent County—Cinter, Shadow's Path, and Black Ashes—were named after the Cinter Stone's cryptic words. Why would they name towns after something so strange? Who knows! Anyway, isn't learning history totally awesome?"

"It is!" Bernadette bellowed, high-fiving her husband.

As dorky and goofy as Bernadette and Arthur acted, October couldn't help but smile at how much they obviously enjoyed each other's company, despite Bryan making sure everyone heard his dramatic sighs and saw his disapproving glares directed at his parents. Bernadette and Arthur were like children, delighted by everything around them.

You'll always be alone, a voice said inside October's head. The smile vanished from her mouth as a wave of overwhelming sadness coursed through her whole body. She pushed the feeling away. Intrusive thoughts sucked. October let her attention drift until she was again staring out of the window.

At last, after about thirty minutes, the bus turned onto a small dirt road and continued for about a mile before they arrived at an unpaved rest area just big enough for the bus to turn around. Once they came to a stop, the bus doors slid open, and Adrianna ushered them all out into the fresh air.

October was the last one off the bus. She gazed around at the forest that surrounded the group. It was beautiful. Compared to her hometown, everything here was just so green, so…alive in such a different way. No police sirens in the distance, no people shouting in the streets, no tires screeching down the road. Just calming silence.

Yeah, October thought, nodding to herself. *I could definitely live around here. Maybe get a place right next to the woods, find a good reading spot under a big tree, all cliché like.*

"Welcome to Arkwright Forest," Adrianna announced, pointing to a weathered wooden signpost. "Named after Joseph Arkwright who was head of the merchant caravan who founded Cinter."

"I'd love to have something as pretty as this named after me," Samira Nazari said to her husband Dara, then giggled. "We have to go discover some unclaimed place."

"What kind of animals can we expect to see around here?" Noel Moss asked. He had gotten his camera out and was snapping pictures of the nearby trees. Soft whirring and clicking noises filled the air. October had no knowledge whatsoever of cameras, but thought Noel's looked expensive.

"I'm glad you asked," Adrianna replied, once again ready to burst with information. "There are all sorts of woodland residents, every-thing from beavers, skunks, and porcupines to deer, woodpeckers, and even flying squirrels."

Arthur and Bernadette leaned their heads together and began to talk in excited whispers, Bryan looking irritated standing next to them.

"Do any dangerous animals live around here?" Samira piped up. Dara seemed eager to know as well.

"Yes, and I'm supposed to warn you," Adrianna went on, nodding at Samira. "While I've never encountered any dangerous animals on a hike, there are wolves, coyotes, cougars, and sometimes even bears that do call this forest their home. While you should never approach *any* wild animal, please make sure to *never ever* approach these in particular. I can't stress that enough. I do have bear spray with me, but they'll leave us alone as long we do the same for them. Does everyone agree to that rule?"

Everyone nodded their acquiescence.

Does playing dead actually work if you run into a bear? October thought. *Can't remember if that was true or not.*

"Good." Adrianna clapped her hands together. "We'll be taking the Lila Trail today, named after Lila Arkwright, Joseph Arkwright's wife. The trail leads us through a gorgeous part of the forest, then wanders down into the Tamáhnous Valley along the cliffs where we'll take a look at Painter's Cave. A security gate has been installed to help preserve the ancient Indigenous wall paintings that were discovered there around the time Cinter was settled. And you're all in luck, because I do have the keys. Then the trail loops around and we'll end up back here. Depending on our pace, the hike should take us, oh, about three hours. I hope everyone brought plenty of snacks, water, and comfortable footwear. You guys ready to start?"

A cave? Shit, she couldn't do caves. Maybe she'd just stay outside and wait for the others while they looked around. And three hours? She hadn't realized the hike would take so long. It'd be fine, she decided. She was in decent shape, after all.

Sort of.

Damn, she should have read everything on that flyer.

CHAPTER FOUR

October

The group had been hiking—walking, really—for about thirty minutes when October could no longer deny that her choice of pants and footwear had been a big mistake. Her tank top felt fine, but her jeans, despite being stretchy, were not meant for this much activity; neither were her boots designed for long walks over arduous terrain. Actual hiking boots wouldn't have so many buckles and spikes or three-inch platforms. Even worse, she had worn out most of the boots' cushioning years ago. She sighed at her own penchant for wearing things she loved until they practically fell apart.

And damn, she was winded. When was the last time she had gone for so much as a walk around the neighborhood?

Only a couple more hours of this....

You really are pathetic, a voice in her head hissed at her.

A sudden chill ran through October's guts, but she quickly forced it down and chastised herself.

Stop it. Those are your own thoughts.

Back when the "voice" had manifested, October never had trouble differentiating it from her own internal voice.

She had dubbed it the Overshadow.

The Overshadow's words not only sounded different, they *felt* different, like something warm and slimy slithering through her brain. It had been a monumental relief when Dr. Iddrisu and October finally discovered the perfect medication combo to muzzle the Overshadow. There had been such a profound sense of wonder and freedom as she gradually came to trust that her headspace was her own again.

Every so often, however, despite her diligent commitment to maintaining the drug regimen, a thought would pop into October's head that sounded...not right.

Dr. Iddrisu had assured her that while her fear of backsliding was perfectly understandable, it was an anxiety she'd be able to conquer as time went on.

October pulled out her phone and checked the time. Speaking of medication, she needed to take her afternoon dose soon.

"Salut. Hello," a thickly-accented voice said, causing October to jump. "Is everything okay?"

October swiveled her head to the right to see that woman walk up beside her; Vior.... Dammit, what was her name? Viorica, that was it. The woman was keeping pace with her.

How long has she been walking right beside me? October had thought she alone had been bringing up the rear.

"Yeah, I'm fine," October puffed, readjusting the backpack on her shoulders and flashing a weary smile. She hoped she was able to disguise how miserable her feet felt at that moment.

Viorica raised a thick eyebrow. "You are sweating profusely." There was a hint of amusement in her voice, though her expression exuded sympathy.

October looked over at her. The woman had pulled her dark brown hair back into a long ponytail and there was not a bead of sweat to be seen on her forehead. October wiped her own moist brow with the back of her hand, trying to get her bangs out of her face.

"No, no," October said with a grunt, forcing as much cheer into her voice as possible. "I'm fine, really. I just don't hike very often. I didn't think about going hiking when I packed for this trip, or else I'd have brought different boots." Discomfort from the sudden attention flustered her. She had to get the focus away from herself. "Anyway, how uh…about you? Viorica, was it? You like to hike? I like your accent."

Stop babbling.

"I am from Romãnia, and yes, I like to hike." Her tone was friendly, but she offered no more words. Perhaps she was trying to let October catch her breath.

"I see," she went on, struggling to make conversation. "So, is that why you're here? Came for the hiking?"

"I'm on vacation," was all Viorica said.

"Alrighty then," October muttered to herself as the conversation died. *Weird lady*, she mused before realizing how grateful she felt to not have to engage in meaningless chit chat. She reevaluated. *Seems nice, though.* She tuned back in to what Adrianna was saying about their surroundings, their guide striding around easily at the front of the little group.

"…and these cool little guys," she was explaining, stopping to kneel beside some white flowers with thin petals hanging from the tops of long stalks, "are fawn lilies. Some people actually cook and eat the bulb, as it's considered a root vegetable. I've never tried it myself, but I've heard it can be tasty."

Noel knelt beside Adrianna, pointing his large camera at the flower and taking several pictures. "Nice." The camera whirred.

Dara Nazari paused beside Noel. "Are you a professional photographer?" he asked.

"I am," Noel answered with a grin, getting back up to his feet. He stood almost two feet taller than Dara. "I used to do photography for weddings and parties and stuff like that. Now I'm doing projects that mean more to me, you know? Right now, I'm collecting shots for a portfolio of beautiful, little-known places across the United States. It's a personal project I've wanted to do for a long while now. Hopefully someone will want to turn it into a coffee table book or something."

Dara nodded and made an approving sound, turning to smile at his wife, Samira. "You know," he said, looking back at Noel. "Our son is a photographer as well. He's currently in Los Angeles setting up a showing of his work."

"Yes," Samira added. "He's been doing photoshoots with celebrities." The pride was evident in the Nazaris' voices.

"Hey, that's awesome!" Noel replied. Even though it seemed obvious that Dara had only asked about Noel's work to have an opportunity to talk about his son, there was no irritation in Noel's voice, and the three of them began an animated conversation about photography as Adrianna got the group moving again down the trail.

Despite the sweat, bugs, and dull ache in October's feet, she had to concede that the forest was truly beautiful. She felt enveloped in the sea of green, the fresh scent of lush foliage wafting over her. The melodic warbling of passing birds overhead was pleasant to the ear. Her thoughts drifted away from her physical discomfort. This place reminded her of the stories Uncle Shane had always regaled her with whenever he babysat her. Some of October's fondest childhood memories were of listening to those stories of fantastical forest monsters, wood witches, shadow creatures, and magic.

The smile that had been forming on her lips vanished at the memory. She hadn't talked to either of her parents or Uncle Shane in far too long. She still had some work to do with Dr. Iddrisu before she could work up the courage to come back into her family's lives.

Mom, Dad, and Uncle Shane would love it here, she thought. *Even if I don't move to Cinter, maybe we could all come up here together sometime anyway. I just need to call them. Talk to them.*

As if she had allowed her mental defenses to fall too far, other thoughts popped into her head: *What if they don't want to hear from you? What if they've written you off already?*

Stop that, she thought, gritting her teeth.

They're tired of dealing with you. Everyone gets tired of you. They're all sick of trying to fix you and getting nowhere.

"Shhh!" October heard Bernadette hiss at the others, shifting her attention back to her surroundings.

October followed Bernadette's pointing finger. The woman quietly indicated a deer grazing just a dozen or so feet off the path to their right in a little meadow of tall grass. The deer raised its head to stare at the group of humans with dark, unconcerned eyes as it munched away, its white muzzle working side-to-side. A calmness settled in October's chest while she watched the animal go about its business. She couldn't remember the last time she had stopped to observe something so peaceful and serene.

She watched as Noel inched closer, his camera whirring. He took dozens of shots. *I should ask him to get a shot of me so I can have a memento of visiting here,* she thought idly. *The family always wants to see pictures.*

It was at that moment that the sharp sound of twigs snapping echoed from among the trees across the clearing, and the deer vanished with a graceful bound into the foliage.

"Wasn't me," Noel said, lowering his camera and putting up his hands. "I swear."

"Nu, that sounded deeper into the trees," Viorica said, studying the surrounding vegetation.

"Maybe there's a whole herd of deer nearby!" Bernadette exclaimed. "Are they herds? Or is it called a pack of deer?"

"Perhaps it's a flock of deer, dear," her husband replied with a corny grin.

"Arthur," Bernadette laughed, pinching his large cheek affectionately.

October could just imagine Bryan's eyes rolling right out of his skull as he tried to stand as far away from his parents as he could, huffing, arms crossed, pretending he didn't know those two dorks. October smothered a quiet chuckle, though she felt a little ashamed when she noticed Bryan staring at her before he looked down at the ground with a beet-red face.

The group began walking once more down the trail.

"Why do you laugh at the blond boy?" Viorica asked October, her voice just above a whisper.

"What?" The question caught October off guard, not realizing anyone heard her. Did Viorica have super hearing or something? She felt her cheeks flush. "Oh, it's just that, I guess he was trying to hit on me earlier." The chuckle that came out of her mouth this time was tinged with a painful awkwardness.

"He tried to hit you?" Viorica said, her tone indignant. A dark look spread over her face. She looked about ready to march over to the teenager.

"No, no." October quickly grabbed her arm. "He hit *on* me. Like, he flirted with me."

"Oh, I see," Viorica answered, laughing. "Îmi pare rău. Sorry. English is not my first language. My grasp is not the best when it comes to American slang. Forgive me."

"No worries." Relief flooded through October at avoiding whatever it was this woman had planned to do to Bryan.

They walked in companionable silence for another few minutes before October mustered up the courage to reopen the conversation. *Don't be afraid to talk to people.*

"Can I ask where you're from?"

"Southeastern Europe," Viorica answered after a brief moment of hesitation. "I am on—"

"On vacation," October finished with her. "Yeah, so you've said."

"So, your name is October?" Viorica asked, changing the subject. "Like the month?"

"That's right," October answered. "That was what the people at SCH—that's the Solumen Children's Home—named me, since I wound up there on Halloween after the cops took me from my biological parents. So creative, right?" She froze for a fleeting moment. The words had just tumbled out of her mouth. She generally refrained from mentioning that she had been in the foster system unless it was both relevant and important for someone to know. She wasn't ashamed of her origin, no. It was just that many people were uncomfortable with the topic. It also seemed too intimate a detail to share, but something about this Viorica's manner invited such confidences. October shrugged, trying to hide her chagrin at the slip-up.

If Viorica had any opinion on what October had just revealed, however, the woman kept it to herself. Instead, she asked, "Are you on vacation too?"

"Sort of," October answered. "I live outside of Los Angeles. I'm thinking of moving, though. The company I work for just offered me a transfer to an office they plan on opening in Cinter."

"What do you do?" Viorica asked.

"I work at Valravn."

"Oh wow, big company," the woman said. "You inventing any new cool technologies? New phones? I heard the Soul-VX 6 will be announced soon. Are you working on that?"

"Ha, no, not really." October adjusted her backpack. "I'm just an administrative assistant. A secretary, basically."

"I see," Viorica said without a hint as to whether she was disappointed in October's lowly position, or if it was what she had expected. With an abrupt change of subject, she pointed to the back of October's right hand. "That's an interesting tattoo."

"Huh? Oh, thanks," October replied, staring down at her hand. She had acquired numerous tattoos over the years. The one inked on the back of her right hand had not only been her first, but the only tattoo with which she had been marked without her consent. "Actually," October continued, "I don't remember getting it."

"You were drunk?" Viorica asked.

"No." Well, she had already told this woman she had been a foster kid. What was the harm in telling her more? "Apparently, my biological parents tattooed it on me when I was two or three. One of the many reasons I was taken away from them, I suppose. I guess the state didn't want to fork out the money to have it removed. Whatever. I don't know why, but I'm kinda glad they left it, even if I don't know what the hell it's supposed to be. It's like a reminder of the bad stuff my parents—not my biological parents, my *real* parents—took me away from."

October's eyes traced the tattoo as they often did—a curving, abstract combination of what might be the letters P and T, with circles on either side.

"You don't know what the symbol is?" Viorica asked, turning an inquisitive look on October.

"Should I?"

Viorica shrugged. "In English, it is called the Sign, no, the *Sigil* of Deep."

"Sigil of Deep?" October repeated. She held up her hand. "Wait. This is an actual thing?"

"Mmhm," Viorica said, and left it at that.

They continued walking side by side. October's mind raced, and she found herself rubbing at her hand. The symbol actually meant something? She had always figured it was a nonsense mark her negligent birth parents had tattooed on her when they were high or drunk or whatever was wrong with them. She was about to ask Viorica what she knew about the symbol when Adrianna asked everyone to watch their footing, as they were now going to descend into the Tamáhnous Valley where Painter's Cave was located. The group murmured with interest as everyone made their way down what turned out to be nothing more than a gentle downward slope. Eventually, they emerged into a sunny clearing where the trees formed a wide circle around an open area of grass with boulders of various sizes here and there that they could sit on for a rest. A calm, bubbling stream flowed peacefully a few dozen yards from the rocks.

"This is one of my favorite spots to stop and take a breather before we get to Painter's Cave," Adrianna said as some people shrugged off backpacks while others found places to sit. "Let's take fifteen, then we'll get moving again. Make sure you're staying hydrated. I don't want anyone passing out on me. The water in the stream over there is clean, but not potable. Please do not refill your canteens and bottles there. I have some extra water bottles in my pack if you need some. And I also have some beef jerky, granola bars, and protein bars if anyone forgot to bring a snack. We don't want to run out of energy. Right? Right!" She smiled at everyone, showing off her perfectly white teeth, then perched herself on a rock. Taking a notebook out of her pack, she began sketching in it, a look of firm concentration on her face while she studied a nearby fallen tree.

After chugging half a bottle of water, October used the front camera on her phone to make sure her makeup wasn't running down her face. She didn't want to look like she had been sobbing the whole way. If she had known the hike would be three freaking hours or anywhere near this strenuous, she certainly wouldn't have wasted time putting all this shit on. Thankfully, everything was still mostly in place, despite her profuse sweating.

Okay, now to go ask Adrianna if it would be okay to stay outside while everyone went inside the cave. The last cave October had been—

"Excuse me."

October looked up to see Bryan's mom, Bernadette, walking towards her.

Oh hell. October's stomach tightened. She felt a grimace overtake her features. Now someone else wanted to come up and talk with her, too? Hadn't she socialized enough for one day? Maybe Bryan had said something about October to his mom. Dozens of dreadful thoughts swirled around inside her brain.

"Hi, dear." Bernadette came to a stop in front of October. "October, was it? I just wanted to ask you something real quick."

"Hmm?" October responded, her mouth feeling dry. "Um, sure. Go ahead."

"Well, I just have to say that your hair is beyond cute!" Bernadette exclaimed. "How do you get it to stay like that? I was just telling Arthur over there, that's my husband, I was just telling him that I was thinking of changing up my style. And I was saying, 'Arthur, look at that beautiful young woman over there. Isn't her hair just so neat with the bangs and that side section that's all like a buzz cut? Maybe I should do something like that!' And Arthur agreed. He's always so supportive. Even though it's not a style I've ever tried before. Gotta keep life exciting, you know?"

"Oh." October fumbled for words. This was not what she had been expecting at all. She almost laughed, but didn't want to discourage Bernadette or make her think she was laughing *at* her. "Thank you."

A piercing shriek from the direction of the stream ended the conversation. All heads snapped up to look around.

"Samira!" Dara called out for his wife.

It was then that October noticed Samira wasn't with the group.

Dara was answered by another scream. Samira came sprinting up to him from just beyond the clearing.

"Samira, what's wrong?" He wrapped his arms around his wife as she struggled to regain her breath.

"Over…by the…stream!" Samira gasped out, clutching Dara's shirt. The others all started to encircle the couple. "There's something dead! It's all mutilated!"

Worried murmuring filled the air around the group.

"Alright, everyone just stay calm," Adrianna said. Uncertainty colored her voice, and her eyes darted back and forth between the group and the grove from which Samira had just come. She looked unsure of what to do. "I'm sure everything's fine. I'll go check it out. Everyone just stay put, please." She didn't move however, as if waiting for someone to object.

"I will go with you," Viorica said after a brief pause. She wasn't asking permission.

"Oh, okay," Adrianna stammered, though she looked greatly relieved. She put away her sketchbook. "Samira, can you show us where it was?" Samira nodded. "Okay, everyone else, please remain here while Viorica and I go check everything out. It's most likely nothing to worry about."

"I'm going too," Dara said.

Viorica, Dara, and Samira set off with Adrianna in tow. Even though instructed to stay put, everyone else followed.

October was only a few feet behind Viorica as they made their way toward the stream when a thick, rotten odor punched her right in the nose. One by one, everyone groaned in disgust, putting hands over mouths and noses to block out the vile stench.

"It's right there," Samira's shaky voice was muffled by the hand over her face. With her other hand, she pointed toward the stream's bank. "I—I was just looking around."

Every eye followed her finger and settled on a large heap of something. The thing looked like a wet, bloody brown rug bunched up and discarded on the ground, chunks of flesh and sinew smattered all over it. Flies buzzed around, and white maggots undulated across its hairy surface and into the greasy folds, enjoying their great feast.

"I think I'm going to be sick." Arthur's face turned green. He backed away a few steps.

"What the hell is it?" Noel asked, his camera hanging forgotten around his neck.

"It looks like it's just a dead animal, folks," Adrianna said, sounding more at ease. Everyone turned to look at her. "There are predators that live in these parts, like I said. One of them probably just left the remains of last night's dinner here. No big deal."

"How did you not smell it?" Dara asked his wife.

"I did," Samira said, looking bashful. "It was gross, but I was curious."

"It's skin," Viorica stated. The group turned their attention back to the stream bank where Viorica was now knelt over the gory heap. She had produced a large hunting knife and was poking at the remains. "It's the skin of a baby bear. Cub bear. See?" She used the knife to flip over a portion of the bloody remains, revealing a deflated-looking cub face. It looked as if everything inside had been removed, vacuumed out, leaving behind only the moist pelt.

"What kind of animal skins a bear cub like that?" Noel asked Adrianna, who shook her head. "Is it even possible for an animal to do that?"

"I don't know what did this," Viorica said. "Whatever happened, this bear cub is, how do you say? Dead as a door."

"Nail," October said, her voice muffled like Samira's. Everyone, save Viorica, had covered their nose and mouth in an attempt to ward off the reek of death. "It's 'dead as a doornail.'"

"Huh?" Viorica rubbed her chin in thought before turning her attention back to the skin heap. "That makes no sense." She went back to examining the pile.

A buzzing and beeping burst from October's hip pouch, causing everyone except Viorica to jump in surprise. October fumbled with the pouch's zipper before finally getting it open and pulling out her phone.

"Shit, sorry!" she said, her face becoming warm. She slammed the screen with her panicking fingers before managing to mute the beeping. "Sorry, sorry. I thought I put it on silent."

Dumbass, she thought, embarrassment flooding her stomach. The alarm meant it was time for her afternoon meds. Returning the phone to her hip pouch, she reached inside for her little pill case.

It wasn't there.

"No." The word crawled out from between October's lips.

"What's wrong?" Viorica asked, leaving the skin and stepping over to her.

"My meds." No, this wasn't right. October dug around inside the pouch. There wasn't anywhere else for the small square case to hide. The hip pouch was a single compartment with room enough to only hold a few things. The pills weren't there.

Fuck! This isn't happening. No, I triple-checked before I left the motel room. They were here! No, no, no!

Had she dropped them somehow? There didn't seem to be any hole in the pouch. What could've happened?

She tried to force herself to calm down. She'd only be an hour or two late. Although she'd never taken her meds so late before. Everything would be fine. It would all work out. It had to.

A loud rustling came out from the overgrown bushes and trees across the stream. Heavy footsteps thudded in a lumbering cadence as leaves crunched and twigs snapped. Gasps filled the air. October looked up just as a large figure emerged from among the trees on the other side of the gently flowing water.

It was the biggest bear she had ever seen.

CHAPTER FIVE

October

O h shit," October hissed. Her body began to shake uncontrollably, and the whole group took a frightened step backward.

Standing across the stream, facing them all, was an enormous grizzly bear. Its head was the size of a car tire. Paws, easily as wide as October's shoulder-width, attached to tree-trunk legs supported a solid body of pure muscle and strength. October had never seen a bear outside of the zoo or TV, but she was positive that this one was far larger than normal.

"Th-that's not possible," Adrianna said, her voice cracking. "Oh God. There aren't supposed to be grizzly bears in this area! Black bears, yes. B-but not grizzlies! They—"

"Adrianna," Bryan interjected, cutting her off. His voice was low. "Shut the hell up."

"Bryan!" Arthur hissed.

"Can we *all* just shut the hell up and figure out what to do?" Noel said quietly through gritted teeth.

Adrianna had just removed the bear spray from her backpack

when the grizzly let loose an ear-shattering roar. The spray can fell from her startled fingers. The bear stepped into the stream and headed toward them, its great paws throwing up water with each lumbering step. The group shrank backward, everyone wanting to get as far away as possible, but no one wanting to break into a run, lest they attract the focus of the approaching killing machine.

Don't piss yourself. Don't piss yourself. October nearly tripped over a log as she took small, terrified steps backward. She couldn't breathe. She couldn't swallow. Cold perspiration coated her entire body, causing her clothes to cling to her skin like they were trying to drag her down. *Don't fall,* she thought as she steadied herself again on shaking legs. *This isn't the way I want to go.* The image of her lying on the ground holding her own disemboweled intestines danced through her head.

The hulking beast stepped onto the near bank and sniffed at the pile of skin that still lay glistening in the sunlight. At first, the grizzly pulled its head back sharply, its large snout twitching. October had the utterly ridiculous notion that the bear was trying to smile.

A second later the bear was pawing and nosing at the grotesque heap. It then swiveled its massive head up at the group of hikers standing ten yards away with what October could now see were strange yellow eyes—the color of sulfur.

Oh no, October thought. *Is that its baby? We didn't do it!*

The bear rose up like a tower onto its hind legs, looming over them all, a mighty colossus of hair and muscle. The thing must have stood eleven feet tall. Thick ropes of saliva hung from its gaping maw as it bellowed another thunderous roar. October found herself locking eyes with the beast. She regarded those sulfurous eyes—was the animal sick?—and felt certain that she could see intelligence and cunning behind them. Was it angry? Definitely angry, if that pile of skin had been its cub. This animal wasn't going to let them leave alive after what had been done to its precious baby.

The bear dropped back to all fours with such force, October swore she felt the ground shake. It charged, rapidly closing the distance. Everyone bolted in blind panic. The bear swiped at the group with its battering-ram paws. Despite a valiant attempt to scramble back, the bear's claws caught Dara in the back. He fell to the ground with an agonized screech, then somehow managed to use his momentum to roll back to his feet. The bear sniffed at the scent of fresh blood that now floated in the air.

What could they do? October's mind raced, searching for an answer. She couldn't see where the can of bear spray had fallen. How fast could a grizzly bear run? Would any of them escape if the whole group decided to bolt in different directions?

"Get out of here," a voice groaned. It was a full second before October realized it had been Dara. She thought he was talking to the bear at first, then saw him lock eyes with his wife. Turning to the group, he yelled again, "Everyone, get out of here now!"

Blood flowed from the deep wounds in his back. His face, now drained of most of its color, was a mask of agony. Before any of them could stop him, Dara turned and faced the bear, picking up a large stick off the ground, brandishing it as a weapon.

"Dara, no!" Samira screamed, her eyes wide and horrified. Her husband had already reached the animal.

Dara dodged around the grizzly and whacked it across the legs with the stick. The bear spun around like a dog trying to catch his own tail. They all watched in absolute dismay as the bear swung its enormous paw with a speed that belied its massive size. Dara went down with a sickening *whack* that caught him along the ribs, blood painting the ground.

He let out a bloodcurdling yowl. Then in an agonized voice, "What are you people doing? Get out of here, Samira!"

Bryan was the first to snap out of it and flee, his parents following after him a second later.

"Oh my God!" Adrianna shrieked when the bear began tearing into Dara's prone form as he lay on his back, still attempting to fight off the monster with futile smacks and punches.

"Dara!" Samira screamed again, trying to get to her husband.

"We have to help him!" October shouted, surprising herself.

"No, we gotta run!" Noel shouted back, holding Samira's arm and dragging her backward. "There's nothing we can do!"

Everything was happening so fast, yet to October, it seemed as if time had slowed. Dara's screams saturated the air. It was one of the most horrible, odious sounds October had ever heard. Screams of unimaginable pain. She knew Noel was right, however. What could they do? The bear roared again, its teeth and claws ripping into Dara's body. Gouts of blood and chunks of flesh flew everywhere. Someone grabbed October's shoulder, dragging her away from where she had stood rooted in place.

"We must go!" Viorica yelled in October's ear, yanking her along after all those who had already made their escapes.

As she ran, October was unable to resist one last glance behind at the carnage. What was left of Dara's mangled body lay motionless on the red-stained ground. The bear's blood-splattered face rose from its kill to glare at the fleeing group, its ears perking up, then flattening. Muscles tensed under fur as the animal prepared to launch itself forward.

"It's coming after us!" she shrieked, her thumping heart feeling ready to explode in her chest. Her legs felt like they were made of lead as Viorica kept her running along.

"Where do we go?" Bernadette shouted.

"Follow me!" Adrianna instructed in a terrified squeak. She had managed to get in front of the group, her powerful legs propelling her quickly forward despite the large pack she carried on her shoulders. "We need to get to Painter's Cave!"

That did not sound like the best idea. Besides October's own reservations about caves, wouldn't they also be trapped inside? Maybe there was a second exit or maybe Adrianna knew something the rest didn't. No one protested the idea, and October certainly didn't want to be left on her own. The sound of enormous paws slapping against the ground and gaining on them spurred her to reach down inside herself to summon more speed, still holding onto Viorica's hand as the woman charged on. A rocky cliff face rose up before them on the left of the trail as they descended even deeper into the

Tamáhnous Valley. Moments later, as they neared the valley bottom, the sheer wall of rock that was the cliff towered several stories above them. Once again, October hoped Adrianna knew what she was doing.

How fast could a grizzly bear run exactly? The question ran through her mind again while bits and pieces of nature documentaries she had seen on TV popped up inside her head.

Don't look back, she told herself over and over. It became a chant in time with her feet. *Don't look back. Don't look back. Just keep going. Don't look back!*

The footfalls faded away, and when October chanced a look behind, there was no bear in sight. October almost yanked her hand out of Viorica's when the ravenous beast came crashing through the trees from their right, plowing directly into Noel and Samira and scattering the group like bowling pins. Samira screamed as the grizzly bellowed its anger at her. The beast raised a dagger-tipped paw, its claws glinting in the sunlight, ready to disembowel.

A blurry shape whizzed past in October's peripheral vision, and a split-second later, she saw a hunting knife lodge itself into the bear's left eye with a sickening *thunk*. She looked to her side to see Viorica lowering her arm.

"Holy hell," October said in stunned awe. She finally released Viorica's other hand, suddenly feeling like a child. Why hadn't she thrown the knife when Dara was being mauled?

The bear bellowed in rage and agony. It stumbled sideways, its flailing claw missing Samira's head by mere inches. Noel took the opportunity to scramble to his feet, yanking Samira up after him. The others managed to run past the bear as it thrashed wildly, trying to get the knife out of its ruined, bleeding eyeball.

As they rounded a corner in the cliff wall, October saw Adrianna frantically waving at them to get to her. Their guide stood beside a dark opening in the cliff face underneath a weathered, green aluminum sign that read 'Entrance to Painter's Cave' in fancy script. Bryan and his parents darted inside, followed by Samira and Noel. October's chest was on fire, her breath coming in and going out in ragged bursts that scraped every inch of her lungs raw. But she knew she couldn't afford to stop or even slow down.

"Do not slow down!" Viorica demanded from right beside her as if she had just read October's thoughts. October felt Viorica's firm hand on her back, pushing her along, refusing to allow her to slacken her pace.

"Wait, wait, wait!" October yelled as the entrance in the cliff approached. "I can't go in there!" Her teeth ground together.

Whether Viorica heard her or not, the woman shoved October into the rocky aperture, Adrianna making sure everyone else made it inside before hurrying into the cave herself.

Panting and gasping, October followed the others deeper into the cave, her eyes adjusting to the darker surroundings. Faded arrows had been painted on the floor to show the way. Bare bulbs, attached to the ceiling and connected with dusty wires, buzzed and flickered, illuminating the rock walls with dim, yellow light. At Adrianna's loud insistence, the group hurried several dozen yards deeper into the cave. They passed a metal security gate that had been embedded and cemented into the rock itself.

Adrianna slammed the gate shut behind them, then retrieved a ring of keys from her pack, looking for the correct one to secure the gate's lock. The keys jangled wildly in her shaking hands, the sound echoing much too loudly in the cave. Above the group's ragged breathing, October heard a snort and a low growl come from the cave's entrance.

"Hurry up!" Bryan urged as he peered through the bars of the fence. "Lock it!"

October would have told him to shut up if her throat hadn't been constricted so painfully from the exhaustion and the overwhelming terror coursing through her body. Through the gate's bars, she could make out the black silhouette of the grizzly bear padding its way toward them, pushing its bulk through the narrow passage, taking its time. It was as if it knew its tasty human prey had no place to run now.

Why did you come on this stupid hike? The question kept burning through October's mind. She had just wanted to enjoy a few nice, relaxing days and check out a small mountain town. Wasn't nature supposed to be serene and peaceful and rejuvenating? *You just watched a man get ripped to pieces and die in front of your eyes. That's going to haunt you. Haunt your dreams forever.* The thought chilled her, though she didn't think she had felt the full emotional impact of everything yet. She would, eventually.

If she lived through all of this.

"I got it!" Adrianna exclaimed, as she slid one of her keys into the lock.

At that moment, a crash sent her stumbling backward away from the gate. Both she and the keys fell to the floor. October couldn't tear her eyes from the bloodied, feral face of the bear where it now pressed against the metal bars, its blade-like teeth bared in animalistic ferocity. Viorica's hunting knife was still embedded deep in the animal's skull, and the remains of its eye dripped down the matted fur of its cheek. The other sulfur-yellow eye glared at them. Was that some sort of gleeful anticipation October saw in the bear's expression?

"Dammit!" Noel yelled as he slammed his body against the gate, trying to keep the beast from pushing through. Arthur and Viorica joined him, throwing all their weight against it.

Adrianna snatched up the fallen key ring as October quickly helped the girl back to her feet.

"Fucking lock it!" Bryan screeched.

"I'm trying!" Adrianna yelled back. She frantically searched for the right key once more. October joined the others in pushing as the bear did the same from the other side. She didn't know if her wimpy body was helping at all. Still, she gave it every ounce of strength she had left. How much did a grizzly bear weigh? Like half a ton?

The bear brought up a massive paw to push on the gate. Its claws passed through the gaps in the bars. Arthur screamed as their sharp points dug into the flesh of his left shoulder where he was using his entire body weight to push back against the gate.

"Got it!" Adrianna announced once more, this time delaying her announcement until the key slid home.

October heard the satisfying click of the deadbolt locking into place. She never thought a lock could sound so amazing.

They all scrambled away from the gate, getting as far back from the bear as they could. Arthur's arm was drenched in blood, and he uttered low moans while clutching the wound.

They pushed several more yards into the cave, the string of light bulbs continuing above them on the low, craggy ceiling, until a bend in the natural passageway led the group into a spacious cavern about the length and width of a basketball court. Even from here, October could still hear the bear growling and rattling the gate. At least they had disappeared from its view for the time being. She hoped being out of the animal's line of sight might encourage it to head elsewhere and leave them alone. Could it still smell them, though? How good was a bear's sense of smell? Predators were adept at smelling blood, weren't they?

Despite danger being literally right around the corner, they all plopped themselves down onto the floor in terrified exhaustion. All except for Viorica. As if nothing untoward had happened, the woman stood studying the cave's walls, which were covered in prehistoric-looking drawings behind plexiglass coverings that must have been installed to protect them from potential graffiti artists.

October could hear Samira's body-wracking, soul-deep sobbing. Nearby, Arthur wheezed for air until Bernadette drew an inhaler out of her fanny pack and gave it to him. Arthur took it with shaking hands and blasted it, taking in a long puff. He gradually managed to regain control of his breathing.

"Oh my God," Adrianna whispered.

"You dumbass!" Bryan exploded, pointing an angry finger at Adrianna. "You led us into a death trap!"

Jumping at the sudden explosion of angry words, October's breath caught in her throat.

"Hey, man!" Noel hissed at the kid. "Are you kidding me? Quiet the hell down!"

"Bryan!" Bernadette snapped at her son, turning her head from where she was now wrapping Arthur's shoulder in the roll of gauze from the first-aid kit in her backpack. "Don't talk that way to her! What's wrong with you?"

"She's trapped us in here, Mom!" Bryan roared. His face contorted in fury. "We're stuck in here with that bear right outside! Look what it did to Dad." He gestured at Arthur with a shaking hand, then clutched at his head. "And how long do you think that weak-ass gate's going to hold up if the bear keeps pushing on it? It's going to tear that thing apart like cardboard. Our little 'nature guide' led us in here to die!"

Everyone looked over at Adrianna, her face dirty and sweaty, her hair a mess, her lip quivering. She looked like she was about to burst into tears.

"I'm sorry!" she said pitifully. "It was the only place I could think of. I knew this place had a security gate. It was close, and I thought we would be safe!"

"Safe?" Samira repeated, looking up, streaks of tears staining her cheeks. "*Safe?* My husband is dead!" She spat every word at Adrianna like venom.

"I can't control wild animals!" Adrianna retorted, finally beginning to cry as well. "You knew that we could potentially run into a wild animal. Besides, there aren't supposed to be grizzly bears in this part of the country anyway."

"What happened to your bear spray? And wouldn't carrying a gun be better?" Bryan demanded, his teeth bared.

"I… I don't like guns," she admitted, looking ashamed. "I've never felt comfortable around them. And no one's been attacked by a bear in this forest in forever!"

"Hey, back off," October snarled, after recovering from some of the shock of the situation. She stood between Bryan and Adrianna. Normally, October would never willingly put herself in the center of a confrontation, but she wasn't going to let Bryan yell at Adrianna like that. October had little tolerance for bullies attacking people they deemed weaker. "This isn't her fault at all. Okay? How were any of us supposed to know we would get attacked by some psycho grizzly bear?" She stepped over and kneeled down in front of Samira. "I'm so sorry about what happened to Dara. That was the bravest thing I've ever seen anyone do. He knew what he was doing. He distracted it. Gave us time to get away. He saved all our lives."

"How am I going to tell our son?" Samira asked, her red, puffy eyes staring pleadingly into October's.

October struggled to find appropriate words. She didn't know what else she could say to the grieving woman. She simply squeezed Samira's hand and sat down beside her.

The group grew silent, and October remembered her previous problem. Where the hell had her meds gone? She was one hundred percent…well, ninety-nine percent certain that the green, plastic pill case had been in her hip pouch as she sat in the motel's parking lot waiting for the bus. She opened the pouch and looked once more. They weren't there.

Fucking fuck.

She needed those meds. Her leg bounced up and down in a frantic rhythm. Never having missed a dose of this particular cocktail of medications before, October had no idea how long she could go without it without repercussions. How quickly would the withdrawal symptoms start? And more importantly, how long did she have before *it* woke up? Days? Or only hours? This life-or-death situation in which October found herself required every ounce of concentration. There was no way she could deal with all this while the Overshadow's loathsome voice was in her head as well.

"Damn, it's busted," Noel said, breaking the funereal quiet and unslinging his expensive camera from his neck. He peered closer at the lens, then looked around. His eyes fell on Samira, guilt written on his face. "Sorry, it's not important right now."

"I haven't had any signal since we started this hike," Bryan snarled, pulling out and checking his phone. "Does anyone have service?"

Everyone checked their own devices. Nobody seemed to have any signal bars.

"Great," Bryan muttered. "Just great." He seemed about to throw his phone onto the ground in anger, then apparently thought better of it.

October surveyed her surroundings. Of all the places to end up—a cave. An extremely cramped and an extremely confined space with tons and tons of rock overhead just waiting to fall and crush you. She would never forget the summer before her freshman year of high school when she had been hanging out with her then-boyfriend Chris in a shallow cave—more of a glorified niche really—down in the ravine behind Chris's house. A sudden earthquake had caused their little hideaway to come crashing down. October had been pinned under the rubble for hours, ending up with only a sprained wrist and a fractured rib. She was the fortunate one. Chris had received severe head trauma which had resulted in a permanent vegetative state. October had attended his funeral a year later.

There had to be something else she could focus on right now.

"Interesting," Viorica said from over by the cavern wall. October looked around to see the woman still examining the cave's artwork, her thick eyebrows furrowed in concentration. October got up, giving Samira one more sympathetic look, and strode over to Viorica's side. The pictographs on the walls—shielded by plexiglass—were composed of ancient, Indigenous-style figures of people hunting and killing animals. Amazing for its antiquity and for what it represented.

"Look, normally I'd be very interested in this," October said, the words coming out in a harsh whisper, "but..." But her own worries and the terror were making anything except survival unimportant at the moment. How could Viorica be concerned with cave art at a time like this? Was it some sort of coping mechanism? Was she trying to distract them from the horror?

Viorica ran a finger over the smooth plexiglass, tracing a humanoid figure on the wall behind it. "What do you make of this one?" she asked, glancing over at October.

October leaned in and looked at the drawing Viorica indicated. "What do I make of it? I don't know." She felt antsy, like a trapped rat with many other things on her mind besides these paintings right now. She forced herself to stop thinking of Chris and to study the wall art.

It was difficult to tell due to the weathered paint what exactly was going on in the scene. It seemed to be a person fighting another person, though while one figure held what she assumed was a spear, the other figure appeared more feral or animalistic. Viorica indicated other drawings with the same animalistic figures climbing trees, hovering over other people who were sleeping or perhaps dead, killing people…eating people maybe? A shiver went down October's spine. What was this art supposed to depict? Maybe it was some ancient folklore? Pictographs forming the story of some early belief system?

A placard beneath read, THESE DRAWINGS ARE ESTIMATED TO BE BETWEEN 5000 AND 6000 YEARS OLD. RESEARCHERS BELIEVE THIS ART DEPICTS A MYTH OR LEGEND OF THE EARLY INHABITANTS OF THIS LAND.

"What do you think it's supposed to be?" she asked Viorica in hushed tones, looking over at the other woman's face.

"It says folk tale, but I am not sure," Viorica answered. "This artwork is stylized and exaggerated. I think there are many depictions of violence. Can you see? Perhaps there are answers among the other wall paintings here."

Turning away from the wall art, October glanced back over at the rest of the group sitting on the cave floor. The Williamsons sat close together in a protective huddle. Arthur's shoulder was now swathed in gauze, and his wife and son were watching him with concern in case he had another asthma attack. Noel was fiddling with his camera while Adrianna sat beside him, holding her head in her hands, tears dripping down her cheeks. She probably felt responsible for everything, though October knew this was in no way her fault. Nearby, Samira had stopped crying. She simply stared at the ground, perhaps in shock. Poor Dara. He had helped them all escape…at the cost of his own life.

October turned back to the cave paintings. It was difficult to focus on them. Instead, she asked Viorica, "So, where did you learn to throw a knife like that?"

"My job," Viorica answered, not taking her eyes off the paintings.

"Okay. And what exactly *is* your job?" October pressed. There was definitely something strange about this woman. October knew she wasn't the best at reading people—and the lack of that skill had burned her several times in the past—but she didn't sense any bad vibes from Viorica. There was just something she couldn't quite put her finger on.

"I don't want to talk about my job. I'm on vacation."

That answer annoyed October, but she didn't question the Romanian woman further. She walked back over to the others and sat down on the cold floor of the cave. Her adrenaline had burned out by that point, and all the physical and mental exhaustion that had been building seemed to hit her all in one giant wave. She reclined against the rough cave wall, using her backpack as an uncomfortable pillow and heaved a big sigh.

How long are we going to be trapped in here? Her eyes fixated on one dim, flickering lightbulb hanging from the limestone roof above her, frigid dread creeping through her body. The idea of being surrounded by an unknowable amount of hard, uncaring rock, under a mountain, scared October to no end. She had no idea how stable any of these structures were. How easily could this one come crashing down, burying them all in crushing stone and eternal darkness?

Trying to distract herself, she counted the seconds between each flicker of the dirty, yellow bulb overhead.

I'm not going to die down here, October told herself. *But what if I do? What if I never make it out of here alive? No, can't afford to think like that. It doesn't help at all. Think of something else.*

You are going to die here, you pathetic piece of shit.

Every bodily system seemed to come to a standstill inside October the instant she heard those words. It hadn't been "spoken" in her usual inner voice. It had been *its* voice.

No. Had the meds in her system really worn off so quickly? How long had they been in this cave? October cringed as she felt the actual physical sensation of something creeping and slithering through her brain's grooves and crevices like a probing, decaying worm. *Oh God, no. Just go away.*

God? No, not really. But I like the sound of it. I suppose inside your head, I am a sort of god. Although I prefer the other name you gave me.

The Overshadow chuckled from deep within October's mind.

CHAPTER SIX

Jordan

Jordan sat back in her chair. She absent-mindedly watched Nathan dig into tiny pieces of carrot that she had put in his little metal bowl next to the computer monitors. The bearded dragon stared up at her while his spiky jaw snapped up and down on a juicy carrot chunk, as if asking, *"What's up?"*

"Not much," she answered the inquisitive animal with a shrug. "Just scouring the world for stuff that could potentially destroy all life on Earth as we know it. You know, that kind of thing."

Nathan kept chewing. *"Sounds like a dangerous job, Jordan. How are you so brave?"*

"It's not about bravery, my reptilian bud." She puffed out her chest. "It's about helping those in need!"

For an extended moment, Jordan and Nathan gazed at one another in silence.

"Or something like that," she said, stroking Nathan's head, taking comfort in the scaly texture under her fingertips.

She sighed. On her computer, she pulled up a program of her own design. Jordan was no hacker, as Wendig liked to call her. She was simply a competent, self-taught programmer and code monkey. And she was pretty good at forging documents. And perhaps she was also rather skilled at obtaining not-so-public, hard-to-come-by information that Lucas often required in his investigations. Okay, maybe she was more than just "competent." She did build the custom rig that sat on her desk like a black obelisk, humming faintly as it made its computations; its double monitors stared back at her like a pair of eyes, judging her poor posture.

The program she was running at the moment was one of several she had created herself, which she liked to remind Wendig of, every now and then. Jordan also very much enjoyed reminding him that he wouldn't have accomplished nearly as much as he had so far in his pursuit for Enigmata if she hadn't been willing and able to lend her bountiful and brilliant assistance.

At the moment, Wendig needed certain credentials to get in to see Caleb Rivas. Her program wormed its way into records and databases she wasn't technically allowed to access. She brought her feet up on the chair, pulling up the hood on her fraying gray Darth Vader hoodie, and began unconsciously chewing on her nails.

It was coming up on three years since Jordan had started working with Lucas Wendig in his search for Enigmata. Time had flown by, yet she somehow felt like she had known him forever. He had saved her life during their first meeting, and since then—though neither of them had ever openly acknowledged it—he had transformed into something of a paternal figure in her life. Or maybe more like a cool uncle?

Either way, Jordan felt she owed a debt to Wendig. That was probably why she was so dedicated to helping him with all the research and fact-finding stuff. And it was a hell of a lot of work.

Who was she kidding? She loved doing this. Having grown up obsessed with *Dungeons & Dragons*, *The X-Files*, Indiana Jones, and so on, it was no wonder that when the opportunity to help Wendig hunt down mysterious creatures and occult objects as his unofficial assistant had presented itself, Jordan had pounced on it. Okay, maybe it had been more like she had relentlessly insisted she be allowed to join him. Either way, she loved the challenging, often-exasperating hunt for all the things Wendig was so hell-bent on finding.

Despite her enthusiasm, she never had been able to root out the real reason Wendig was so determined to locate and contain every existing Enigmata in the world.

Well, whatever. She refrained from digging into what might be delicate topics as long as he allowed her to accompany him on this wild ride. Wendig didn't want to bring up some things? That was fine with her. Hey, who was she to complain?

Now if only she could think of a way to convince him to let her out into the field with him instead of being stuck behind a screen.

"Sidekick, pfff…"

Bored with unfathomably dull Omaha, Nebraska, Jordan longed to join Wendig and work by his side—and maybe see the glamorous sights in California. If only he would let her.

Jordan could fly over there anytime, though. What if she surprised him by showing up in person one day? She could afford a plane ticket and a hotel room. Wendig paid her plenty, and she had saved up a nice nest egg.

Where did Wendig get all his money from anyway? She often wondered. He'd told her he came from money. That was as far as he went on the subject. She could dig into it, although she would never violate Wendig's privacy. It would come up at some point, maybe.

At that moment, there was a knock at her bedroom door. She quickly minimized the window displaying the progress of her search program on the computer monitor, switching it out for a "Cats Getting Scared by Cucumbers" compilation video on YouTube.

"You may enter," Jordan stated in a regal tone.

The door swung open, causing Nathan's beard to puff out in surprise as he scrambled into her lap. Her roommate/brother, Gabe, strode in like he owned the place.

"Hey, beotch," Gabe said to her, wonderfully belching the words.

Jordan slowly swiveled around in her chair to face him while she caressed Nathan's scaly head like a Bond villain.

"Good evening, Mr. Dickhead," she answered suavely.

"Just wanted to check in on you." Gabe leaned against the door-frame. "I'm going out tonight. Gotta make an appearance at Steve's party. So, riddle me this: Is your bony ass going to come with me? Or are you and the lizard going to have another quiet date night together?"

"Don't those parties usually start pretty late?" Jordan replied, glancing at the time on her computer. She scratched Nathan's chin. The very thought of a social gathering filled with loud, drunken people unnerved her more than any Enigmata ever could.

"Yeah, and?" Gabe said. "I want to go get drunk and possibly high. Plus, you stay up all night anyway."

"Touché," Jordan answered, shooting him finger guns before swiveling back around to face her computer so he couldn't see her biting her lip again. She hated to disappoint him, but she just couldn't bring herself to attend a party with all that noise and all those people.

"There's going to be karaokeeeee," Gabe sang.

"Oh, hell no."

Gabe threw up his hands. "Come on. You used to be in the school choir. You'll show everyone up."

"That was a long time ago. Nah, Nathan and I are going to stay in. No partying for us. We have *muy importante* work to do. You know how it is."

That familiar desire to share everything about her work threat-ened to burst forth. Jordan desperately wanted to spin back around in her chair, sit her brother down, and tell him everything—to talk to him for hours about the fascinating artifacts she was helping find and the utterly crazy adventures she had—remotely—been a part of.

She knew she couldn't. She had promised Lucas.

"What a surprise," Gabe said as he made to leave, then turned to look back at her. His eyes narrowed. "If you're going to be living with me in my apartment, you could at least do me the favor of joining your wonderful brother on a night out every once in a while. Get out of your stinky-ass room occasionally. Smells like lizard shit and nerds in here. And here's a thought: maybe you could take all the dirty dishes in here out to the sink. Maybe even *wash* them."

"Soon," Jordan said without taking her eyes off her monitors to look back at him. "And my room doesn't smell. Girls don't stink." Nevertheless, she raised an arm and sniffed.

"Yeah, yeah, whatever you say," Gabe answered, pulling her bedroom door shut as he left.

The closing of the apartment's front door was the signal that it was safe for Jordan to get rid of the cat video and return to her work. The program had been successful.

"Well, Nathan." She placed the bearded dragon back on her desk. "We're in."

Nathan said nothing.

CHAPTER SEVEN

Wendig

Wendig's blue Toyota Camry pulled into the gravel parking lot of a three-story, red-brick building nestled in a remote wooded area, far from the prying eyes of the residents of Fulgent County. The lawn that surrounded the building sprawled out around the back and sides like an ocean of grass, green and expansive.

A few children, closely supervised by doctors and orderlies, dotted the scene, incongruous against the mostly uniform landscape. Wendig could sense all eyes turn to him as his car rolled past before they returned to whatever activity they had been engaged in.

"Were you able to do it?" Wendig asked, bringing the car to a halt and putting it into park.

"For shame, Lucas. Are you questioning my divine abilities?" Jordan's voice came through the cell phone, dripping with mock indignation. "Well, I never! Have you lost faith in the almighty Jordan? I am the goddess of digital forgery! I am the queen of—"

Wendig sighed. "A simple 'yes' or 'no' would do." He massaged the bridge of his nose.

"Yeah, yeah," Jordan answered with a laugh. "Your new credentials have been in their system since this morning. You shouldn't have any problems. At least, not from my end. It's all up to you and your acting skills now."

"Thank you, Jordan," Wendig said, a sense of partial relief washing over him. "I'll let you know how everything goes once I'm finished."

"Roger, roger. Good luck, Lucas," Jordan replied and hung up.

Wendig peered out through his windshield once more. A large wooden sign in front of the building identified the place as the Forestleaf Juvenile Behavioral Health Center, a mental health hospital that looked after and treated male patients under the age of eighteen. It looked like a nice place, surrounded by beautiful trees that sprouted up everywhere the lawn's vast reach ended, forming a barrier around the property. A large pond with a bubbling fountain shaped like a rearing horse directly in front of the pathway led to the solid oak doors of the entrance. Peaceful. Very peaceful.

I suppose that's the point, Wendig mused.

A new thought formed unbidden in his mind: Rowan being committed to a place like this. If she somehow ever returned, how scarred and traumatized would she be? Would she require help from a facility such as this one?

For a moment, closing his eyes, Wendig reviewed the grisly crime scene photos in his mind. If only he had the resources for a large team of investigators to scour the world. He was well-off enough to have a nice home in a nice neighborhood. He could afford what many people couldn't. And he was able to travel all over the world, bribe people when he needed to, pay Jordan well for her work. Still, it wasn't enough.

If only.

If only he had possessed the knowledge and skill that he had today back when Rowan had been taken from him.

Rowan...

His hands tightened their grip on the steering wheel. Wendig had never forgiven himself for bringing Rowan along with him on his hunts. He had been such an idiot back then. Nothing more than a glory-seeking treasure hunter. He and Rowan had worked so well together, though that didn't excuse the danger he had put his own daughter in.

The world faded from his consciousness as Wendig was mentally catapulted back to that awful day. The chill, musty ruins of that medieval cathedral. A cacophony of furious shouting, guns firing, stone walls cracking. Rowan reaching into the sarcophagus they had opened. Then there had been that horrible noise: a gut-wrenching clamor that had been seared into Wendig's mind like a brand—the sound of reality itself being torn open as something forced its way through the veil.

Then…nothing.

Whatever horror had been emerging from the sarcophagus had disappeared into thin air, taking Wendig's daughter along with it, as if neither had ever existed.

The event had crippled him for the better part of a year. After recovering back to a functional level, Wendig made a solemn promise to his daughter that he would never quit. Not only would he never give up on finding her, he would never stop hunting every Enigmata in the world to contain them. Every death and every irrevocably damaged life he prevented made each investigation worthwhile, despite the continuous danger to himself, both physically and mentally. Plus, there had to be some Enigmata out there that could help bring back Rowan.

Shutting the engine off, he finally let go of the steering wheel. Wendig thought about Rowan all the time. Despite his subsequent years of work and the vastly greater understanding he had acquired, he still hadn't figured out what, exactly, had happened on that day in the cathedral. All he knew was that the cathedral was gone, buried under tons of rock, and that something had taken Rowan from him. Wendig hated to admit it, but he sometimes preferred to think that his daughter had died. The thought that Rowan was at peace was better than the alternatives his imagination could conjure. Who knew *what* had been inside that sarcophagus?

With a sigh, he got out of the car, taking a moment to stretch and get his mind back in the game. Straightening out the suit he wore for such occasions, he listened to some birds in the tree above him for a moment, singing and chattering to each other, before he headed toward the building, the gravel crunching under each step. When he reached the heavy-looking double doors, he pressed the button on the intercom to their right.

"May I help you?" a polite voice crackled out of the speaker almost immediately.

"Dr. Luke Connor," Wendig replied. It was an alias he had used a few times before, but he still always felt weird when pretending to be someone he wasn't. Deceiving people wasn't something he derived any joy from. But in his line of work, tactical deceit was often essential. Wendig looked at the time on his cell phone. "I have an appointment with Dr. Sommers in five minutes," he said.

The door buzzed and clicked open after a few seconds, and Wendig walked inside. The interior was a mix of sterile, white hospital walls and furniture that looked to be from the Victorian era. A large foyer greeted him, with a high ceiling from which hung an iron chandelier. A double staircase curved upward on the right and left of the room, leading up to the second story. In front of him, a wide front desk was positioned in the middle of the floor, overseeing everyone who entered, and was currently staffed by a young woman with short blonde hair wearing teal scrubs.

She flashed a friendly smile at Wendig. "Hello, Dr. Connor, was it?" Her nametag read: "Carol."

"That's correct," he answered with a smile of his own.

"And you said you had an appointment with Dr. Sommers?" Carol asked, looking at her computer, clicking a few things then typing something.

"Right. My assistant called yesterday and spoke with Dr. Sommers directly."

"Yes, I see you here," Carol said, looking up from her computer screen. "Come on, I'll escort you to Dr. Sommers's office." She stood up, gesturing for Wendig to follow. "Sorry, can't have you walking around here by yourself. Not that any of the kids here are dangerous. We just can't have strangers just wandering about, for their safety. You understand."

"Of course." Wendig nodded as they climbed the left-side staircase, then turned down a hallway when they reached the top. They passed several unmarked rooms with closed doors. Through small windows set in the doors, Wendig could see a kid inside most of them, lying down or reading. One boy just stared at the bare wall, eyes glazed over and unblinking. A hollowness manifested in Wendig's chest, and he averted his eyes. The pair made their way through a recreational area where several boys played old board games or watched a television that was bolted high up on the wall. Animated superheroes were battling a hulking monstrosity on the dusty screen.

A brief memory swept through Wendig's consciousness: he and a ten-year-old Rowan watching cartoons on the couch and eating big bowls of Cinnamon Toast Crunch on a long-ago Saturday morning. The hollow feeling in his chest grew.

Wendig observed the kids watching the TV for a brief moment before stepping away. At last, at the end of a long hall, Carol brought him to an office door that stood ajar.

"Dr. Sommers?" Carol asked, knocking on the frosted glass that made up the upper half of the door. "Your three o'clock is here."

A woman in a white coat, about the same age as Wendig, with thick-framed glasses and wavy bronze hair that fell across her shoulders, pulled the door open for them. Carol took her leave as the woman invited Wendig inside a spacious office, the walls of which were lined with shelves of books ranging from the expected psychology textbooks to more colorful titles about dragons and spaceships.

"Dr. Amanda Sommers." The woman held out her hand. Her steel-blue eyes studied Wendig's face as if trying to quickly determine his character.

"Dr. Luke Connor," he responded, shaking her hand, finding her grip firm and authoritative. "It's a pleasure to meet you."

Dr. Sommers invited Wendig to sit in a leather chair. She seated herself back behind her large mahogany desk, which was cluttered with dozens of folders, each crammed with documents. "So, you're the one I received the call about yesterday. I talked with your assistant, a Miss..." She looked at a sticky note stuck to her computer monitor. "...Ellen Ripley, I believe it was."

Oh hell, Jordan, Wendig thought, trying to keep his expression nonchalant. *You couldn't have picked another damn name? I swear to God.*

"She said," Dr. Sommers continued, unconcerned, "that you would be stopping by today to speak with one of my patients." She paused. "So, tell me. Who exactly are you, Dr. Connor? What's your field? And why do you wish to speak with Caleb Rivas?"

Wendig looked into the doctor's eyes. He hadn't been expecting the doctor to be so aggressively blunt. He composed himself. "I'm a psychologist, and I'm investigating the events Caleb Rivas was involved in a couple of months ago."

"I see," Dr. Sommers said. "Are you some doctor friend of the family who doesn't think the police or I am doing a good enough job? Or are you some sort of private investigator?"

"Something like that. To the second question." Wendig gazed at her with dark, unblinking eyes. "I investigate special cases like Caleb's. Mr. Rivas hired me. I'm afraid that's all I can tell you."

"Very well," Dr. Sommers said after a long moment of silent staring that made Wendig think she wouldn't buy it. "I did receive a fax this morning with written consent from Caleb's father allowing you to talk with his son. Although I'm not very fond of being kept in the dark regarding why you're here, I won't go against Mr. Rivas's wishes." She paused, tapping a pen on her desk. "And truthfully, just between you and me, I'm sort of glad you've come. I would be interested in what another doctor has to say. Also..." She paused again. "Can I be frank with you, Dr. Connor?"

"Of course," Wendig said.

"You see, Caleb doesn't get many visitors. Or, I should say, any visitors. It's unfortunate. Sad, really. The first week he was here, both his parents came to visit him almost every day. In the last month and a half, though, I've only seen them visit him two or three times. To be honest, I think they're afraid of Caleb."

"Afraid of him?" Wendig asked, concern furrowing his brow. "Afraid of him in what way?"

"Obviously, having a child put into a mental health care facility is not a happy thing to happen to any family," Dr. Sommers explained. "And, as ridiculous as it sounds, I think people in general have an innate fear of 'madness,' as if they can be somehow infected by it just by being in proximity to an individual with a mental illness or who is experiencing mental trauma. People are afraid of what a layman would refer to as a 'crazy person,' even if that person is part of their own family." She sighed. "Anyway, I'm sure you know all this already. Sorry, I sometimes ramble on, even to other doctors." She shook her head. "From what I've observed on those occasions when Caleb's parents have come to visit, they've been distant. It's almost like they expect their son to suddenly jump up and attack them."

"Caleb's parents don't think he had anything to do with Evan's death, do they?" Wendig asked. *How could you fear someone you loved?* he asked himself. It was difficult for him to imagine it. He could never have feared Rowan under any circumstances, could he? The very notion appalled him.

"It was certainly suspected in the beginning," Dr. Sommers answered, leaning back in her chair and steepling her fingers. "I assume you've read all the reports?" She stared at him as if he should already know this, then continued. "The police eventually ruled him out since it was beyond Caleb's strength to pin his poor friend to the wall like that."

Wendig nodded, those awful crime scene photos flashing through his mind's eye.

"I think his parents still suspect that he had *something* to do with it," Dr. Sommers continued. "According to what I was told, those boys used to be inseparable. They'd been friends practically since the day they were born. The best of buddies. Caleb was with Evan the day before Evan's body was discovered."

"Terrible," was all Wendig could say. "Suspecting your own kid of something like that. Just awful."

"It is," Dr. Sommers agreed. "After many sessions with Caleb, I'm positive he had nothing to do with what happened. Although, as to who did commit that crime, I can't even fathom a guess. Caleb did have a wild story at first, but I believe that was his own subconscious trying to deal with what he witnessed in that room."

"Mr. Rivas sent me a copy of all the police and psychological reports he could acquire. I read Caleb's story." Wendig shook his head. "That poor boy."

They both sat in silence for a moment, the grisly photos once again running through Wendig's mind like some horrible slideshow.

"Caleb should be done with his group session," Dr. Sommers finally said, checking her watch. "I can take you to meet him now."

She led Wendig out of her office, through several long hallways, and into a large, sparsely furnished room with half a dozen folding chairs set up in a rough circle. Several boys were leaving as the pair walked in. Dr. Sommers nodded to the staff member who had just finished conducting the session, then walked over to a short, slim boy of about twelve or thirteen years, with brown, tousled hair and dark circles under his eyes that stood out sharply against his ashen complexion.

"Hello, Caleb," Dr. Sommers said to the boy in a friendly tone, bending down to be at his eye level. "This here is Dr. Connor. He's come to talk with you, if you're up for it. He just wants to ask you some questions. If you're uncomfortable, you can stop at any time. Okay? Do you feel like chatting with him?"

"Sure," Caleb said in an emotionless voice and shrugged his shoulders. He sat back down in one of the chairs. Wendig pulled a seat over so he could sit in front of the boy.

"I'll just be over here if you need me," Dr. Sommers told Caleb with a wink, then glanced briefly at Wendig.

"Thank you," Wendig replied as Dr. Sommers went to stand by the door. He then realized the doctor had been talking to Caleb.

"Hi, Caleb." Wendig turned back to the boy. "My name is Dr. Luke Connor. You can just call me Luke."

"Hey," Caleb replied. The poor boy had a haunted, dull look in his brown eyes. The youthful spark that Wendig believed all kids should have was just not there in the kid's flat gaze.

"How are you doing today?" Wendig asked in a casual voice, trying to get the boy to relax.

"Tired," he said.

"Not sleeping well?" Wendig asked. He stared at those dark circles under the boy's eyes.

Caleb shook his head. "No," he answered. "I haven't slept good since…since Evan…since he…since the Watcher." He looked away as if he had said too much or had said something wrong. One hand grasped the other, wringing it.

"I see." Wendig made mental notes. He couldn't press the boy too hard too quickly. "I'm sorry for everything that you've had to go through recently. I can't even imagine what—"

"Do you work for the police?" Caleb interrupted, looking back at Wendig.

"No," Wendig answered. He decided to be as honest as he safely could with the boy. That might get him to trust Wendig more. "No, I don't work for the police. But I do investigate things. Things that aren't normal and are hard to explain."

Caleb stared down at his slippered feet and didn't say anything. Wendig would have liked to have known what was going through the boy's head at that moment. He cleared his throat and inched his chair closer to Caleb.

"Can you tell me about this Watcher you just mentioned?" Wendig said in a voice not so low as to be a whisper, but not loud enough that Dr. Sommers would likely overhear. "I'd like to hear more about it. Is it a person?"

Caleb raised his head slowly, inch by inch, until his dull eyes looked straight into Wendig's. "It's not real," the boy said. "Dr. Sommers said it was all in my head. My mind concocted a monster to help me deal with Evan's death." This recitation of words certainly sounded like something that would come out of a doctor's mouth. "There is no Watcher, and there never was. The only monsters are the ones that live inside you. In your imagination." He placed a finger on his skull and gave it three slow taps.

How I wish that were true, Wendig thought.

"I believe you told the police you saw this Watcher even before Evan was...before what happened to him. Isn't that right?" Wendig waited patiently until Caleb nodded his head before continuing. "Tell me the truth, Caleb. Don't worry, you can trust me. Do you believe this thing was really all in your head?" When Caleb remained quiet, Wendig leaned in closer. "I've seen things too. Things that no one else would believe if I tried to tell them. I've seen things that other people only see in nightmares. They're real, and I try to stop them."

Caleb hesitated, then looked over his shoulder at Dr. Sommers, who was chatting with the group session counselor. "It wasn't my imagination," the boy whispered, looking back at Wendig. "I know what I saw. That thing came to kill Evan because he took something from that cave we found."

"I know this might be difficult." Wendig's blood throbbed in his ears at the kid's answer. "But it would really help my investigation if you could tell me the whole story. Tell me what really happened. I'll believe you. I promise."

Caleb said nothing, his hands wringing themselves again in his lap.

"Please," Wendig said. "If I can put a stop to whatever you saw, it will prevent more people, other kids, suffering like Evan did."

Caleb looked Wendig in the eyes for a long moment. "Okay," he finally whispered.

"Thank you." He took out a notepad and pen. "Take your time, and go back to just before anything strange happened."

"We live in Shadow's Path," Caleb began, gesturing vaguely to his right. "Evan lived next door to me all my life. He was my best friend." He paused, as if to arrange his thoughts. "So, Evan came over one morning and told me he'd found something out in the woods. He wouldn't tell me what it was because he liked to surprise me. Our houses were close to where the woods start, so we used to go over there and explore a lot. Sometimes Evan went by himself since he was always hunting for, like, weird stuff. Cool rocks, animal bones, things like that. That day, he took me to an area I'd never been to before. It was pretty far in the woods. We eventually came to a hole."

"A hole?" Wendig repeated, taking notes. He was eager to know where the story was going but was determined to let Caleb tell it at his own pace.

"Yeah. Just like a small opening at the foot of a hill, all blocked up with rocks and stuff. And sticking out between the rocks was a hand." He gulped. "A dead hand." The last part came out in a near whisper. The memory must have still frightened Caleb greatly.

"Did you tell anybody about the hand?" Wendig asked when the boy remained silent.

Caleb shook his head. "No. I was scared, but Evan said we should move all the rocks so we could uncover the body that the hand was attached to. Evan said he wanted to see what a real dead body looked like. I didn't even want to touch any of those rocks at first. Evan kept begging me and was already moving stuff, so I ended up helping him. I didn't want him to know I was really scared. It took us hours to move enough rocks so that we could see inside. There was a tunnel that led inside, under the hill."

"And was the hand attached to anything?"

"Yeah." Caleb nodded. He took a deep breath before continuing. "The rest of the body was inside the hole, under the rocks. It was some dead guy. I don't know who. The dead guy looked so weird. He was squished and broken, but there was something else. It was like he wasn't real. He didn't look like what I thought a dead person would look like. You know, like from TV and movies and stuff. I remember thinking that his skin looked weird. Or maybe he was just too rotted. I don't know."

Caleb went silent for a moment.

Strange, Wendig thought. There hadn't been any mention of this corpse in any of the documents Jordan had sent over to him. Did the police ever find out about an unidentified body in the woods? Or had something happened to it?

"Anyway," Caleb started up again, "Evan wanted to see what was at the other end of the tunnel. I kinda did too, even if I was really scared. He'd brought a flashlight, so after we looked at the dead body for a while, we went deeper inside. I remember it getting colder and colder the longer we walked. And we walked for a long time. Then we found a big room at the end of the tunnel."

"A room?" Wendig continued scribbling notes. "What kind of room? You mean like a cave?"

"No, caves are natural," Caleb replied. "Someone had definitely *made* this room because it was very round, and the walls were all really smooth. Anyway, the walls had paintings on them. I remember we watched this video in school once about this cave in Italy called Mug…Mug…something."

"Magura Cave?" offered Wendig.

"I think so, yeah. It has these paintings in it. You know what I mean? Like stick-figure type drawings? Well, the drawings in the room we found under that hill reminded me of those from the video. Sort of a different style, but kinda similar though. But the art we saw…they weren't paintings of animals or people."

"What were they of?" Wendig asked.

Caleb bit his bottom lip. "Monsters."

The word hung in the air for a minute, harsh against Wendig's ears. He suppressed a shudder. "Can you tell me more about the room?"

"There were shelves along the walls too. They were covered in these metal…tools, I guess. I don't really know what they were. Kinda looked like the knives and things you'd see a surgeon use on TV. These ones were really rusty and old looking, though. Like maybe they were what was invented way before the tools doctors use today."

In his notebook, Wendig wrote, *possible Relic Enigmata?*

"And then there was this big thing made of rock in the middle of the room that Evan said must be an altar. My grandma took me to church a couple times. The altar there didn't look anything like the one in that room, but Evan insisted it had to be an altar. He knew more about that kinda stuff than I did. He liked to read about it on the internet. On top of the rock altar was some thingy."

Wendig's ears pricked up at this, and he felt a flutter in his chest. An object on an altar in the middle of an underground chamber really sounded like an Enigmata. He needed more information.

"What was this 'thingy'?" he asked, careful not to let his eagerness color his voice.

"I'm not really sure. It was like some sort of metal disc thing, like a small frisbee or something. It was, like, perfectly smooth if you looked at it one way. Then if you looked at it from a different angle, you could see that it had a bunch of lines and symbols carved into it, real faintly. It maybe looked like it could be a puzzle or something. I just remember Evan being really interested in it. Almost hypnotized by it."

"I see." Wendig wrote down more notes. "Go on, Caleb. What else do you remember?"

"Evan and I went back home after that. I didn't say anything to my parents about the dead body. I was scared about getting in trouble. Evan didn't say anything to his parents either. I didn't sleep good, though. I kept thinking about the dead man. The next day, I went over to Evan's house. His mom let me in. She said Evan wasn't feeling good. I went upstairs to his room, and he was just laying in bed. Told me he didn't get any sleep and that he shouldn't have brought it home with him. He pointed to his desk, and I saw the disc-thing from the underground room. It made me nervous. I asked him why he took it, but he didn't answer. He just started mumbling about something with yellow eyes watching him through his bedroom window all night, and that's why he couldn't sleep. It went on for a few days. Every time I went over, Evan looked worse. You could tell he wasn't sleeping good at all. His parents took him to doctors and stuff. I don't know what the doctors said. All I know is that he kept looking worse and worse, and he kept talking about the Watcher when I would go over."

Wendig scribbled in his notepad: *Watcher? Could this be a bonded pair of Enigmata? An object and an entity?* He had dealt with such things before. He recalled a djinn imprisoned in a stone statue that had nearly killed him years ago.

Caleb swallowed. "One night—I don't remember exactly how long it was after we went in that cave—I was in bed, and it was really windy. I thought I heard someone talking outside. I kept telling myself it was only the wind, but it kept getting louder. I don't know how my parents didn't hear it. I finally had to get up and look. I had to. My bedroom window faces Evan's room next door. We're both on the second floor. I saw his bedroom light on, and he was standing at his window. I could tell he was really scared. I waved at him and was going to get my phone to text him, but then I saw what was stuck to the outside of his house, and I knew why he was so scared. It made me scared too. There was some light from the streetlamps, and I could see there was this person on the wall right above his window." A pause. "No, not a person. It was shaped sorta like a person, but it was just…wrong. Its skin looked pure black—not black like yours, but coal black. Middle of the night, room with no lights on black. And it had pieces of rags or something hanging from its arms and legs. I'm glad it was so dark so I couldn't see all of it. It was sticking like a spider to the outside wall of Evan's house, staring in at him.

"And then it looked over at me."

Caleb wrapped his arms around himself as if he were cold. When he continued, his voice was just above a whisper.

"I don't know how it knew I was there. It twisted its neck so that it could look at me with its yellow eyes. And it smiled. I dropped down to the floor under the window and waited there for what felt like hours. It was probably only a couple of minutes. When I looked back up, the light was off in Evan's window, and I couldn't see anybody. I ran to bed and hid under the blankets for the rest of the night. It was hot and hard to breathe, but I was too scared to take the covers off."

Wendig cleared his throat. This was quite a story. "And the next morning was when you…" He let the question drift off.

Caleb nodded. "I woke up, so I must have fallen asleep at some point, right? I woke up to a lot of shouting and sirens. I remember not even being drowsy. I jumped out of bed and had the worst feeling in the pit of my stomach. I just ran outside, following all the noise. Next door, I saw Evan's mom crying in their front yard, and Evan's dad was crying too. There were lots of police and neighbors standing around."

Wendig nodded grimly. Picturing the crime scene photos again, he could imagine the police presence that would have showed up at Evan's house. Awful questions flitted through his mind. Who had discovered the boy's mutilated body? His mom or his dad? Which one of them had called 911? How had the poor parent even described the situation to the emergency operator?

Caleb continued on, his eyes misty. "I ran into Evan's house. I didn't think about going in there, my body just did it. I got past a policeman at the door and got up the stairs into Evan's room."

Tears began slipping down Caleb's face. Wendig put what he hoped was a comforting hand on the kid's shoulder.

"So much blood everywhere," Caleb said in a hoarse whisper. "It was all sticky under my feet. I saw Evan stuck on the wall. And his face—"

"You don't have to talk about that part," Wendig interrupted. There was no way he wanted to make this kid relive any part of this. However, if the information could help him find the Enigmata and put a stop to whatever evil it had unleashed, then it would have been worth it.

"That metal disc from the cave was still on Evan's desk when I went up there that day," Caleb said. "I don't know why, but I took it before the police came in and made me go outside. It was so crazy, they didn't even notice what I was holding." He met Wendig's eyes. "I don't know why I took it. I just felt that I should keep it. Now I don't think that I should have."

"And why is that? Did something else happen?" Wendig asked. It took him a moment to realize how softly he was speaking now as well.

"Ever since..." Caleb started. His eyes were red and he chewed his lip. "Ever since I touched it, I've felt strange. And..."

"And what, Caleb?"

"And ever since then, I've seen Evan," Caleb choked out. Tears flowed freely down his cheeks. "I see him every night."

"Is that why you're not sleeping well?" Wendig asked. "Do you keep having dreams of that day? Nightmares where you see Evan? You know none of this is your fault. You did nothing wrong. And you—"

"They're not nightmares," Caleb interrupted with a whimper, wiping at the tears on his face. "I see the Watcher every night. He watches me through my room's window and smiles. He…"

Terror welled up in his eyes.

"He wears pieces of Evan's skin like a costume."

Message (papyrus)

Written by a citizen of the Kingdom of Aksum to her brother (names unknown)

Date: Approx. 400 CE

Translated from Ge'ez to English by Dr. Negasi Kiros

Brother,

As you may have gathered from our previous exchanges, my marriage [TEXT ILLEGIBLE] *... Jahi has finally returned from across the sea from the Kingdom of Saba. As you know, he has become quite a successful merchant, trading in all manner of spices. Our first year together as husband and wife has been a joyous time. I could not have asked for a better life full of happiness. I felt truly blessed. But Jahi's return from his travels has changed all of that, and as much as I hesitate to write this down, I fear for my life. I am not sure what to do. He* [TEAR IN PAPYRUS] *...*

*...the man who returned is not the same man who left. Jahi never speaks to me any more except in short, whispered commands when he wants me to do some chore or to fetch him something. The sound of my own husband's voice chills me to my very spirit. He stays out all night, doing what, I cannot begin to fathom. There have been reports of attacks recently. I dare not think Jahi has anything to do with such things. I cannot believe such a thing. The man I married was of the sweetest kind. I just... * [TEXT ILLEGIBLE]

...and the most curious, and perhaps most frightening, habit he has adopted, is his constant insistence of wearing a thick veil around his face, as if to shield his eyes from my view so that I may not see them. I do not know how he can see through that cloth. The servants are afraid of him now. I must

admit that I am afraid of him as well, though it pains me to think such things, let alone write them down.

I wish to look upon the gentle eyes of my husband again.

It is as if something else has replaced my Jahi. I know my words sound mad, though if you were here to see him, we would be of the same mind. Tonight, while he slumbers, I will try to peek under his face-cloth. I haven't dared do such a thing yet. But I must see them. I must confirm they are the same eyes I know. I confess, however, that I fear what I may discover under that cloth. If only I could [REST OF PAPYRUS LOST]

CHAPTER EIGHT

October

The itsy bitsy 'tober crawled down into the cave.
Down came death to send her to her grave
Out came the screams, and the shrieks, and the howls
Her blood painted the floor as she was disemboweled.

Shut up, shut up, shut up! October screamed at the other voice in her head.

What? Are you not enjoying my rhymes?

"Come on, people." A stern voice rang out in the cave, bouncing off the walls.

October opened her eyes to the dim light. The mind-clearing breathing exercises that she had learned from a YouTube yogi had obviously been unsuccessful. Her mind was still a storm of screams, fear, and nightmarish images.

And the Overshadow.

You pathetic excuse for a human being, the Overshadow hissed in her ear with its fetid, greasy voice. *You're going to die. You're going to suffer. You're going to rot in here for all eternity.*

As October focused, she attempted to push the vile words from her mind. Slowly, everything came into view around her. They were all still trapped in the cave.

This is going to be your tomb. The Overshadow wouldn't shut up. *This is a coffin of rock, and you are the corpse that will lie in it until your very essence is nothing but dust and forgotten memories.*

October bit her lip.

Why? Why did she have to forget her meds and allow the Overshadow to awaken now of all days? No, that wasn't right. She didn't forget. The meds *had* been with her in her pouch. She distinctly remembered putting the pill case in there. Something wasn't right.

That didn't matter at the moment, however. The Overshadow was here. Refreshed and raring to go; eager to resume its mission of ruining October's life.

Worthless. Your corpse is going to be food for the insects that crawl in this place.

"People, people," Viorica was saying. She pulled Samira to her feet. "Get off your asses. I have an important thing to show you."

October shook her head and gritted her teeth, trying to tune out the Overshadow. She watched as Bryan suddenly bounced up like a springboard. It seemed he had actually fallen asleep.

"What?" he shouted, looking around like a cornered mouse. "What's going on? Is it the bear? It got inside!"

"Nu, the bear did not get inside," Viorica reassured him. She pulled October to her feet. Once everyone was standing up, she continued. "Everyone, come with me. I have found something good."

Taking a deep breath, October walked with the others as they all followed Viorica. She led them toward a far dark corner of the cave where the dim flickering light of the dusty lightbulbs overhead didn't reach.

"What did you find?" Noel asked, looking at the rocky wall with curiosity. "I don't see anything."

"Do you feel that?" Viorica asked, looking from one person to another in expectation. She held out a hand a few inches in front of the wall.

They all stood silent for a few moments trying to discern her meaning. It was then that October did feel something. Something moving across her cheek like a whisper.

"I feel a breeze." October lifted her hand in front of her face. Yes, she definitely felt the soft tickle of a cool draft coming from the wall.

"Da, I felt it as well," Viorica said. "I've been studying the paintings for some hours while you people sat around. Very interesting artwork. But that is beside my point. When I stood over here, I felt a cold wind very soft on my skin." She produced a heavy-duty flashlight, shining its beam onto the granite wall. In between two drawings of wolves, a large crack, about three inches wide, ran deep into the rock.

October peered into the small, stony aperture. She couldn't see anything, only pitch blackness. A twitching sensation ran through her body at the sudden nightmare image of cave bugs squeezing out of there and leaping onto her eyeball. She quickly pulled back. The gouge in the wall exhaled cool air that carried an earthy scent. A draft coming out of this rocky wall meant one thing.

"Are you saying that there's a way out behind here?" October asked, pointing at the crack. A warm hope rose in her chest.

No hope. Only despair, the Overshadow said. *You really think you're going to escape? Don't be even more fucking stupid than you already are on a day-to-day basis.*

"Da, very likely." Viorica rubbed her chin, smudging some dirt on her jaw.

"A way out?" Bryan piped up, his eyes staring at the wall as if trying to bore through the rock with sight alone. "Well, hell yeah! Let's knock this down right now!"

"And how exactly do you expect us to do that?" Noel asked. "We have no idea how sturdy that wall is. What if knocking it down brings the whole cave down on us? And do you happen to have a pickaxe in your pocket, or do you plan to go at it with your fingernails?"

"Please don't talk about cave-ins," October pleaded in a whisper. An image of them all trapped under tons of rock and boulders flashed through her mind. She could almost feel all that weight pressing against her, smothering her, each inhalation causing the constricting debris to crush her more and more, little by little, until she couldn't even draw an ounce of breath into her chest. Nausea roiled in her stomach at the thought.

Squeeze, squeeze, the Overshadow hissed. *All the air will be pushed out of your lungs. You won't be able to breathe. You'll suffocate. And your blue, oxygen-deprived carcass will never be found.*

Shut up! October bellowed inside her head.

"Hey, I'm just trying to get out of here!" Bryan spat, rounding on Noel, his hands clenching into fists. "Step off!"

As the two continued arguing, October watched Viorica take a step back, lift a booted foot, and thrust her heel into the wall. She must have thought the wall to be thicker than it actually was, because she emitted a startled grunt as her foot sank through the wall with ease, causing a large vertical section to come crumbling down, revealing a low narrow passageway on the other side. October hoped no one had heard the involuntary squeak she had let out as she waited for the cave ceiling to come crashing down. Everyone stood there in stunned silence as the dust settled and the last bits of debris clattered onto the floor.

"Shit!" October exclaimed when her voice deigned to return. A brief blaze of anger flitted through her. They could've all just died. But they hadn't, and now a potential exit from this nightmare presented itself. Getting a hold of herself, October stared at the hole Viorica had opened with a single kick. That must have taken some strength. *Okay, okay, I really need to hit the gym when I get back home,* she mused, trying to focus on thoughts other than those of being crushed to death. *Pack on a little muscle. Not get winded on a damn nature walk. Yeah, let's do that. That'd be nice. Yeah.*

"Wow, how did you do that?" Arthur asked Viorica with wide eyes, as if he had never seen anything so amazing.

"That was some kick," Bernadette said.

"You certainly have some, uh, powerful legs," Arthur said. He seemed to instantly regret his own comment and began to turn red. "I mean, uh—"

"Shall we go through?" Viorica's jaw clenched as she shone her flashlight into the darkness beyond. "If we're all finally done chatting away, that is. We can't stay here in this cave forever. This might be our only chance. Unless you want to go back out the front, although I am sure the bear is still out there somewhere."

"Is there really no other way out of here?" Samira asked, trying to get a good look into the tunnel beyond the wall that led off into unknowable darkness. The draft was stronger now, and cooler, as if it came from deep within the earth instead of from the outside world.

"The only exit I know of is the way we came in," Adrianna said, eyeing the tunnel nervously. "I have no idea where this could lead to. I didn't even know the cave extended beyond this one chamber. Who knows where this system will go? I mean...maybe ...maybe it goes nowhere?" She paused. "Well, actually if there's a draft coming out of it, there has to be an exit somewhere. That makes sense, right? Right?" The expression on her face was one of internal conflict and fear. "Under normal circumstances, I would never, ever, recommend going into an unmapped cave system. In fact, I would explicitly advise against it. But we can't contact anyone from here, and that bear's still out there. And it's gotten our scent and a taste for blood. I... I don't really see any alternative." She took a shuddering breath and clutched the sides of her head. "Don't listen to me. I don't know what I'm doing."

She looked like she might start crying again. October felt bad for the poor girl, wishing she could comfort her in some way.

A sudden metallic shriek made them all jump, the noise echoing down to them from the cave entrance.

Noel slipped away, then came jogging back a few moments later. "The bear's almost through the gate!" he whispered in an urgent voice. "It pulled the bolts about halfway out of the rock already."

"Oh, jeez," Adrianna whimpered. Her whole body shivered. "I hope Phil will notify the police if we don't show up at the pickup spot on time. He'll do that, right?" She looked around the group for reassurance. "I mean, that's what people do when someone doesn't show up. Yeah, Phil will call the cops to come look for us. He'll do that." She answered herself, nodding.

"I don't know about this." October mumbled as she contemplated at how low and claustrophobic the tunnel appeared. She couldn't see past the first couple of feet due to a darkness so thick it seemed they might have to somehow break through that as well. The thought of Chris and of cave-ins flashed in her mind once again, and she began to feel as if she were in a straightjacket, arms pinned around her, the thick material constricting her chest, making it hard to inhale air into her lungs. "I have to admit, I'm not super comfortable when it comes to small, confined spaces like caves. And this looks even smaller and more confined."

A serpent of rock and darkness constricting, forcing out the oxygen from your weak lungs, the life from your flesh. Your defiled body will decorate this tomb until the years wear you down to nothing but a few slivers of bone and regret.

Shut the fuck up, October growled inside her head.

"Don't be such a wimp," Bryan said, a smirk on his face. "It's easy, see?" Without another word, he got onto his hands and knees and crawled into the opening, using his phone's flashlight to make his way.

"Bryan, wait!" his mother cried out. Obvious fear welled up alongside the tears in her eyes.

"He'll be alright, Bernie." Arthur put his uninjured arm around his wife. "It's just a tunnel. Let him be brave."

"You're right," she said in an exhausted tone, leaning into Arthur. "I just worry about him sometimes."

They all listened to Bryan shuffling along through the tunnel, the light from his cell phone flashing back out occasionally as if he were checking his progress from the entrance. After a few long minutes, Bryan called back to them.

"I'm on the other side of the narrow part." His voice floated back to them in triumph. "The tunnel is pretty straight and opens up much more over here. I can stand up all right. Uh, let's see. There are a couple of branching passages that I can make out. I can feel a stronger draft coming out from one of them. I'm going to go scout ahead down that one to see if I can find anything."

No one else made a move toward the tunnel.

"Well, I guess we should try this," Adrianna whispered after a protracted silence. She stood there a second, like she was hyping herself up, then unshouldered her pack and threw it into the tunnel, crawling in after it on her hands and knees. She was directly followed by Samira and Noel.

"Okay, your turn," Viorica said to October. "Are you ready?"

"I…" was all October could say before her voice seemed to desert her. The tunnel looked so tiny. There was no way she could fit through there. *Noel did,* she told herself. *And he's twice your freaking size. Just do it.* Still, she could get stuck halfway through and asphyxiate. What if there was an earthquake and the thing collapsed on top of her, crushing her to death? What if—

What if you end up trapped like that soccer team in Thailand? the Overshadow asked, the words implanting their festering seeds inside the folds of October's brain. *What if you end up like those miners in Chile?*

Those groups both made it out!

Not by themselves. You think anyone would mount a rescue party for you? Please. Who would care?

"I can't. I-I can't do it." October croaked out. She started to hyperventilate and put her hands on her knees to try to take in oxygen with short, rapid breaths. It wasn't working.

Ever heard of John Edward Jones and Nutty Putty Cave? Wedged head-first into a fissure and unable to turn around. Just awful, don't you think?

"Hey, hey." Arthur patted October on the back, distracting her from the voice. "Just breathe, just breathe. Nice and easy. Need a puff from my inhaler?" He chuckled, but not unkindly. "Bernie's a bit claustrophobic herself. Isn't that right?" He unhooked his fanny pack from around his large belly, his wife wordlessly taking the item out of his hand as she nodded. "We've been in caves before in our travels. It's always helped Bernie to watch me go first." He patted his stomach with a grin. "Because if a big guy like me can make it through, then *she* can definitely make it through. And if she can, then you can. Am I right? You'll see that you'll have no trouble at all."

Her throat was too tight to allow words to pass through, so October nodded in response as she tried to calm her breathing.

"Okay then," Arthur said. He got on all fours, wincing as he put pressure on the arm that had been clawed, then flat on his belly, stuffing himself into the tunnel, slowly pushing and pulling himself along. It was a tighter squeeze for him than it had been for the others, but he seemed to be making it through just fine, until they heard him grunt. "Just a little hitch. I'm okay. Keep on coming down!"

Arthur's last word echoed out of the tunnel and throughout the cavern, bouncing off the granite walls and roof. Viorica opened her mouth to say something, but before she could, a loud crash ricocheted from around the cave's bend, coming from the entrance.

There was no mistaking what that sound had been.

"Was that the gate?" Bernadette whispered, the words coming out in a sort of gasp. "Oh God."

"Futu-i!" Viorica hissed to herself. "Let's go." She grabbed October's clammy hand. There was a forced calmness in the woman's voice.

"Listen, October," Bernadette said. "Viorica will go in first, you follow her and stick close to her. She'll lead you through. I'll go in last and be right behind you. I… I'm not great with tight spaces either. But we can do this. Everyone's waiting for us on the other side."

Trapped like a rabbit, the Overshadow said with glee. *Now let that animal tear into your body with its teeth and claws so that it can put you out of your misery once and for all, you worthless cow. You're slowing them all down. You're going to get them all killed.*

No, fuck off! October shouted internally.

"Okay," she said, a bit too loudly. With massive effort of will, she followed Viorica, scrambling into the tunnel after her. The rough floor scratched at her palms, but October hardly noticed. She tried not to think of what she was doing or what was behind them. She just had to get to the other side.

"Come on!" Viorica hissed back at Bernadette.

"I'm coming!" Bernadette yelled and it sounded like she practically threw herself into the tunnel. "Oh God! Oh God!"

Continuing forward took all the resolve and fortitude that October could muster. She kept forcing herself forward, deeper into that stone passageway, not paying attention to whatever poison the Overshadow was pouring into her mind's ear. She hit her head painfully on the tunnel's roof several times, but fear kept her moving through the darkness. Suddenly, her face collided with Viorica's backside.

"Wh-why did you stop?" October asked, her words frantic. She brought out her phone and turned on its light to see what was happening.

"Futu-ti ceapa matii!" Viorica growled. October could see her trying to dislodge the man blocking the tunnel. "Arthur's stuck! Come on, suck it in, pulete!"

"I'm trying!" Arthur's muffled voice bellowed.

"No, this can't be happening. This can't be happening." October bit the inside of her cheek so hard she tasted blood.

I've missed watching you suffer.

"Leave. Me. Alone!" she hissed.

"Keep moving!" Bernadette implored from behind October. "What's happening? Don't stop now!" There was a pause in Bernadette's pleadings, followed by a sharp intake of breath. Then, "Oh no…"

Those two words sent a chill down October's spine. She twisted her body to look behind her, shining her phone's light. A dreadful sight greeted her. Bernadette hadn't removed her blue fanny pack, and the thing seemed to have caught itself on something as she had crawled into the tunnel.

"I'm fine, I'm fine!" Bernadette shouted when she noticed October's light in her face. She tried to dislodge the fanny pack's strap that was stuck on an outcrop of protruding rock. "Keep going. I'm right behind you. Keep going!" The ever-rising panic was evident in her voice.

Time seemed to slow as more and more terror pumped through October's veins.

You took advantage of this woman's kindness, the Overshadow said. *Because of you, she went in last. Now she'll probably die because of it. Shame. Real shame.*

No, October couldn't let this happen. She couldn't just leave Bernadette behind to struggle by herself. The woman had made October go in before her. And there had already been one death today. October couldn't endure seeing yet another heroic person being left to perish.

Despite her own overwhelming panic and fear, October managed to twist and contort herself enough so that she could turn around and crawl back to Bernadette.

"What are you doing, honey?" Bernadette squeaked. "Go out the other way!"

"We're not leaving you behind," October told the other woman. She could see the fanny pack's buckle on Bernadette's waist, but couldn't reach it due to the tight confines of the tunnel. "Bernadette, the buckle is on your left side. Keep reaching." She kept her light as steady as she could and watched the woman's fingers probe for it. "Just a little farther. You got this. Almost. Yeah, it's right there!"

Bernadette's fingers found the buckle and fumbled with it, trying to unclip the pack from her waist. There was a click and the pack finally dropped off her waist. "I got it! October, keep—"

Bernadette's words were cut off and immediately replaced by a harsh wheeze, her mouth opening so wide, October thought it might unhinge. A sickening crunch met October's ears, and Bernadette let loose a throat-rending scream before coughing up thick, viscous blood onto the floor. The woman was jerked backward like a rag doll.

"No!" October shrieked. She flung herself forward and grabbed Bernadette's arms. The wind was knocked out of her as she fell flat on the ground, but she clung to Bernadette's wrists with all her strength. "No! No! No!" October shrieked.

"October, we are clear forward!" Viorica shouted from somewhere behind her.

What the hell is this? Bravery? Just let go of her. Why are you holding on? Don't you want to save your own worthless life?

"God dammit, shut up!" October yelled as Bernadette's sweaty skin slipped ever so slowly from her grasp. The poor woman continued to scream in terror and agony as she and October were pulled along toward the tunnel's entrance. October dug the toes of her boots into the ground, but the floor was too solid and smooth. She couldn't gain any traction.

A pair of hands wrapped around October's ankles. It had to be Viorica.

"I won't let go," October said to Bernadette. *Don't do this. Don't fucking do this.* October didn't know who she was pleading with. God? The bear? The uncaring universe?

Bernadette said nothing. Her tear-filled eyes locked with October's. The woman's blood-stained mouth opened as if to speak. "Bry —" she managed before her voice faded into a rasp. Bernadette's eyes lost focus, her head falling to the floor with a thud.

With a vicious strength, Bernadette's body was dragged backward, all the way out of the tunnel, her limp hands ripping free of October's grip.

The next few moments were a blur. October was only vaguely aware of Viorica awkwardly turning her around and pulling her along into the depths of the lightless passageway. The tunnel seemed to go on forever. October wasn't sure if she was actually crawling or just being dragged.

She couldn't help but take one last look behind her.

Bernadette's head rested on the ground at the mouth of the tunnel. She looked wrong somehow.

Of course she looks wrong! October screamed inside her own head. Or was it the Overshadow yelling? *She was just mauled to death! Killed! Murdered! You let go of her! You let her get dragged away!*

You let her die.

Bernadette's slack face watched with lifeless eyes as October was forced to leave her behind.

CHAPTER NINE

October

W
h...where's Bernie?" Arthur asked as Viorica and October emerged from the other side of the tunnel into a bigger passageway where the others waited.

Everyone turned on their phone's light while Adrianna brought out a flashlight.

Even in the scattered illumination, October could see Arthur's stricken face was drained of all color. "Those screams," he went on. "What happened? Tell me what happened!"

Viorica stood up, but looked down at her feet, her face an emotionless mask as she refused to meet Arthur's eyes. October sat on the ground, her heart unwilling to quell its hammering, like it was trying to break through her ribs and escape this place without her. She stared at Arthur who looked back at her with terrified expectation etched into every line on his face. October had no idea what to say or if her voice would even work at that moment. Her mind was filled with the image of Bernadette being wrenched away; the feeling of sweaty hands being ripped out of her grip; the sound of agonized screaming.

Bryan came jogging back from one of the passages he had been exploring. The boy looked around at the group. Only some looked back at him in silence.

"What was all that noise?" he asked. He looked from one person to another before awful realization dawned on his face. "Where's my mom?" Childish innocence tinged his voice. No one said anything, and he asked again, sounding frightened. "Guys, where's my mom?"

Tell him. The Overshadow let out a putrid laugh. *Oh, please tell him what happened to his sweet mother. I want to watch his fucking soul shatter with despair. Tell him!*

"The bear..." October managed to rasp out. The image of Bernadette's lifeless eyes flashed inside her mind. "Bernadette...she tried... I'm so sorry, Bryan... Arthur..."

"No," Bryan whispered, his eyes doubling in size. For a moment he stood paralyzed, hands raised before him as if reaching for something before turning to a nearby wall and kicking it. Once, twice, three times. October winced at each kick. "No! No! No!" he shouted. Pieces of rock crumbled to the ground in a dusty heap with the impact of each kick. If he had hurt his foot, he showed no signs of pain.

"Bernie... She's gone?" Arthur let out a choked gasp before his face froze in a confused grimace. He wheezed as if he had just inhaled a lungful of acrid smoke. Clutching at his chest, he attempted to draw in a series of ragged breaths that seemed to catch painfully in his throat.

"Dad?" Bryan turned to look at Arthur. He scrambled over to his father, kneeling down beside him. "Dad, breathe! Breathe! Where the hell's your inhaler?"

"Y-Your—" Arthur tried to say between gasps. "Your m-mother..."

"It was in mom's pack?" Bryan asked, his face falling. "Fuck!" Tears welled up in his panicked eyes. "Dad, just breathe! Come on! Deep breaths, remember? Just like the doctor said. Sit up and take deep breaths. In through your nose, out through your mouth." Bryan tried to calm himself and demonstrate his instructions, trying to get his father to imitate his breathing.

As October watched, one thought dominated her mind.

I'm not going to let this happen.

Without another thought, October threw herself back into the tunnel, ignoring the surprised shouts from behind her. Her attention was laser-focused. No extraneous data was being processed. Her mind was locked on one thing: Get the inhaler. Get it now. Bryan wasn't going to lose *both* parents.

You're an idiot, October. She's dead. Do you really want to die too?

Fuck you, October thought at the Overshadow. *Watch me die. Then where will you fucking live?*

The Overshadow didn't respond.

Although the tunnel had seemed impossibly long just moments before, the entrance came into view in less than a minute as she crawled back through on her hands and knees. Where was Bernadette? Had the bear...eaten her? October couldn't think about that now. She saw the blue fanny pack lying just outside of the passage. It was almost as if it had been placed right there to lure her. Bears didn't have the mental capacity for such tactics. Did they?

With the utmost caution and care, October peeked out of the passageway. The bear lay a few feet from the tunnel, facing toward her, eyes closed. And it was...dead? No, that couldn't be. That made no sense. Maybe it was just sleeping? That wasn't logical either. How could it fall asleep in a matter of minutes, especially after all the previous excitement? October didn't know much about bears, but something was off.

She inched closer. Was that Bernadette's blood dribbling out of the animal's mouth? A shudder ran through her. And its body looked wrong. Like its abdomen had sort of collapsed in on itself, like there was nothing inside holding its shape.

An image of the bear cub pelt they had found earlier flashed through her mind.

Who cares! October thought. *Just grab the damn pack!*

Why are you risking your life for this? the Overshadow asked her.

Why don't you go the hell away? October spat back.

Gathering her courage, October reached out toward the fanny pack. A bead of sweat trickled from her forehead and onto her nose, making it itch. She did her best to ignore it. As soon as her fingertips brushed the straps, October's hand gripped the pack and whisked it back into the relative safety of the tunnel.

She had done it. She had actually done it. Now she just had to make sure the inhaler was inside. After backing up several feet deeper into the tunnel, October opened the pack, trying to muffle the noise of the zipper. It was difficult to ignore the nauseating patches of blood that had splattered all over the blue nylon.

Once the zipper had glided all the way open, October dumped the contents onto the ground.

A scream swelled in her throat, and she had to clamp her teeth down on her lip to keep herself from shrieking in horror. A dismayed groan escaped instead as her body instinctively pressed itself against the tunnel wall.

The only thing that had fallen out of the pack were two small, bloody orbs.

Eyes.

Bernadette's goddamn eyes.

There was no mistaking them. October had seen the life in these very eyes extinguished mere moments ago.

Who could've done this? Had she gone crazy? Had the world?

She flung that fanny pack away from her in disgust and panic. It hit the wall of the tunnel with a soft smack and slid to the ground. "What the hell?" she whispered. "What. The. Hell?" *This whole thing has to be a nightmare!*

This was some horror movie, serial killer shit right here.

The killer is probably creeping up on you, the Overshadow whispered. *He's going to end your life. Where could he be? Hmmm, maybe....right behind you!*

A hand grasped her shoulder and October finally let the building scream burst out, her body reflexively throwing an elbow backward.

"Bag pula-n gatu tau, curva!" Viorica spat, as October's elbow connected with her cheekbone.

"Oh my God!" October choked out. "I'm sorry! I'm sorry!"

"It's fine," Viorica said, rubbing her bruised cheek and flexing her jaw. "I've taken harder hits than that before. Don't worry." She massaged her jaw again before pointing at the bloody eyes on the ground that were, thankfully, not staring at October. "Listen to me now, and listen well. We will not tell the others about this. Do you understand what I am saying? We are *not* going to tell them about this. At least not yet. I don't know what did this, but that is not what's important at this moment. We don't need to panic the others any more. Do you understand me?"

October nodded, thoughts tumbling over one another inside her head. Viorica could obviously handle such insane situations much better than she herself could, so October would follow the woman's lead. That definitely seemed the best course of action for the time being. Feeling numb, she followed Viorica back down the tunnel, and they emerged back where the others still waited.

They were all watching Arthur in silence. The big man seemed to have calmed down somewhat, and his breathing had returned to a more normal rhythm. He lay there, eyes closed, his chest rising and falling in a smooth motion. Bryan had an arm around him and was weeping quietly.

"Sorry," October said, her voice catching in her throat. "I'm so sorry. I couldn't find the inhaler."

The image of Bernadette being yanked out of her grasp replayed in October's mind like some awful movie.

Slipped right out of your hands, the Overshadow taunted. *You could have saved her. Why didn't you save her?*

No! October thought. *Bernadette was already dead when she was pulled away. I tried to save her. I tried to hold on to her. It's not my fault!*

"What now?" Noel asked after a long moment of silence. He turned to Viorica in the same way a soldier would look at his commander.

"Well, we keep moving forward," Viorica pointed into the yawning blackness that sprawled out before them. "We can't go back. Definitely not now." She didn't elaborate on that last part.

"So, you want us to wander around in some uncharted cave system," Samira said with no emotion. Her tears had dried, and her eyes were now bloodshot. "Not knowing where we're going. Not knowing what's in here. Not knowing if there's even another exit."

"I don't want you to do anything," Viorica responded, firmly but not unkindly. "I am going to continue forward, following the air that must be coming from somewhere. I know October will be coming with me. If you wish to stay behind, that is your choice. I want to leave this place alive. If you don't want to accompany us, then you can stay right where you are. As soon as I reach the town, I promise to send help back this way."

"And you think that's the best option we have?" Noel asked. "Do you think you can actually lead us out of here?"

"Da, I do," Viorica answered. The confidence in her voice boosted October's sense of hope.

Noel gazed down at the broken camera in his hands, turning it around several times before speaking. "Fine," he said, putting the camera back in its bag. "I guess I'll come with you. There's no point in just waiting around here."

Nodding, Samira grunted her acquiescence. "Okay, let's get out of here," she said with steely eyes, striding over to stand next to them.

"Well, I'm definitely coming with you too," Adrianna joined in, rising to her feet and brushing off her shorts.

"I'm not going anywhere with her," Bryan growled, glaring at Adrianna. "This is all her fault. She was in charge. Look what happened to my dad because of her! Look at...what happened..." He glanced at October. Her stomach clenched at the boy's words. "...to my mom." He began to weep again.

"Bryan, stop it," Arthur said softly, opening his eyes. "Help me up." Bryan helped his father to his feet. The big man swayed for a moment before recovering his balance. He put a hand on Bryan's shoulder. "Now listen. Stop blaming Adrianna. This is nobody's fault. No one can control nature." October felt that Arthur was trying to convince himself as well as Bryan. "And you know we can't stay here." His voice cracked with emotion, and he cleared his throat. "Your mother wouldn't want us to fall to pieces right now. She would want us to do anything we could to survive. Don't you think so?" His fingers flexed on his son's shoulder.

Bryan continued to weep, but nodded his head. He let his father sling an arm around his shoulder for support, and they began shuffling deeper into the large tunnel at a slow pace, using Bryan's cell phone light to illuminate the path before them.

Yes, October thought, still sitting by the tunnel. *Survive...I'm so sorry, Bernadette. I'm so sorry. I'll help them. I'll help Arthur and Bryan. It's the only thing I can do to make up for letting you go. Helping them get back to safety.*

You'll fail in this, the Overshadow said. *Like you fail at everything.*

Viorica replaced her phone with a small flashlight from her pocket. "October, you are coming with me, right?" she asked, extending a hand to her.

"Yeah, I will. Of course." October grasped the hand to be pulled upward off the ground. The shock of everything that had happened was taking its toll on her mind and soul, and she felt utterly exhausted. She couldn't let it overwhelm her. She couldn't let the fear, the despair, and the Overshadow sink their claws into her and bring her down into the mire. That would spell her doom. She had to stay strong, at least for the time being, despite the horrors she had just witnessed.

They all caught up with Bryan and Arthur and headed down a passage that wound its way through the rock as if a giant worm had once burrowed itself into the mountain. Many side-passages branched out from the main one, leading off to abyssal depths October would rather not imagine. Viorica led the group, her flashlight bouncing off the walls. Despite no blockages in the main passageway, she would take a look inside every nook and cranny they came across. From there, Viorica led them down turn after turn in a confusing and tiring game of follow-the-leader. Every so often, when faced with a fork in the tunnel, she would pause to pull something out of her pocket and shine her flashlight on it—October couldn't see what exactly it was. Viorica would study the object she held for a few seconds at a time before returning it to her pocket and picking a direction to head in.

A compass or something, October mused.

The others had their phones out, using their small flashlights to help penetrate the blackness. October could hear water dripping somewhere far off, and she could have sworn that they were gradually descending deeper into the earth. She had to trust that Viorica knew what she was doing.

Fiddling unconsciously with her nose ring, October became lost once again in her own thoughts. *What am I doing here?* she asked herself. *I should have just stayed in the hotel room or gone to that little park I saw down the street to read a book. Or better yet, I should have just stayed home.* She couldn't get the deaths out of her mind. Dara's and Bernadette's screams kept replaying in her brain on a horrible loop that she couldn't shut off no matter how hard she tried. There had been so much blood. How could a human body contain so much blood? It didn't seem possible. And would she have had the courage to sacrifice herself like Dara did? Or to let everyone go ahead of her when danger was fast approaching, like Bernadette had?

Obviously not. Just look at how long it had taken her to get into that damn tunnel.

She shook her head to dislodge the thoughts. There was no point in dwelling on what she should have done. She was here, and she was determined to get out of this situation.

If she got home—no, *when* she got home—October decided that she would have to memorialize Dara and Bernadette's sacrifices. Somehow. She had no idea what she would do. For now, though, she had to get out of this awful place, then reach the safety of town. In the short term, surviving and getting their loved ones home safely would honor their sacrifices the most.

October brought up the rear of the group as they trudged along. She kept shining her phone's light over her shoulder every time she thought she heard a noise behind her in the passage. *Stop being para-noid. Probably just a bat. And bats are cute. Bats and mice and other little animals live in caves. The bear could never have fit into that small tunnel. We're safe in here. At least, safe from the bear.*

You're never safe. Life is easily lost. Just like dear Dara and Bernadette. Just like you and everyone else soon.

Shut up, October told the cruel voice in her head. When she had been a teenager, October had tried several times to knock herself unconscious so she wouldn't have to listen to the Overshadow's slimy words. The urge to do so again swelled within her, and she had to fight to resist.

The claustrophobia October had felt since squeezing herself through the crack in the wall and coming out the other side had eased up only a little. The passage they now travelled through was nowhere near as confining as the initial one. In most places, there were several feet between her scalp and the ceiling, allowing her to walk upright without fear of banging her head, though she had to dodge a stalactite every now and then. And even if she stretched her arms out as wide as possible, she wouldn't have been able to touch both of the cold, craggy walls that glistened with cool moisture.

I don't want to die down here, she kept telling herself.

October inhaled deeply, performing her YouTube breathing exercises. She let her breath out in a quiet, full exhalation, then inhaled again, the moist, earthy scent of the cave's innards all-encompassing. They weren't working.

The group traveled for what must have been several miles. October had no idea how long they walked down there in the darkness, the only sounds being their footsteps echoing off the walls around them. The tunnels were expansive, and just when October's feet could take no more, Viorica halted the group. The passageway they had been navigating had opened up into a cavern, wide enough for three cars to easily drive through it side-by-side. Despite that, the air felt more oppressive here, and October could detect a faint and unpleasant odor that she couldn't identify.

"Are we taking a rest?" Arthur gasped. "I could really use one."

October shook her head at herself. If an asthmatic like Arthur could make it this far, she had no right to be so tired.

"I see something ahead," Viorica said.

"What is it?" Samira asked, shining her phone light in front of her.

Viorica's answer was to move forward again, striding to the other side of the cavern.

They all followed Viorica, curious whispers floating through the otherwise silent caves. The walls narrowed again into a more symmetrical passage as the group reached the far end. Shining her phone's light on the walls around her, October realized the surrounding rock was covered in drawings and some sort of strange markings that could have been writing. This wasn't like Painter's Cave, however. This artwork, while still ancient-looking in style, was different from the pictographs she had seen earlier, as if an unknown culture from the other side of the world had come here and made these paintings. Instead of hunting and battle, these paintings depicted scenes of people kneeling or prostrating themselves before a group of eight figures with large eyes, spider-limbs, and sharp talons on their hands. The people were offering bundles of something to the taloned figures. In other scenes, these eight figures were dressed in the apparel of different cultures. One depiction showed them in flowing garments and turbans, while in another they had donned leather armor and helmets. Another tableau had them wearing something like Egyptian headdresses. Did that other one show them dressed as samurai? October couldn't make out much more due to the strobe effect of the group's phone lights flashing here and there.

"That's different," Samira said.

Every flashlight and phone light joined Samira's on the wall before them. This wall was most definitely not part of the natural cave. A nine-by-six-foot rectangle had been carved into the stone. The entire surface within this rectangle was a skillfully sculpted bas-relief resembling an organic latticework of ribs, femurs, vertebrae, and other bones. A body-shaking tremble caused October to break out in goosebumps as her mind raced with possible explanation for what she was looking at.

"Are you kidding me?" Bryan demanded. "Did we hit a dead end?"

"What the hell is that?" whispered Noel.

Viorica reached forward and ran her hands over the wall, as everyone shone their lights on it and held a collective breath.

"Well," she finally said, looking back at them from over her shoulder. "It is not a dead end. I think we have found a door."

CHAPTER TEN

Jordan

Unbeknownst to Dr. Sommers or Caleb Rivas, Lucas had recorded his entire conversation with the boy and sent it over to Jordan for her to listen.

"He wears pieces of Evan's skin like a costume."

The voice of Caleb Rivas went silent, and Jordan closed the audio file on her computer. She had listened to the full recording four times already, and Caleb's words had given her dreadful chills every time. She rubbed at the goosebumps that covered her arms and legs. They weren't going away.

"Poor Caleb," Jordan muttered to Nathan. "I can't even imagine."

Nathan opened and closed his scaly mouth as if preparing to speak. She waited, but he just stared at her with his half-closed eyes.

"What the hell is this Watcher, though?" she asked him. Some awful hallucination that Caleb was suffering from? Some psychotic person tormenting the poor boy for kicks? Or perhaps it was something worse? Something actually supernatural?

As was her tendency, Jordan's mind initially rejected that possibility. She was a logical person and had always viewed mysteries through a lens of facts and evidence. Sighing, she shook her head. After working with Lucas, though, she could no longer deny the existence of the supernatural.

No. By now she knew she had to be willing to consider all angles.

After that first encounter with Lucas almost three years ago, Jordan couldn't rule *anything* out when it came to dealing with Enigmata.

Leaning back in her chair, Jordan gathered Nathan into her hands, feeling every bump and ridge of his tiny scales under her fingertips. As she caressed the little dragon, she recalled the night she'd met Lucas Wendig.

Her late-night shift having just ended—and reeking of all the cinnamon rolls she had made that day—Jordan had been leaving the Westroads Mall in her hometown of Omaha. The moon had already been high in the sky for some time, the wind had an autumn chill to it, and the parking lot was mostly deserted at this late hour. She remembered admonishing herself for having parked so far away, and she quickened her pace to her car.

Out of the corner of her eye, Jordan spotted a woman struggling to open the trunk of her own car. The woman had a cast on her left arm and half-a-dozen heavy-looking bags in her right hand.

Jordan should have known better than to fall for such a transparent ploy. She *did* know better. Later, she would beat herself up repeatedly for ignoring the risk. Would she have so freely agreed to help if it had been a large, burly man asking? The mall had been closed since 8:00 p.m., so there wouldn't still be shoppers carrying bags to their cars. But she had been naïve and felt a need to be helpful when she could.

"Excuse me!" the woman called out to Jordan, sounding tired and frustrated. "Think you could just open my trunk for me? I'm having some trouble here."

"Of course!" Jordan said, not thinking twice about the situation. The woman looked harmless, innocent.

As soon as she had approached the woman with the arm cast, a fetid odor of sunbaked garbage smacked Jordan in the face. In the blink of an eye, the woman had dropped all her shopping bags and wrapped her vice-like right arm around Jordan, spinning her around and pressing Jordan's back tightly against her chest like a human shield. It was only then that Jordan spotted another stranger, a tall black man, approaching them, a gun drawn and pointed in her direction. Lucas Wendig, though she'd had no idea who he was at the time.

"Get out of here!" the woman shouted. "Leave me alone already! I don't fucking know who you are. This doesn't have anything to do with you. Why do you keep coming after me? I just want to be left alone!"

"Let the girl go," Lucas demanded, his gun trained on the woman, his eyes unblinking. "Let her go, and we can work this all out. There's no reason to hurt her. We can figure out what the artifact did to you, okay? I can help you. All you have to do is let the girl go."

"I-I can't," the woman holding Jordan uttered. "I can't. I'm just so hungry. You don't understand. You can't understand what it feels like. This constant gnawing in my stomach. It hurts. It hurts so much, no matter what I do. No matter how much I eat. It won't go away. I'm so hungry!"

The grip on Jordan had tightened, and she could feel the woman's heart pounding against her back. *What is going on?* Jordan remembered thinking, unable to form the words into speech. *Am I going to die? What does she mean, she's 'hungry'?*

Just then, Jordan felt something sharp press against her neck, and a trickle of warmth slid down her skin. A scream lodged in her throat, and a split second later, a deafening gunshot shattered the silence of the night.

Jordan was immediately released from the iron grip, and she took the opportunity to scramble away, gasping for air. Another gunshot rang out. The woman who had been holding her hostage fell backward.

Every detail of what had happened next would be forever burned into her mind with perfect clarity. Before Jordan had been able to regain any composure, her attacker had sprung back to her feet. In the glow of the parking lot's sodium lights, Jordan saw that the woman now sported two large, gaping gunshot wounds, one in the chest, the other through the left cheekbone. The holes that had just been blasted into the woman's body oozed, not blood, but a viscous, pus-yellow sludge.

Jordan was positive those were fatal wounds, yet there her attacker stood, glaring at the man with the gun, burning, primal fury writ large on what was left of her face.

Before Jordan could scream, her rescuer had pulled a glass container from out of his coat. Uncapping it with a flick of his thumb, he threw it at the creature standing before them. The contents of the container doused the woman in what looked to Jordan to be simply water. However, she watched in stunned horror as her attacker melted into a puddle of festering ichor mere seconds after the liquid had splashed her.

"I'm sorry I couldn't save you," Lucas murmured to the sickening pile that had once been a person.

The bones that remained lying on the asphalt were not entirely human, though Jordan could never recall what exactly struck her as off about them. Among the ribs and sternum was a fist-sized pyramid, carved of a deep green jade. Jordan had only stared at the strange object and the bones, her thoughts muddled in a fog of disbelief, before her savior donned latex gloves and carefully scooped everything into a thick trash bag.

"We need to get out of here," Lucas had told her.

That had been the night her life changed forever. Her fingers subconsciously touched the little scar on her neck. An unwanted souvenir from her first encounter with an Enigmata.

Something nibbled at the skin of her palm, bringing her out of her reverie. Jordan glanced down to see Nathan staring up at her, his head tilted at an adorable angle.

"Hungry?" she asked before gently setting him back onto her desk and heading to the kitchen. She took the box of mealworms out of the fridge. Gabe hated that she kept the little buggers in there. Said it always ruined his appetite whenever he saw the "writhing container" even though nothing was visible through the closed lid.

Returning with the box of goodies to her bedroom, she dropped several mealworms into Nathan's little bowl. The lizard immediately scurried over when he heard the plink of the insects hitting the metal.

"What would I do without you, Jordan?" she said in her Nathan voice.

"I don't know, buddy," Jordan told him with a grin. "And slow down. Don't gobble." She plopped herself in her computer chair and swiveled back to her dual monitors. She examined the results of her automated search, which had popped up on one of the screens. "Now what do we have here?"

A few rabbit holes and a half hour later, Jordan was looking at the scanned images of old letters and documents, along with their English translations or summaries, from the archives of museums all over the world.

"Interesting." This was more documentation than she usually found on a specific Enigmata. It looked like Caleb wasn't the only one who'd had to deal with this Watcher being. No surprise there, seeing how far back the dates on some of the documents went. She clicked through them, reading carefully. Nathan watched with apparent interest as Jordan downloaded more and more files.

Her brow furrowed as she started to realize a repeating detail that stood out to her. A worrying detail.

"Oh hell, Nathan. I think that the Watcher might actually be Watchers."

CHAPTER ELEVEN

October

Nope," Noel said. He pointed at the macabre door before them with its latticework of bone carvings. "Mm-mm. No way. Nuh-uh. Screw that."

"That's impossible." Arthur craned his neck to get a better look at what lay in front of them. "How could there be a door here? I thought these caves were unmapped?"

"Not mapped by modern people," Viorica answered, shining her flashlight up and down the intricate, skeletal bas-relief that made up the door's face. "This door looks ancient."

"Everything in these damn caves looks ancient," muttered Bryan.

"It gives me the creeps," Samira said.

October stared at the door in front of them. The latticework of bone shapes carved from the rock cast stark and disturbing shadows each time someone's light passed over them. She thought she could discern some form of writing inscribed here and there. Still, even if it had been in English, would October want to read whatever it said? She quickly decided that she would not.

"This wasn't carved by the people who made the pictographs in

Painter's Cave." Adrianna touched the door with light fingers. "Not that I'm an expert or anything. But I'm positive this wasn't made by the same people."

"Did people live down here?" Samira asked. "Or was this for something else?"

"We shall see." Viorica placed both her palms against the door and pushed, grunting with the effort. October thought she saw the stone move an inch.

"What are you doing?" Bryan asked, worry in his voice.

"What does it look like I'm doing?" Viorica snapped at him. She immediately seemed to regret her harsh tone as Bryan flinched. She continued in a softer voice. "There is no handle. So I thought I'd push instead of pull. We must go forward, unless you want to stay here or retrace our steps all the way back." She went back to pushing on the door.

"God, I'm going to regret this," Noel said as he stepped up next to Viorica and threw his weight against the strange door to help.

For a few seconds, it seemed that the door wouldn't budge any more than it initially had. Perhaps it wasn't a door at all? *If this isn't a way forward,* October thought, *then we really are screwed.* Moments later, to her great relief, the sound of rock grinding on rock reverberated around them, and the door moved reluctantly inward. Plumes of stale air and dust wafted over them like a giant's exhalation after a thousand years of entombment.

Coughing and sneezing, the group followed Viorica through the dark portal. October found herself standing in a large circular room the size of her own apartment. Everyone shone their lights about, trying to dispel the blackness that threatened to overwhelm them with its crushing shadows.

"What is this place?" Arthur asked, adjusting the dusty glasses on his sweaty face.

"What the hell?" October murmured, turning her cell phone flashlight this way and that. The phrase "ritual chamber" immediately came to mind. She couldn't think of another term that would better describe the room in which they now stood. The door they had come through appeared to be the only way in or out. The uneven walls were pockmarked with dozens upon dozens of shallow niches, most of which held a strange metal instrument of one sort or another. The weird instruments were of all different shapes and sizes, contraptions composed of dark iron and constructed of stained blades, rusted hinges, and large handles. October didn't know what purpose these evil-looking tools served, but she could vividly imagine, and it made her stomach tighten.

In the center of the room stood what October could only describe as a cylindrical altar, about four feet high, its center etched with indecipherable symbols, and its sides featuring the same osseous aesthetic as the door they had come through. What October assumed to be a stone box or chest rested right on top of the altar. She wasn't sure she wanted to know what was inside and was inclined to just leave the thing undisturbed. There was probably a booby trap inside it. These sorts of things were always booby trapped.

However, there was something else far more disturbing. Something that seemingly verified October's hunch regarding the metal instruments resting in their little niches. Evenly spaced around the altar were five stone slabs, each standing about waist-high. On one of the slabs rested—

"A dead body?" Samira gasped, her hand shooting up to cover her mouth as her cell phone spotlighted a prone figure.

October's light joined with the others to illuminate the skeleton that lay on one of the stone slabs. Its eyeless skull was turned to the side, staring sightlessly toward them, as if pleading for the newcomers to take it away from here. Its bony jaw stretched open in a silent scream of agony. The remnants of shredded, disintegrating cloth lay piled around its fleshless body, like they'd been viciously torn off. Stuck in between the bones, seemingly at random, were sharp metal instruments akin to those resting in the wall niches around them.

Had they been used after or before the victim had perished? October wondered. She didn't want to say what she was thinking aloud. She sensed an overwhelming pall of evil hanging in the air, threatening to suffocate her.

A glimpse into your future? the Overshadow asked. *I desperately hope so.*

"Oh damn," Noel said, eyes wide. He stepped closer to the skeleton, putting on a brave face, though he swallowed loudly. "I wonder how long this guy's been down here? Man, this is one messed up place. Why did they do this to him?" A horrible realization seemed to dawn on him, and he voiced the same thought that October had swirling around in her own mind. "Was this dude, like, some sort of sacrifice?"

"I don't know." Adrianna stared with unblinking eyes at the skeleton. "They estimated the drawings back in Painter's Cave to be around five to six thousand years old. So, who knows how old *this* place is? And I don't think any Indigenous tribes around here performed human sacrifices. Not that I know of." Her words faltered as if her topic of discussion left a bad taste in her mouth. "I know that people like the Mayans, Incas, and Aztecs performed human sacrifice. Maybe a group of them migrated up here for some reason? Though the architecture here doesn't really look like Mesoamerican." She looked around at the group of tired eyes. "I'm sorry. I'm babbling. I'm sure this place has been abandoned for a long time and there's nothing to worry about." The quaver in her voice betrayed the certainty of her words.

Gathering her courage, October crept over closer to the skeleton on the stone slab. Something had caught her attention; something that seemed out of place peeked out from behind the stone. A messenger bag? Curiosity replacing her apprehension, October knelt down and carefully opened the bag to look inside. "Uh, guys. I don't know how ancient this room is, but I don't think this person is that old, unless he's a time traveler."

"What do you mean?" Viorica asked, looking over at October.

October held up an object from out of the bag. "This guy had a cell phone." The heavy, blocky phone was covered in dust and scratches. "I don't think they had those in ancient times."

"That's an old-ass flip-phone," Bryan said, shining his light on the phone that October held aloft. "That thing must be from like twenty years ago."

October nodded in agreement. "Looks like it. So, whoever this is, they haven't been here for very long, assuming this bag belonged to them. I don't see anyone else here. So, this person may not be super-modern. Definitely not a thousand years old, though. What were they doing in here?"

"Maybe this fella was some kind of researcher," Arthur suggested in a wheezy voice. "Like an archaeologist? That would be the type of guy who'd willingly come down here. This place looks like it would be an archaeologist's dream."

"Would a researcher carry a gun?" October brought another item out of the satchel, holding it up for everyone to see. She held the gun awkwardly by the grip. Never having held a firearm before, it felt strange in her hand.

Guns, dead people, Bernadette's eyes in the fanny pack. Was there really some killer on the loose here?

"Let me see that." Viorica strode forward and took the handgun. She examined the weapon like an expert, dropping the magazine and clearing the chamber before ensuring the safety was on. "A Browning Hi Power semiautomatic pistol. A little dirty, but in good shape. Thir-teen-round capacity magazine. Four rounds already fired or missing."

"Maybe I should carry that," Bryan said.

Viorica looked as if she wanted to snap at him again. She held her tongue. "Nu. I would not want you to hurt yourself accidentally," she said instead. She put the gun and the magazine in her pants pocket then turned to October. "Is there any more ammunition in there?"

October looked through the satchel once more and shook her head. "No, sorry. Just what looks like it used to be food. I think there's also a notebook here. Noel, can you shine your light here a sec?" Noel nodded and walked over, shining his phone light down so that October could use both hands to flip through the small leather notebook, the pages faded and brittle. "Most of it is still legible. Let's see. Names, some dates, nothing that means anything to me." She turned the crackling pages. "Wait, here's something." She squinted at the spiky handwritten text on a dirty page near the back of the book. "I shouldn't have taken this damn job. Fuck all of this. Fuck these caves. Fuck the damn binding Wheel. Wheel of Kurkoth, whatever it's called. No amount of money was worth coming down here. I'm never getting out of this place. I swear I'm walking in circles. I'm running out of food and water. No more batteries for the light." The handwriting became shakier. "You know what's weird? When it really sinks in that you're going to die. The idea that your life is going to end goes from some abstract idea to a reality. No one's going to miss me. Maybe someone will find my corpse one day down here. Well, if you're reading this, I assume you're looking for the wheel too. Why else would anyone come the hell down here? I never found it, so it's all yours. There's a fork in the passage that I've been staring at for about an hour now. I think I'll just flip a coin. Also, I think something lives down here. I thought I heard something moving. Could be just a rat. Maybe I'm just going crazy. Whatever. — Seth Monahan.'"

October paused for a moment. A thought flitted through her mind: How was Viorica able to lead them here when this guy got so lost he died? She shook the paranoid thought away.

Focus.

On your certain death.

"Looks like this guy was searching for something called the 'Wheel of Kurkoth.' Whatever that is," she said.

"It doesn't say what it is?" Samira asked. "Besides being a wheel."

"Not that I see." October flipped through some of the earlier pages, scanning for the words "Wheel" and "Kurkoth."

"Guess the answer died with this guy," Noel said.

Died, the Overshadow murmured. *Die, dying. I like those words. Death. Muerte. Almawt. Shi. Ölüm. Dauði. Oti. Marwolaeth. Kifo. Moarte—*

I get it, October thought.

"Kurkoth? I've never heard of such a thing," Adrianna said. "I took some local history courses at the museum in town before I decided to start the hiking tours. I've never heard of anything like this. At least there's no reference to it in any of the museum's exhibits."

"Wait," interrupted Bryan. "So this guy wrote that he was lost in those tunnels and that he was staring at a fork in the tunnel. Does that mean he finally found his way here? Or did someone *bring* him here from where he died?"

The group all turned to look at the skeleton on the stone slab. The budding silence was broken when Arthur fell to one knee in a fit of wheezing. In a blink, Bryan was at his side

"Not that I relish staying here any longer than necessary," Arthur said as he was helped into a sitting position by his son. "But do you think we could rest here for a short while?" He drew in a ragged breath. "I could really use a break from all the walking we've done. Please?"

October looked at Viorica. All the others did the same. It seemed that they had collectively decided, without a word, that Viorica was the leader of their little group now. She had led them this far and was going to get them all to safety. Even Bryan waited for her to speak. The woman was mysterious, but October was glad to have her.

"Da." Viorica nodded, shrugging off her pack. "Let's take a break for a little time. Rest your feet while I look around. Maybe there's another way out of this room."

They all plopped down once again on the cold, hard floor. No one wanted to sit on the slabs or be near the skeleton. October breathed a sigh of relief for her feet. She was dead tired, although she hadn't wanted to be the one to ask for a break. She considered removing her boots to let her feet breathe for a few minutes. With one glance at all the straps and buckles, she thought better of it. If something were to happen—she didn't know what, but if something did—she wanted to be ready to run.

Half the group turned their phones off to conserve battery. Arthur's phone had run out of battery. October looked at her own phone, bringing the screen to life. The power indicator sat in the red at 11 percent. "Great," she said, biting her lip.

Powering down her phone for the moment, October stared out from the darkness at the other hikers, their worn faces barely illumined. Samira's tears had stopped hours ago. She just sat motionless, a stony expression on her face. Noel sat next to her, his cell phone held between his teeth with the light shining down as he tinkered with his broken camera again. It looked like the lens itself wasn't cracked, so perhaps he thought he could fix the camera's other parts and get it working again. Bryan sat with his arm around his dad. Arthur was trying to take steady, deliberate breaths, though his lacerated arm obviously pained him.

If only she could have found Arthur's inhaler.

Adrianna sat a few feet apart from the group, staring down at the ground.

"Hey." October scooched closer to Adrianna. Although October was generally reluctant to strike up conversations, she felt she had to say something to the girl. "How are you holding up?"

"Not that great," Adrianna said, trying to chuckle but groaning instead. She brought her knees up to her chest and hugged them. "Nobody's ever going to want to go on my nature walks again, that's for sure." It had probably been meant as a joke, but the pain and guilt were audible.

October snorted. "I don't think that's something you need to worry about right now. Nobody can blame you for a bear attack." Despite being adopted into a loving family, showing any sort of affection had never come very easily to October. She wanted to comfort Adrianna, put an arm around the girl or whatever people did in these situations. "Let's just focus on getting out of here for now, yeah?" She decided to put a hopefully reassuring hand on Adrianna's shoulder. "That's all that matters right at the moment."

"I needed this job," Adrianna said, putting her face in her hands. Apparently, the reassuring hand hadn't worked. "I was trying to save up money for college. I wanted to get out of this damn town. Get a degree. Graduate. I wanted to go out and see the world. Travel. See different countries. Eat exotic food. Meet awesome people." She sniffled. "What if we can't get out of here? What if we all die down here?"

"Hey, hey." October paused as she hunted for the right words. "We'll make it out. Okay? You'll be able to go to college. You'll be able to do all that stuff you wanted to." October wasn't used to being the reasonable one, the one to give reassurances and advice. At this moment, Adrianna needed someone to be on her side, however, and tell her things were going to be alright. It felt oddly nice to step up and be that person. "We're going to get out of here and back to town just fine. Viorica will lead us out of here. Have you seen that woman? She's kick-ass. I'm positive she knows what she's doing. She's been navigating this maze, choosing the right paths. We'll get out of here."

"Really?" Adrianna looked up at her. "You promise?"

No, there's no way I can promise that, October thought. *Though I did already tell myself that I was going to get Bryan and Arthur out. I vowed to Bernadette, wherever she may be now.*

"October?" Adrianna asked, her moist eyes wide in the darkness.

"I promise," October said, swallowing her apprehension at saying such a thing. "We're going to get out of here."

Oathbreaker, the Overshadow hissed the word in October's head.

"Has anyone checked this out?" Noel asked the room. It seemed he had given up on his camera for the time being. He now stood next to the center altar that held the stone chest on top of it. "Could be something useful inside."

When no one said anything, he shrugged.

October watched as Noel cautiously reached for the stone lid, a wave of apprehension tingling in her skull.

"Be careful," Arthur said from where he lay on the floor.

The lid easily opened at Noel's touch, and he jumped back. When nothing sprang out from inside the box, he cautiously peered within, then reached his hand down into the chest. He withdrew a dark, round disc, a little smaller than a teacup saucer and as thick as a deck of cards. It reflected a blue sheen when light hit its smooth, glassy surface.

"What's that?" Arthur asked. "Please be careful."

"It's just some metal plate thing," Noel answered. The object fit perfectly into his palm. "Maybe it's that wheel the notebook talked about. What was it called? Kur-something?"

"Kurkoth," Viorica said.

"Yeah, that." Noel studied the item in his hand, turning it this way and that. "There're markings and little indentations on it, like parts of it should be able to move. Maybe it's a sorta puzzle, you know? My mom got me this wooden puzzle for Christmas once." He poked at it, tried to twist it at various angles. Nothing happened. "Damn, this thing's small, but it feels really heavy."

Bryan stood up. "Let me see."

Noel tossed it like a frisbee over to Bryan, who let out a quiet "oof" when he caught its full weight.

"Ah, shit," Bryan muttered.

"What happened?" demanded Arthur, trying to get up. He only managed to prop himself up on his elbow.

"I don't know. Stay down, dad. I'm fine. The thing just cut me somehow."

October hadn't realized she had gotten to her feet until Bryan glanced over at her. She watched him examine every inch of the disc. There didn't seem to be any sharp or protruding pieces on it. Still, Bryan's thumb was undoubtedly bleeding. He stuck the wound into his mouth.

"I wonder what it's for," Adrianna said to October. "It was obviously valuable to that guy." She indicated the skeleton. "Worth enough to risk his life coming down here. Well, I guess he changed his mind toward the end, though." She reached into her pack for an alcohol pad and a Band-Aid, holding them out for Bryan. "Here."

"Thanks," he muttered, taking the items, but not meeting her eyes.

"Who knows what it's for," October said. She gave Adrianna another gentle squeeze on the shoulder, then strode over to where Viorica was still studying the weird, bladed metal instruments nestled inside one of the wall niches. "Cutting implements" was the term that kept coming to mind every time October laid eyes on one of them.

"Any idea what these are?" she asked in a low voice. She didn't want the others to listen in. "It doesn't look fun. Are they for sacrifices?"

"Perhaps. Or it could be some sort of torture device." Viorica gingerly picked up one of the objects, avoiding its sharp edges. "Though it's like no torture device I have ever seen before." She turned the thing over in her hands, feeling its edges, sniffing at it, bringing it uncomfortably close to her eyes to examine its blades.

"Weird." As a big fan of horror and dark things, October had seen plenty of torture devices, all in movies, museums, or online. In her present situation, though, she didn't really care to think about more death and horror. She did agree with Viorica. She had never seen torture implements like these things before either.

"Okay," October heard Noel say. "Going to conserve the rest of my phone's battery."

"I'll keep mine on," Samira told him. "It still has juice left."

October turned back to look at the instrument and its niche illuminated by Viorica's large flashlight. She thought she saw something else in there.

"Find anything?" a voice asked from behind them. October jumped, and both women turned around to see Bryan standing there. "Find any way out yet?"

"Not yet," Viorica answered. "I was studying these devices, hoping one of them would provide an answer."

"An answer to what?" Bryan asked, but Viorica didn't respond. "A way out of this hell hole, I hope."

"Viorica," October said. "Shine your light back here a moment." October peered into one of the lower niches as Viorica redirected her light. October was right. There was indeed something here. Was that a wooden handle?

"What is it?" Viorica asked.

"I think there's a lever in there," October told her. Excitement bubbled inside her, though she tried not to get her hopes up.

"Pull it," Bryan said without the slightest hint of hesitation.

Yes, throw the lever. Pray to the gods.

October wasn't sure pulling a random lever in a strange ritual chamber was the best idea. They had to get out of here somehow. Who knew what this mechanism did though?

"No," October said. "Maybe we should look around some more before we pull any mysterious levers. We don't know what it might do."

"We have to get my dad to a hospital," Bryan said. He reached past them and pulled the lever before either of the women could stop him.

There was a cacophony of noisy grinding right above their heads. The ceiling trembled, dust and small debris falling down upon them. Everyone except Arthur leapt to their feet.

"What the hell did you do?" Noel yelled from across the room, shielding his head.

"Shit!" October shouted, a small chunk of stone hitting her ear. Fear immediately replaced the excitement. Had Bryan just doomed them all?

Everyone looked upward as a panel in the ceiling, measuring about five feet by five feet, slid to one side with a shriek.

And out poured bones. Dozens of bones. Hundreds of bones. Remains, both human and animal, poured out of the open panel, skeletonized rain clattering onto the floor in a dirty white torrent of morbidity. Adrianna and Noel gasped as the ground around them became an open grave.

After the dust had settled and everyone had finished coughing their lungs out, they all stood there in utter silence as the last few bones trickled out of the ceiling, clacking down onto the giant pile that had formed underneath. Among the myriad bones, October could see remnants of clothing, some modern, most older looking. Much older looking.

Bryan huddled next to his wheezing dad. "What. The. Hell." He held a hand to his dad's spasming chest.

"That is not what I was expecting to happen," Viorica muttered.

October felt an angry heat rising in her chest as she surveyed the chamber. Bryan could have just killed everyone. What had possessed him to pull that lever without knowing what it did? October had told him not to.

Yell at him! the Overshadow demanded. *Scream at him! Tell him how utterly stupid he was! Better yet, tell him how disappointed his mother would've been. Tell him!*

No, she couldn't yell at him, despite how angry she was at that moment. October forced herself to swallow her rage. Bryan's mom had just died in a horrible way. His dad was in bad shape. The kid wasn't in his right mind and was desperate to get out and get his dad to safety.

"I'm sorry." Bryan's voice was barely a whisper. October realized she was glaring at him.

October expected the group, especially Viorica, to be furious at him for his stupidity. But no one said anything. Perhaps they were all too stunned by what had just come out of the ceiling.

"This is good," Viorica said unexpectedly into the silent chamber, walking around the pile of bones. "This might be good."

"How is this *anywhere* near good?" Noel demanded, his hand running over his head. "This is the opposite of good. There are freaking bones in here! Human bones! And not just one skeleton lying on a table. Look at all this! Now, tell me how this is good?"

"October found a lever," Viorica said. October felt herself redden even though it hadn't been her hand that had pulled the switch. "Bryan pulled the lever. It opened that panel above. There's a good chance there are other mechanisms in here. And one of them will open the door that gets us out of here."

"We already have a door!" Noel practically shouted. "It's right there. The one we came through into this damn room. We can walk right back out of it!"

"I have to agree with Noel," Samira said. "We can just go back. There could be other passages we didn't see. And if we have to go all the way back to the bear, then so be it."

October shivered at the look on Samira's face.

"As I said before, you are free to go back," Viorica stated while she searched the other niches for any similar levers. Every time she shoved aside one of the metal instruments, October feared that the woman would cut her hand open on those evil, rusted blades. "However, I led us here, and I'm not going back. Do you remember every turn we took to arrive here? Every fork in the road I chose? Because I don't think I could tell you how to get back without going with you."

Noel and Samira glanced at each other but said nothing. October could tell that they knew they'd have no chance of navigating the maze of tunnels back to Painter's Cave. October knew that *she* definitely couldn't find her way back. She was going to stick with Viorica for now.

"Ah, I found one," Viorica announced. "Actually two." She indicated two dusty wooden levers side-by-side inside another low niche. "I've seen things like this before. I believe this will open an exit. Just to be safe, everyone be alert and shout if you see something begin to happen." She proceeded to mumble something to herself, studying the two levers. After a moment, she pulled the left-hand one.

Another grinding noise met their ears, but nothing appeared to be happening.

"Oh no!" Samira exclaimed from behind. They all turned around to see the door they'd come in through slowly shutting. Samira tried to make a run for it but was held back by Noel.

"Stay back," Noel said. "You might get caught in it and crushed." He let go of Samira. "Hopefully, we can just open it again if we have to. For now, I think we should stick with the lady."

Bryan began to tear up. "Mom's still back there," he said.

The large stone door shut with a definite *clunk*. Everyone looked back at Viorica. "Hmm." She made to pull the lever again but struggled with it before the wood splintered and it broke off in her hand. "Oh." She shook her head and tossed the broken piece aside. "I guess let us try the other one." She wrapped her hand around the remaining lever, paused for a split-second, then pulled it down.

As the sound of grinding stone rang through the air again, October felt a faint rush of wind behind her. Before she could turn around, however, she heard a loud smack, and saw Samira's phone sail through the air.

"Hey!" Samira yelled. "What the hell?"

Viorica's flashlight was yanked out of her hand as well, illuminating beams flying through the air.

"Futu-i!" she shouted.

In the brief moment before the flashlight and phone clattered to the floor, October glimpsed a flash of large orbs on the ceiling above them, like eyes reflecting light. The phone went out, most likely broken, leaving Viorica's flashlight as the only source of illumination as it shone on the skeletal remains that littered the floor. It sputtered out and died seconds later, plunging them all into a darkness so profound, October couldn't see her own hand in front of her face.

As she fished for her own phone in her pocket, she heard something drop from the ceiling beside her, followed by a loud, agonized gasp.

In the utter lightlessness, Adrianna began to scream.

CHAPTER TWELVE

October

Octobers phone wouldn't turn on, no matter how many times her shaking, sweaty fingers pounded on the power button.

Adrianna continued to scream, a horrific, agonized shrieking that made October's chest physically hurt. She heard the others rushing around in confusion and calling out in the darkness, but she couldn't tell who was where or what was being said. Every voice and footstep echoed in that black chamber, creating a din of unintelligible sounds like they were sitting in the middle of a stadium at some sporting event.

A light suddenly flared to life, blinding October for a brief second. Viorica had managed to find her flashlight in the darkness and get it working again. The beam illuminated a section of wall that had slid open, revealing a new exit before them.

A way out.

Viorica's flashlight died again, its bulb fading to dim orange before winking out. They were all plunged into that awful, encapsulating pitch once more.

In that same brief second, Adrianna's screaming was cut short as if something had blocked her windpipe. The girl uttered a desperate choke, which was immediately followed by the sickening tearing sound of something wet and fleshy that filled the room before everything returned to a hideous silence. The only thing October could hear now was her own heart throwing itself against the inside of her chest.

After several loud whacks, Viorica got her torch working again, then turned with the light, aiming the beam directly on the section of darkness from which Adrianna's screams had been emanating.

In the circle of light, October saw the young hiking guide lying on the floor, motionless. October raised a shaking hand to her mouth—whether to prevent herself from screaming or vomiting, she didn't know. Adrianna was a mangled mess. Her clothes were torn to shreds. Large gashes and rips marred her skin like a morbid tapestry of gore. She was covered head to toe in streaks and splatters of blood. Blood everywhere. So much blood. Adrianna's blood.

"Oh my God," someone whispered. October wasn't sure who had uttered the words, or if it had just been in her head.

The visceral horror of seeing Adrianna lying there momentarily distracted October, so that at first she didn't see the figure standing close to the prone girl, partly obscured by the shadows. The figure then took a step into the light. It was a woman wearing no clothing. Her skin was covered in a spiderweb of gashes and splotches of dried, caked blood. There was also, however, fresh blood, Adrianna's blood, dripping from the woman's hands where black claws had sprouted through the flesh of her fingertips.

"Bernie," Arthur said in such horrified awe that his voice was almost unrecognizable. "Bernie, is that you?"

"Mom?" Bryan's squeaking voice reminded October he was essentially still just a child.

Bernadette stood over Adrianna, strips of ragged skin hanging off her body like peeling wallpaper. The top half of a bear's head, *the* bear, sat upon Bernadette's own like some sort of perverse hat, dripping gore down her face. She stared at each of them in turn without saying a word, her pallid, blood-streaked face starkly illuminated by the single beam of light from Viorica's flashlight.

No, this couldn't be.

Oh, but it is, the Overshadow said. *This is real.*

October's mind was reeling so hard, it hurt. She had watched Bernadette die. She had seen the light snuffed out of the woman's eyes. She had seen the corpse dragged away.

Yet, here she was. Bernadette was clearly alive. Had they left her behind while she had still lived?

I abandoned her back there, October thought in horror. *I left her even though she wasn't dead!* That couldn't possibly be, though. She had seen Bernadette's lifeless eyes. Eyes in the fanny pack. But now... God, those eyes! As more details became clear, October's chest constricted. Those were not the same eyes she had seen before. Alive or dead. Attached or disembodied. The Bernadette that stood before them now had the eyes of a beast. The right one was yellow, inhuman. Evil. And the left eye looked damaged, mangled.

"B-Bernie," Arthur sputtered, getting to his feet. "You're alive? Jesus, you're alive!"

"You said she was dead!" Bryan shouted, rounding on October. "You made me think my mom was dead!"

"Sh-she was," October spluttered. Her mouth didn't seem to want to form any words properly at the moment. Her brain was refusing to accept the situation before her.

"What did you do to Adrianna?" Samira interjected. "Christ, Bernadette. Did you do that? You mutilated her! You killed her!"

Bernadette stepped closer to them, bare, blood-covered feet slapping against the floor. It was then October noticed the same sort of black claws that grew from Bernadette's fingers had sprouted from her toes as well.

An amused grunt escaped Bernadette's mouth, and she tossed something on the ground at the group's feet. It was the hunting knife Viorica had thrown into the eye of the bear.

October stared down at the knife on the ground. An uncomfortable twitch raced through her at the implications.

Noel was the first to move. Managing to pull out his phone and turn it on, he shined its light over at Adrianna. With slow, steady steps, Noel quietly made his way around Bernadette—who paid him no heed—and over to the still girl. He crouched beside her.

"She's still alive," Noel muttered after putting his ear close to Adrianna's face. "She's breathing. We need to get her to a hospital. And I mean right now." He lifted the bloodied girl into his arms with care. Bernadette still did not seem to care as she smirked at Bryan and Arthur.

"The exit is open," Viorica stated, the beam from her flashlight never wavering from Bernadette. "We should leave this place right now."

"Mom, we need to get you to the hospital too!" Bryan extended a hand toward his blood-covered mother. "Come on!" He reached out to take Bernadette's hand.

Having finally figured out how to control her body again, October caught Bryan's arm, pulling him away from Bernadette.

Oh, come on, the Overshadow said. *Let him touch his mother. Let him run over to her. Whatever she's become, I'm sure she only wants to hug her son.*

"No." October breathed out, ignoring the voice in her head and tightening her grip on Bryan's wrist. "Bernadette. Your eyes. Is that you?" She knew it wasn't. It couldn't possibly be. "No. It's not you. It can't be. What did you do to Bernadette?"

Bernadette's eyes widened as if to revel in the fear their appearance caused. They all groaned at the sight of the one yellow, animalistic eye and the other destroyed eye now set within Bernadette's skull. Bryan allowed October to pull him a step backward, away from the thing posing as his mother.

"Bernie," Arthur said plaintively. He started to sob. "What happened to you? What did this to you? Can't you answer me?"

"We need to leave," Viorica repeated, taking a backward step toward the open passageway as Noel, carrying Adrianna in his arms, inched closer to the exit as well.

Bernadette leaned forward, then lifted her black-clawed hands to her face. If any of them had failed to notice her inhuman digits before, there was no avoiding looking at those unnatural talons now. Bernadette hooked her two forefinger claws into the corners of her mouth, then yanked savagely, tearing the flesh all the way back to her ears. October gagged as the bile rose into her mouth at the sight and sound of ripping skin.

The Bernadette-thing smiled at them.

Rows of sharp, jagged teeth that sprang from glistening, coal-black gums—far too many teeth for a human mouth to contain—glinted at them like dirty razor blades. The Bernadette-thing smiled literally from ear-to-ear in a display that disturbed October down to the very core of her sanity.

October's mind had been slowed and clouded by the abhorrent scene unfolding before her. She noticed too late that Bernadette's body had tensed like a large cat preparing to pounce on its doomed prey.

Thankfully Viorica was there.

As Bernadette leapt toward Arthur, a deafening crack exploded within the chamber, and her body stumbled backward, crashing into the center altar, her gruesome bear hat flying off her head. Ears ringing, an acrid smell filling her nostrils, October quickly turned to see Viorica holding her flashlight in one hand and the gun they had taken from the corpse on the slab in the other.

Muffled voices were yelling. October couldn't understand the words. It was like her ears had been stuffed with cotton. But she knew what they must be saying. She watched as Bernadette stood back up, still smiling that awful, too-wide smile. A large patch of skin on her right shoulder was now missing, revealing bloodied, obsidian-black flesh underneath.

October didn't have time to comprehend what she was seeing as another gunshot rang out and a hand gripped her shoulder, yanking her away from the scene. She didn't realize she still had hold of Bryan's arm and pulled him along as well.

I can't leave her again! October's conscience screamed, despite her rational mind knowing it couldn't possibly really be Bernadette.

Fortunately, her body refused to listen to such nonsense. She just ran, sprinting after Viorica's light which bounced ahead of her down the newly opened passage. She could just make out the form of Noel carrying Adrianna in his arms farther down the tunnel. She fervently hoped Arthur and Samira were right behind her.

"Arthur!" October yelled out over her shoulder. "Samira!" She didn't slow down. Her legs refused to even consider it.

They're probably dead, the Overshadow whispered in her ear. *You left them behind to be killed by Bernadette. You know. The other person you left behind to be killed today. Remember that?*

October tried not to listen. She just ran. And ran. And ran.

She didn't let go of Bryan. She didn't stop. She couldn't stop. Pure, unadulterated terror kept her legs pumping. There were many times in her life when she had heard the term "fight or flight." Perhaps she'd even experienced it before in short, small bursts; an unexpected door slamming from the wind, thinking she felt something crawling up her leg as she sat on the couch, or that moment when her socks lost traction on the kitchen floor and slid for a brief moment. But nothing compared to how much adrenaline surged through October right then and there as she fled from the monster.

What had happened to Bernadette?

The cave tunnels were an endless twisting labyrinth of granite and shadow. Slick walls, uneven floors. October tripped more than once, somehow managing not to fall. She didn't know if Bernadette was right behind them. Either way, October had seen enough horror movies to know that falling down would be the end of her. She had to get Bryan and herself out of this hellish maze of rock.

Shadows danced everywhere, only kept at bay by Viorica's flashlight aimed directly ahead. A beacon of hope. October couldn't lose sight of it. *Turn when Viorica turns. Just watch the light. Keep your eyes on the light! Don't even blink!*

Not until she was absolutely certain that her chest was going to crumple in a fiery implosion, did October stop running to take in deep shuddering lungsful of air.

"Wait!" she gasped out. Viorica and Noel came back for her and Bryan, entreating her to keep going.

"We have to keep going," Viorica said, her voice somehow calm, yet determined. "We're almost out. I can smell the fresh air."

"Come on." Noel shifted the unconscious Adrianna in his muscular arms. "If I can keep running while carrying her, you can keep running too!"

October tried to say something, but Viorica grabbed her hand and resumed running. Bryan was launched into flight as well by October's unwavering vice-like grip on his wrist.

She had no idea how long they ran, or how far. October only knew that she could barely lift her knees, and her toes were going to fall off sooner or later. Viorica would pause ever so briefly, look at something in her hand, then yell directions. Turn after turn, twist after twist. Were they just running in circles? Had she died? Was she now in hell? Was her eternal punishment to listen to the Overshadow cackle in her mind as she ran through the bowels of this lightless earth trying to escape, only to be forever trapped in despair while holding onto that sliver of hope that made each instance of disappointment that much more painful?

October didn't realize it at first, but the air that she was attempting to get into her tattered lungs had become lighter, fresher, cooler. The faint scent of pine needles accompanied her desperate breaths as a jagged portal of light in the black wall appeared in front of them.

Then they were out. Viorica had actually led them to an opening. It was more of a crevice, really. A narrow crack that a passerby outside would never have noticed had they not known it was there. October pushed Bryan and then herself through, not caring how the sharp craggy edges of the cleft snagged her clothes and scratched at her skin.

In a single, miraculous moment, the earth vomited them out of their underground hell and into a sunken pit with tree roots poking through the earthen sides.

They were out.

Great gouts of fresh air, of free air, filled October's chest. Finally letting go of Bryan's arm, October ran both hands through her hair. She looked up at the orange-red clouds that hung in the darkening sky, wanting to embrace them. Outside had never once looked so lovely to her as it did at that moment.

"Where's my dad?" Bryan panted.

October looked around at the others. Arthur and Samira were not with them. Did they fall behind? Did that Bernadette-thing catch them?

I've left someone else behind, October thought, her stomach sinking. "I-I thought they were with us." Tears spilled from her eyes. "We have to go back!"

"I saw them right behind us!" Noel said. "I swear I saw them!"

You let both of Bryan's parents die today, the Overshadow said in a voice so soft and intimate it felt like a tongue licking the inside of her ear canal. *That's quite the feat. Actually, you created an orphan, just like you. Ha!*

"My dad can't run that fast!" Bryan shouted, his voice rising in pitch. "He has asthma, you moron!"

Viorica shushed him. "Listen," the woman said, her attention focused on the crevice they had all just squeezed out of.

There was a sound. October could hear it now. It was emanating from out of rock. It was someone, something, crawling. Coming closer. Was that breathing she heard?

"Screw this." Noel heaved Adrianna's catatonic form out of the pit and pulled himself up. Bryan scurried up after him.

"Viorica, let's go!" October hissed.

A hand shot out of that dark aperture and gripped onto the rocky edge.

7/23/2006

Dear Mr. Seth Monahan,

I know you have been eagerly awaiting this letter. I apologize for the delay in its reaching you. But, with all due respect, as you most likely anticipated, my people had to perform an extensive background check on your, shall we say, colorful past. Do not fret. This is customary procedure for any individual I consider for employ, whether the position be on my staff or as a freelancer such as yourself.

You have passed the review and are now officially under contract with me. Since you were able to gain access to the unusual circles where my name and reputation may be known, then I expect you are familiar with this type of work. And even though you have already signed the contract with its strict non-disclosure provisions, I must stress at least one more time the importance of confidentiality. Save for the list of contacts you have been given, you are to speak to no one about your activities relating to this job, especially any person associated with Valravn Technologies. Under no circumstances, however dire, may you reveal the nature of your work to any person or any law enforcement agencies. The consequences set out in the contract are not discretionary and will be immediately enforced for any breach. There are no second chances when it comes to this point.

Now on to the details.

My staff have informed me that the object we seek is called The Wheel of Kurkoth, likely located somewhere in the Pacific Northwest of the United States. Focus on the region in and around Fulgent County in the state of Washington. My sources suggest you should begin your search in a town by the name of Cinter. Your task is to locate and obtain the Relic Enigmata for me. You may accomplish this in any way you see fit. I am only interested in the results.

That is all the information I can provide you at this time. I am certain that a man such as yourself can get me what I want. Your $3.5 million is waiting for you, provided you find the Wheel of Kurkoth and deliver it t

[REST OF LETTER BURNED]

CHAPTER THIRTEEN

Wendig

Have you eaten today?" Jordan asked, peering at Wendig through the screen on his phone. "You need to eat." She slurped some steaming ramen out of a blue plastic bowl, using chopsticks to stuff the noodles into her mouth.

"You know how much I hate listening to people eat," Wendig said with a frown, sitting in his idling car. *Misophonia* it was called, the agony and extreme irritation some people experience when listening to others eat, breathe, or make other disgusting sounds. He tried to ignore Jordan's loud eating and looked up into his rearview mirror. He could see the sky, burning with red clouds that resembled the dying embers of a fireplace. The sun would be completely set in a minute or two.

"Sorry." Jordan put down the chopsticks. "Anyway, don't change the subject."

Wendig felt a sense of relief wash over him at the cessation of eating noises.

"You always do that. I know your ways, Lucas. Now listen, you need energy. With all that running around you do, you need to eat more. I know how wrapped up you can get in your work and that you forget to get some food. I'm supposed to be your assistant, not your mom. But I do worry about you, you know? Now tell me, when was the last time you ate today, Mr. Wendig Boss-man, sir?"

Wendig sighed, looking out at the driver's side mirror, then back at his phone. "Seven," he finally admitted with reluctance.

"Seven? Like, seven this morning?" Jordan sputtered, startling the lizard who had been dozing on her shoulder and almost spilling her ramen all over her cluttered desk. She pulled her webcam closer to her face so that Wendig was able to clearly see the spots of black that flecked her brown eyes. "Dude, Lucas. It's almost, what, nine p.m. where you are? You need to freaking eat, like right now. Don't make me fly over there and drag you to some fast-food place."

"I wouldn't allow you to fly over here anyway," Wendig replied. "If you did, I'd fire you."

"What? Really?" Jordan said, taken aback. She then chuckled after a moment. "Oh, you're joking. It's a joke, right?" She gave him a suspicious side eye. "Anyway, go get a slice of pizza or a burger. Now! Or else." She wagged a finger at him.

"I will," Wendig said, and he meant it. "After I talk to Mr. and Mrs. Rivas."

"Promise?"

"I will," he answered.

"Say that you promise," she insisted.

"I promise, Jordan."

"Good." Jordan gave a satisfied smile. "Now what was I saying? Oh yeah. I found interesting documents from lots of different countries like Japan, Ethiopia, Turkey, Mexico, even here from the U.S. Many just detailed myths and folklore. There was also some old, personal correspondence I found. They were all pretty creepy. And they sounded very similar to what Caleb said when you spoke with him. Anyway, I won't keep you. Now remember, according to what I've been able to uncover, this Relic Enigmata most likely looks like a solid metal wheel or disc of some sort. Like it said in my email, if you remember."

"Metal wheel, got it," Wendig interrupted her. "I need to get moving again on this investigation."

"Okay, okay," Jordan said. "Be careful in there." She gave him a solemn salute and made Nathan wave goodbye, then terminated the connection.

Jordan reminded him of Rowan a lot of the time. The thought always caused him mixed feelings; both happiness and sadness. Why had he involved Jordan in all of this? They had only been working together a few years. Not that long at all. He could end their partnership easily.

Could he?

He didn't know. She probably wouldn't let him cut her off. Jordan felt that he had saved her life and she now owed him a great debt. Plus, she loved the work and was incredibly stubborn.

Just like his daughter.

"Rowan," Wendig breathed.

Shutting off the engine, he stepped out of the car into the cool evening air. The sun had dipped below the horizon to slumber as he regarded the house, a modern two-story Craftsman with a lawn that had sprouted numerous weeds. He double-checked the address just to be sure. This was definitely the place: 433 Marlow Lane, Shadow's Path, Washington.

Reviewing relevant notes and topics in his head, Wendig made his way up the concrete walk, stepped onto the covered porch, and knocked on the blue door. He inhaled deeply as he waited, almost as if he were nervous. Perhaps he *was* nervous. A little.

Footsteps sounded on the other side of the door. A moment later it opened to reveal a thin man dressed in a shabby collared shirt. He had an unshaven face, and a head of brown hair that looked like it hadn't come into contact with a hairbrush all day or been washed in a week.

"Can I help you?" the man asked in a monotone, not opening the door all the way, his dull green eyes inspecting Wendig without much interest.

"Mr. Rivas?" Wendig tried to sound as friendly as possible. He put on a smile.

"Yeah," Mr. Rivas answered, narrowing his eyes. He still didn't open the door any farther. "Who're you? What do you want? Is this about the car payments? You people already called me yesterday."

"No, Mr. Rivas. My name is Dr. Luke Connor. I believe you spoke with my assistant—er, Ellen, yesterday evening, about your son? I'm the investigator she works for. You agreed to let me talk with Caleb, over at Forestleaf. You signed the consent form, remember?"

"Oh, right." Mr. Rivas scratched at his stubbly chin with a sloth-like movement. "I didn't know you were going to come here, too, though. Or did I just forget? Is everything okay with Caleb?" He let the door open a few more inches, his eyes becoming more alert. "Is he alright?"

"Oh, yes," Wendig reassured the man. "Caleb is fine. He seems to be benefitting from his rehabilitation and therapy. Nothing to worry about, Mr. Rivas. I came here tonight to talk with you about some important details that would really help my investigation along. May I come inside?"

Mr. Rivas stared at him for several moments. Wendig could see the gears sluggishly turning behind the man's eyes, as if the machine of his mind needed a tune-up.

Nodding, Mr. Rivas said, "Yeah, okay. Come on in." He opened the door all the way, allowing Wendig to step inside. After securing the locks on the door again, he led Wendig into a living room strewn with used paper plates, empty fast-food wrappers, and dirty laundry. "Can I get you anything to drink, Dr. Connor?"

"No, thank you," Wendig answered, moving aside two old pizza boxes in order to sit himself down on a beige sofa. Rivas sat down across from him in a well-worn armchair.

"So, you said Caleb is okay." Rivas stared at Wendig, scratching at his stubbly jaw once more. "That's great. That's great." A pause. "Caleb's a good boy, you know? Never was a troublemaker. Almost always did the chores his mom told him to do. Got good grades for the most part. Except for math. He hated math with a passion." He made a throaty sound like the beginning of a chuckle. Instead, he drifted off into another pause, staring off into space.

"Seems like a great kid," Wendig said with a smile. He had to be careful to balance keeping the conversation on track while also offering compassion and empathy.

"Mmhm, yeah." Rivas seemed to finally snap back to reality. He cleared his throat. "I'm sorry. What did you need to talk to me about? It must be something important if you felt the need to come down here all this way. Did Caleb say anything? Give you any insight into this whole crazy situation our family's found ourselves in?"

"He may have. We will certainly see." Wendig quickly went over his mental notes once more, trying to see how best to word what he was about to say. "I know this may be painful to talk about, but I need to ask you about that unfortunate day when Caleb stumbled into the room of his friend, Evan, and saw what he saw. Do you know if Caleb took anything from Evan's house? Brought anything home with him? Think hard, please. Maybe you didn't notice that day. You certainly had plenty of other matters on your mind, I'm sure. Maybe you saw something later in Caleb's room? Something that looked out of place among his stuff?"

Mr. Rivas's eyes widened a fraction, providing all the evidence that Wendig needed. Caleb had been telling the truth. The boy had indeed brought the Enigmata home with him. A regrettable, foolish move that embroiled him further in this mess. At least Wendig was on the right track for the Enigmata's location. Hopefully, Caleb hadn't messed around with the thing too much. Who knew what this particular Enigmata was capable of? It seemed just having it was enough to summon the presence of this "Watcher" being. Wendig hoped that by studying the item, he could free Caleb of the presence that haunted him.

"Does anything come to mind, Mr. Rivas?" Wendig asked, leaning forward. "Do you know what I might be talking about?"

Mr. Rivas swallowed, his Adam's apple bobbing up and down in a loud gulp. "I..." he began, but the word trailed off.

"Are you alright, Mr. Rivas?" Wendig asked. The man had paled, and his hands seemed to be shaking. "If there is something you want to say, then please tell me. If you have seen such an object among Caleb's stuff, I can help you."

"You know about that thing?" Mr. Rivas blurted out in a harsh whisper. He balled his fists to stop their uncontrollable trembling. "Is that why you came, Dr. Connor? You know about that round metal plate?"

Matched the description Jordan gave me. Good job.

"Yes, that's why I'm here, Mr. Rivas. Do you think you could show me this metal plate?" he requested, rising from his seat. "It's very important that I examine it. It might provide valuable clues that could help your son in his recovery."

Mr. Rivas opened his mouth as if to say something but then closed it again, remaining silent. It appeared to Wendig that several dozen thoughts were running simultaneously through Mr. Rivas's mind before the man nodded his head and stood up. He led Wendig to the stairs and began climbing with tentative steps up to the second story of the house.

A thought struck Wendig as they went up. "Is Mrs. Rivas out for the evening?" he asked. He realized he hadn't seen or heard another person in the house since arriving.

Mr. Rivas halted mid-step on the stairs, his hand holding onto the railing in a claw-like grip. "We're separated for the time being," Mr. Rivas answered without turning to look at Wendig. He let out a long, lamenting sigh. "We've had some problems. Ever since Caleb was sent to the mental health center, our marriage started to crumble and deteriorate." He finally turned around, looking down at Wendig on the step below him with tired, weary eyes. "We didn't talk anymore. It was like one evening she said goodnight to me, then the next morning the silence started. All she did was cry about Caleb while lying on his bed. I heard her mumbling to herself all the time about how he was stuck in that 'looney bin.' I tried. I really did. I was in a dark place too. Didn't know what to do. Didn't know how to help." He sighed. "I didn't stop her when she eventually moved out. I didn't have the energy. And I think that I felt it would be better for her to get out of here. She's staying with her parents in Rhode Island." He turned back around. "It's for the best. I kind of wish you had contacted me sooner. Maybe you could have helped us with all this and saved my marriage. Could still be salvageable, don't you think? If Caleb can get better, things might work out."

A lump formed in Wendig's throat. He said nothing, and they resumed the climb to the second floor in silence. Mr. Rivas opened the door to Caleb's bedroom. It appeared that his parents had left everything exactly as it had been when Caleb was last here. Literally. There were action figures and graphic novels on the floor, the bed was unmade, a video game controller sat on a chair, and a dirty dish had even been left on the kid's nightstand, now growing mold in a lovely shade of pale green. That was probably a health hazard.

Wendig surveyed the room until his eyes fell upon a blackish-blue object lying on Caleb's desk beside his computer.

"There it is." Mr. Rivas indicated the dark circular item that Wendig had already spotted.

Wendig walked over to the desk, kneeling so that he was eye-level with the thing. The wheel was about as big as his fist. It seemed to be made of a black metal with a deep blue tint, so polished he could see his reflection. At first glance, the object appeared to be completely smooth. When Wendig studied it up closer, however, he saw indentations, grooves, faint etchings of glyphs, and thin lines that wound around the shiny surface in several concentric circles.

He had to relocate this thing to a safer place. He pulled a pair of gloves from his coat and slipped them on. A special metallic microfiber had been woven into the very fabric of the gloves, and special symbols were meticulously stitched on the interiors. Both helped protect against malevolent energies such objects frequently possessed. These gloves—courtesy of a friend from Iceland—had been one of the best acquisitions during his early years of hunting Enigmata.

"Mr. Rivas, have you touched this object at all?" Wendig asked, flexing his fingers inside the gloves. They fit snug against his skin.

"Yeah, I did," Mr. Rivas said mournfully. "And I'd tell you not to do the same."

Before he could reach out for the Enigmata, Wendig heard a distinctive click behind him. He spun around to see Mr. Rivas holding a pistol, pointed directly at him.

"Mr. Rivas," Wendig began, raising his hands. Confusion suffused his mind for the briefest of moments. "Whatever you think you have to do, you don't."

"Shut up! Just don't...say anything..." Mr. Rivas started to sob, losing all composure, the weapon wobbling disconcertingly in his hand. "I-I can't let you take it. Don't touch it! It's evil...so evil." Tears streamed down his cheeks. "I put my son in an insane asylum because of what he told the doctors. I put him in a prison for crazy people!" The man's voice rose to a shrill pitch.

"Just listen." Wendig kept his face in a neutral expression. His mouth felt like sandpaper. "Your son is not crazy. I'm trying to help him. Trying to help you too. There's no need for any of this. Let me help your family. Whatever it is you're going through, you don't have to go through it alone."

"Stop with all the bullshit!" Mr. Rivas shouted. "Just shut the hell up. I let them take Caleb away and lock him up. But after I found this thing in his room, I took it. I touched it. I... I saw it..." His eyes went wide, the memory of whatever he had seen obviously replaying inside his head and terrifying him. "I saw it. Do you hear what I'm saying? I saw the fucking thing! I thought my son had lost his mind." The man sobbed openly. "He didn't. No. Caleb was telling the truth."

The pistol swayed dangerously in front of Wendig. "Mr. Rivas, please," he said, hands still raised. "I can help. Just put the gun down and listen to me. I can help you. I can help Caleb. I promise I can."

"How?" Mr. Rivas asked, the pistol lowering for a second, before coming right back up. "This thing, this Watcher Caleb talked about." He shook his head. "It's not human. I-I don't know what it is. It's not something that should...be. Do you get it? It shouldn't exist!" He rubbed sweat and tears out of his wild eyes. "It visited me the same night that I touched that disc. I thought I was having a nightmare at first. I couldn't wake up, though. It was outside my damn bedroom window, staring in with that awful face. It kept visiting me until one night it was, poof, gone. The next day, I went to visit Caleb in the hospital. He whispered to me that he had started seeing the Watcher again. You know what I did? I bought this gun the very next day from some shady hustler down on Second Street. Paid three times what it cost in a store so I didn't have to do all that paperwork and then wait. I needed it right then. I got this gun so that I could kill it. Kill that unnatural thing! But it showed me the truth. Do you know what the truth is, Dr. Connor?"

Wendig said nothing.

"The truth is that it's all my fault Caleb is where he is. And it's true. His mom didn't want to put him in that place at first. I insisted. I convinced her."

For a brief moment, Mr. Rivas looked down. Wendig took the opportunity to get closer to the man. Mr. Rivas's head snapped back up, and Wendig halted in his tracks.

"Stop," he pleaded. "Just stay there. Stay where you are and don't get any closer. Just tell me." A pause. "Can you really help Caleb?"

"I can try." A hard knot had formed in Wendig's stomach that threatened to squeeze the life out of all his organs. "I will do my best. I've dealt with unusual situations like this before. I can't say I know what this Watcher is capable of. What I can tell you is the same thing I've been saying. I will do whatever I can to help you and Caleb."

"It came to my window last night," Mr. Rivas said, snot dribbling down from his nose, tears leaving stains on his cheeks. "It was like it knew what I was planning and came to mock me. I think it enjoys misery, Dr. Connor. The Watcher loves to watch others wallow in fear, misery, and sadness. I think it craves those negative emotions like it needs them to live. Do you see? Do you see how it smiles?"

He glanced out the window, then turned back to Wendig.

Icy fingers ran their frigid touch up Wendig's spine at Mr. Rivas's words. He slowly turned away from the distraught, gun-wielding father, and looked out of the bedroom window just above Caleb's desk. A body, as black as the night that surrounded it, clung to the outside of the glass. A lighter-colored, mask-like face, withered and slack, yet smiling a far too-wide smile, stared at him. Animalistic eyes the color of sulfur peered through ragged eyelids.

The Watcher.

The thing was only there for the briefest of moments before scurrying away in a soft clattering of claws that went up onto the roof.

"Mr. Rivas." Wendig turned back around. "We can't let it get—!"

"It revels in the misery of others," Mr. Rivas cut him off, turning the gun on himself.

There was a deafening bang as Wendig watched the man shoot himself in the head.

CHAPTER FOURTEEN

Wendig

It was a laugh, Wendig realized.

After the ringing subsided, Wendig's hearing returned some-what to normal. He had reacted quickly, covering his ears with his palms just as the gun had gone off.

Now he stood immobile, staring at the limp, motionless body of Mr. Rivas where it had crumpled to the floor. Bits of bone, blood, and brain lay splattered across the wall and bedroom carpet. Ice spread out from his core as the shock of what he had just witnessed fully embraced him in a freezing hug.

Still, that wheezing laughter rasped from behind him. It penetrated his mind like a scalpel, slicing through every layer of tissue to stab at the depths of his consciousness.

Wendig spun around when he heard the glass break. The abhorrent Watcher held the Enigmata in a clawed hand. It stared at him with those sulfur eyes, dangling upside down from the edge of the roof outside. The leathery skin that covered its face—strangely tanned and ragged and contrasting with the rest of its obsidian body—stretched into an expansive smile that leered at him with malicious enjoyment. It continued to laugh like a maniac. The monstrous abomination was enjoying the scene that had just unfolded before it. With one last cackle and an obscene licking of its lips, it disappeared from view, taking the Enigmata with it.

Too many thoughts sped through Wendig's mind. Dashing out of the bedroom, he flew down the stairs, and out of the house. He felt a twinge of guilt leaving Mr. Rivas on the floor upstairs like that, but someone was bound to find the poor man soon, even if he had to call it in himself. Sure enough, as Wendig jumped into his car, he saw a few people peering out of their windows across the street, no doubt alerted by the blast of the gun that had echoed through the night moments ago, shattering the peace of the quiet street.

Wendig wasn't paying much attention to the people, however. He was focused on the dark shape that crouched on the roof of the Rivas house like a life-size grotesque made of black stone and obscured by shadow. If it hadn't moved, one would have thought it *was* a statue.

As Wendig watched, the Watcher shot off into the night, bounding from the roof of the Rivas house to the dwelling that lay directly behind it in one giant, graceful leap. Wendig brought his car to life and sped after the thing, only turning on his lights after he had roared around the corner of Marlow Lane onto Night Willow Avenue. He hoped the people watching from their windows hadn't seen his face. He couldn't worry about that now, though. At least he was able to quickly hide his license plate with the flick of a switch. Or more accurately, the use of an app on his phone that would obscure a pane of special glass mounted over the license plate. Another point to Jordan for obtaining that for him.

The lanky horror leapt from house to house with incredible speed and agility that no human being could have ever achieved. It moved like a frog. No, more like a cat. No. It was nothing that made any sense. If the circumstances were different, Wendig might have spared a thought to wonder how this foul creature could move the way it did. In the present situation, he didn't care. All he knew was that he had to follow the Watcher, wherever it went.

He had to deal with it. He had to end this abomination before it caused any more misery. This creature was tied to Evan's Enigmata somehow. An obviously dangerous Enigmata. Just as dangerous as the one that took Rowan.

Who was he kidding? All Enigmata were dangerous.

Speeding through the streets of Shadow's Path, trying to keep the creature in view, Wendig got his cell phone out of his coat pocket and had to yell "Call Jordan!" three times before it accepted the command. The phone rang once before being answered.

"Hey, Lucas," Jordan's voice said through the speaker. "I was just heading out for some sustenance of the chicken nugget kind. What's up?"

"Jordan, listen carefully," Wendig said through gritted teeth, steering around another corner with one hand on the wheel. The car's tires screeched in protest. "I need you to call the police department in Shadow's Path immediately. Tell them there's been an accident at 433 Marlow Lane. Don't give them your name. Don't give them my name. Hang up before they ask you any questions. Do whatever it is you do so they can't trace your number."

"Oh crap. An accident?" He heard a door slam shut from her end. "Did something happen? Are you okay?"

"Jordan, just do as I say." He tried to maneuver around an oncoming car on the road, dinging its fender and almost hitting a postal box. The other car blared its horn at him. "I'll answer questions later. Just please call them for me."

"Yeah! I—"

And he hung up on her, tossing the phone into the center console. The phone immediately started to ring. He ignored it. *Sorry, Jordan,* he thought. *No time to talk.*

He caught quick glimpses of the creature here and there in the glow of streetlights as it bounded across rooftops in the deepening night. The Watcher was heading for the outskirts of town. Opening the car's glove compartment, Wendig reached inside and pulled out his Glock 19, dropping it on the passenger seat within easy reach.

A car he sped past honked at him, and the driver flipped him off. A late-night jogger flailed arms at him, most likely shouting at him to slow down. Wendig didn't care. They didn't see the evil thing he was chasing. He couldn't let this foul monstrosity escape. Where was it headed? Where was it so eager to go?

The unbridled glee in those yellow eyes as they peered out of that mask of leathery skin flashed in his mind. The Watcher had visibly reveled in Mr. Rivas's suicide like a child seeing all his presents on Christmas morning. It had laughed at the poor, anguished man pulling the trigger and ending his own life right in his son's bedroom. Whatever this Watcher-creature was, it wasn't just some mindless animal. Animals didn't enjoy the suffering of others. Animals didn't laugh at death.

Car speeding down the roads, Wendig tried to follow the Watcher out of town. He lost it for a few panicked moments before he saw its black silhouette barely defined against the night sky as it escaped the city limits and darted into the surrounding forest. At the pinnacle of a tree, it turned back to look at him with a grin. Had it just been playing with him? Allowing him to chase after it for its own amusement?

The tree swayed forward and backward as the creature flung itself deeper into the forest like a cannon shot.

It disappeared into the darkness.

Wendig could discern no more movement among the trees save for a small breeze that rustled leaves and pine needles in a gentle caress. No, no, no. He couldn't lose it. He couldn't let the Watcher go free to hurt someone else.

Pulling over to the side of the road, Wendig grabbed his pistol and got out of the car. He stared fixedly up at the trees that surrounded him, his index finger resting on the gun's frame, itching to slide onto the trigger.

Nothing. There was absolutely nothing. He knew it was futile. The creature was long gone by now. The Watcher had eluded him. He had lost the trail, letting the monster slip through his fingers.

"Dammit!" Wendig shouted, pounding the roof of his car.

Who was he kidding, though? The Watcher had been playing with him. Leading him on a little jaunt before it went off to more interesting things.

And now someone might just die because of him.

Turning away from the car, Wendig studied the dark mass of trees that spread out before him. He considered venturing out into that forest but then thought better of it. What would he accomplish besides getting lost in there? There was no way he could follow the Watcher on foot through the shadowy tangle of woods. The most probable scenario would be him getting turned around, then walking in circles until the sun rose.

He reluctantly got back into his idling car, tossing the Glock onto the passenger seat. He ripped off his gloves, then grabbed the steering wheel, gripping it tightly, the faux-leather cover squeaking under his fingers. His phone that lay in the console between the seats pulsed with the notification light.

Turning it on, he saw that he had several texts from Jordan. He unlocked the phone and selected the message.

lucas r u ok?

called cops like u said, on their way

please answer

whats going on?

LUCAS

Sighing, he tapped on the call button right below Jordan's name. The phone barely rang once before it was answered.

"Lucas!" Jordan exclaimed. "I called the police like you said! Are you okay? What's happening?"

"I'm fine, Jordan." Wendig rubbed his temples. "Nothing to worry about."

"Nothing to worry about?" Jordan cut him off, catching Wendig by complete surprise. "You think you can just pull something like that, do you?" Wendig's voice faltered in his throat. She went on. "You think you can just call me, saying there's been some sort of accident? Telling me to call the police? Then just hang up on me without another word? Not even telling me if you're okay or if you're hurt?"

"Jordan, I was—"

"I was worried about you, you jerk!" Anger rose in her voice. "You know, I was about to go for food. I was having a nice evening. Then you call and pull this crap. You expect me not to worry when you say things like that? What is wrong with you? What if something had happened to you?"

"Jordan." Wendig was unsure of what else to say. What had just happened? He had never heard Jordan talk like this before. He fidgeted, adjusting the phone against his ear. "Are you...angry at me?"

"What gave you a freaking clue?" Jordan spat through the phone. Wendig thought he could almost feel spittle hit his face. She was silent for a moment before saying, "I'm going to demand a hell of a raise. You hear me?"

"Well, uh," Wendig sputtered, confused, his mouth dry. "If you think—"

"Never mind, Lucas," Jordan said. He could tell she was speaking through gritted teeth now. "I just...urgh!"

At a loss for words, Wendig just sat there in his car. He would have thought Jordan had hung up if he didn't hear her breathing. He said nothing, not wishing to provoke her further. What could he say?

"Okay, I'm done. I'm done," she finally said. "I'm calming down." She inhaled loudly, then exhaled, her breath coming out in a whoosh. She cleared her throat. "I'm sorry. I know how dangerous our work is. I was just super worried. I didn't know what was going on, and my anxiety started going through the roof. I'm sorry. Maybe I wasn't totally joking about that raise, though." She let out a weak noise that was half chuckle, half sigh. "Okay, I'll be fine. I'm fine. Let's talk. What happened over there? You spoke to Caleb Rivas's parents, right? You said there was an accident. Is everything alright?"

"Um," Wendig fumbled over his words. His mind was drawing a blank. Was Jordan still angry at him? Should he ask if she was still mad at him? No, that would be the wrong thing to say.

"Are you still there?" she asked.

"Uh, yes," he stuttered, then cleared his throat. "I spoke to Mr. Rivas. He showed me the Enigmata." He sighed. "I almost had it, but I lost it. This is a mess."

"Oh," Jordan said. "Wait, what was this accident? Who got hurt?"

Wendig rubbed his eyes with his thumb and forefinger as despair settled over him. The horrible image of Caleb's father shooting himself refused to fade away. "Mr. Rivas is dead. I just watched him shoot himself while we were talking."

"Oh my God," Jordan whispered. There was no longer any trace of anger in her voice. "Why did he do that?"

"The Entity that Caleb talked about," Wendig said. "The one he called the 'Watcher.'" Jordan made an affirmative noise. "I saw it. The creature was here, Jordan. I saw it watching us through the window. Mr. Rivas killed himself because the Watcher was tormenting him. Haunting him. Just like it's haunting Caleb still. Just like it haunted his friend Evan before it killed him. I chased it in my car, but I think it was just playing with me. I lost it when it got out of town."

"Holy hell." Jordan paused a moment to take everything in. "Look, I found some interesting things on this Enigmata. Evan and Caleb and you aren't the only people to have seen it. I've found references to similar incidents that go back a very long time."

"Tell me." Wendig closed his eyes.

A thought suddenly popped into his head then, blocking out everything Jordan was saying.

"Wait. I know where the Watcher's going," he said. Throwing the car into reverse, he backed onto the road and sped off. How had he not seen the obvious answer?

"What? Where?" Jordan asked.

"I need to get to Caleb. Now."

He hoped he wouldn't be too late.

DATE ENTERED: 6-29-2021
OFFENSE REPORTED: MURDER
REPORTING OFFICER: SERGEANT CASSANDRA B. HALE
LOCATION OF INCIDENT: 431 MARLOW LANE, SHADOW'S PATH, WA

NARRATIVE FOR SERGEANT CASSANDRA B. HALE

On June 28, 2021 I was called to the scene of an apparent homicide at 431 Marlow Lane. Officer P. Redland and I were dispatched at approximately 0700 hours. Dispatch received a call from Kyle Brooks (age 39) stating that his son Evan Brooks (age 13) had been murdered.

Officer Redland and I arrived at approximately 0715 hours. Rita Brooks (age 37) was outside on the porch of the residence, crying and in obvious distress. Kyle Brooks sat with her on the steps, crying as well. When we approached, the couple were too distraught to speak with us. Mr. Brooks just pointed Officer Redland and me up toward the second floor of their home. Officer Redland took point as we ascended the staircase and conducted a search of each room until we entered the bedroom of Evan Brooks.

We found Evan Brooks, deceased, in his bedroom. The victim's body was pinned to the bedroom wall with what appeared to be old bladed instruments of unknown origin. The victim's torso had been slashed open and the entrails spilled onto the floor. CSI commented on-scene that the skin on the victim's entire body appeared to have been "removed with disturbing efficiency." No portion of the skin was found at the scene nor in the immediate surrounding area. The single bedroom window was open. At this time, no DNA evidence or fingerprints have been found, other than those belonging to the residents of the house, as well as those of Evan Brooks' best friend, Caleb Rivas (age 13).

Caleb Rivas, neighbor of the Brooks', managed to get past Officer Redland and enter the crime scene where he witnessed the victim's body on the wall. He was promptly escorted out of the house. Recommend the boy attend counseling along with Kyle Brooks and Rita Brooks.

No additional subjects identified or apprehended at scene.

CHAPTER FIFTEEN

October

Samira and Arthur were both alive and safe.

October had been beyond relieved when the pair had emerged from the rocky crevice that led deep underground, leaning on one another like injured soldiers returning from a battlefield. October didn't know if she would have been able to take any more death that day. For a split-second, as a hand emerged from that dark portal to hell, October thought the murderous and crazed Bernadette-thing had found them again.

Thankfully, that was not the case. It was Samira, pulling herself and a wheezing, choking Arthur out of the rock. Arthur was in rough shape, and as badly as October wanted to get moving, she knew the group couldn't leave until Arthur was able to breathe at least somewhat normally again.

If only Bernadette hadn't been the one carrying his inhaler for him, October thought. Shouldn't Arthur have had a backup? If he did, Bernadette had probably been carrying that one for him as well. It wasn't like Arthur would have been expecting his wife to be killed today.

Or to return from the grave and try to kill him.

He would have his medication if it weren't for your cowardice, the Overshadow said, cackling.

That's not true, October shot back. *I tried! I tried to get Bernadette's fanny pack! All that was inside was her own eyes. Jesus.*

Lame excuses, the Overshadow spat, its coils squeezing October's mind. *You're afraid of eyeballs? I hate to tell you, but you have some eyes socketed in your own skull at this very moment.*

Don't talk to it, October reminded herself. *Don't engage with it. You have to remember that nothing good ever comes from engaging.* She tried to tune the voice out.

Once the group was back together and Arthur had sufficient rest, they got far away from the cliffs, delving deeper into the dense forest. A light drizzle began misting them as they trudged through gloomy trees that reminded October of an overgrown, prehistoric jungle she had once seen in a movie. The sun was already setting, hiding behind the verdant wall around them, and sinking lower. Night would arrive soon.

The group really had no idea where they were going. Even Viorica wasn't sure which way to go. She kept pulling out and glancing at the device she used to navigate the cave system, but each time she would only sigh after a moment. Perhaps it had gotten damaged? Only Adrianna might have been able to determine their location, and she was unfortunately unconscious in Noel's arms. Still alive, though, thank God. Any maps Adrianna might have had with her would have been in her pack which now lay on the floor back in that creepy chamber somewhere among the pile of bones that rained down from the ceiling. Everyone else's cell phones were either dead, broken, or back in the cave as well, which prevented them from using their lights or digital compasses. Only Viorica's flashlight remained. A lone beacon.

October had lost all sense of how long they'd been walking when Viorica finally made them halt. They gathered under a thick part of an overhead canopy of leaves to protect them from the worst of the drizzle—which was quickly turning into a heavy rain. Not the best shelter. Still, any defense against the cold, wet weather was better than nothing.

"We'll stop for now," Viorica announced to the group, wiping rain out of her eyes. "We can't go any farther tonight."

"What? Why?" Bryan asked. He had been supporting Arthur while they walked, and now lowered his father down, setting the man against a fallen tree. Arthur looked pale and shaky. His breathing was ragged, and he hadn't said anything in a long while.

"Look at your father." Viorica waved a hand at Arthur. "He needs to rest to recover some strength. We all do."

"He needs help! Medical help! We can't stay in this forest," Bryan protested, waving his arms around. "It's starting to pour! And it's cold and dark."

"Yes, exactly." Viorica stood with her arms folded like a schoolteacher lecturing a recalcitrant student. "It's dark, and it will be much darker soon. We won't be able to see where we are going when my flashlight dies. Its batteries are going to run out soon." She held up her flashlight, which had dimmed considerably since the caves. She turned it off. The rising moon, partially obscured by rain clouds and mist, offered the only illumination now. "There's no point in wandering around in a forest at night. Unless you want to become even more lost than we already are. We have no compass. We have no operating phones. We have no map to navigate by. And soon, we will have just weak moonlight to guide us. We have no choice. We have to stay here for the night. I don't like it either, but it's the better option."

"I agree with Viorica," Noel said as he gently laid Adrianna's small form against the fallen tree, close to Arthur. The girl still hadn't made a sound or shown any signs of returning to consciousness. October was so glad she could at least see Adrianna's chest rising softly with each shallow breath. "Oof, my arms are tired." Noel shook his arms out to get the blood flowing back through them. "My whole body needs a rest."

"We can build a shelter for tonight," Viorica stated. She turned her flashlight back on. "We need to do it now before the rain gets worse."

Everyone agreed, though Noel and Bryan did so reluctantly.

Following Viorica's instructions, they got to work building something to help keep the rain off of them while they rested and slept. Not that any of them were going to get much sleep after everything they had witnessed that day. Within a fairly short time, they had gathered up enough deadfall to make a good-size lean-to big enough for everyone to huddle under. They set up the shelter around Adrianna and Arthur, using the fallen tree they rested against for additional support. Pretty soon they had a modicum of protection against the rain that showed no sign of letting up. Though they had covered the floor in leaves and brush, it was still uncomfortably wet to sit on.

Bryan sat beside his dad, watching Arthur rest. Every once in a while, the man would start coughing and gasping for air. October would find herself holding her own breath until he quieted again. Samira had done what she could to tend to Adrianna's plethora of awful-looking wounds without a first aid kit. October had heard the woman mutter, "no one else is going to die," as she wrapped one of the nasty, blackening gashes on Adrianna's leg, using strips of cloth that Noel handed her, tearing them off an extra t-shirt he had brought in his backpack.

They rested there in the dark. Viorica turned her flashlight off again to conserve the remaining battery. Faint beams of moonlight found their way through the heavy, black clouds, illuminating the falling raindrops and making them look like glass beads falling toward the earth.

October, shivering from the cold, sat next to Viorica. She usually wouldn't relish the thought of having to sleep while touching someone to share body heat, though as the night grew colder—the wind biting at her exposed face and arms—her desperation for warmth overrode any reluctance.

Viorica scooted closer to October. "How are you doing?" she whispered.

Awful, the Overshadow wanted her to say. *You are pathetically scared, cold, exhausted, in pain. Basically a pile of useless shit. Tell her the truth. Tell her how you haven't helped this little group at all.*

"Oh, I've been better," October whispered back without a hint of humor, trying to block out the voice in her head. "I can't wait to finally get home. I don't know if I'll ever want to be around trees again after this. And my therapist is going to be seeing even more of me, at least for a while."

"You're a tough woman." Viorica cleaned some dirt out from under her fingernails. "We can make it out. I'm worried about Arthur and Adrianna, however. Arthur needs, how do you call it in English?" She mimed putting something to her mouth and breathing in.

"An inhaler," October answered.

"Da, inhaler." Viorica nodded. "And Adrianna needs a hospital very bad. Poor girl. She didn't deserve what happened to her." She lowered her voice. "To be honest, I fear for her."

"Bernadette," October lowered her voice even more, not wanting Arthur or Bryan to hear her. "How could she have done that to Adrianna?" She shook her head then turned to look at Viorica's undefined silhouette in the darkness. "Do you have any idea what could've happened to her? Did she get infected with something? It was like she went crazy. Rabies? Did that bear have rabies, maybe? No, that doesn't make sense. The bear attacked and killed her. I *watched* her die. I swear, she was dead." October didn't want to think about these things anymore, but her mind was stuck in a loop. "What can explain her standing right there in front of us after she died? I'd call myself crazy if everyone else hadn't seen her too."

Viorica was silent for a while before responding. "I don't know what happened to Bernadette," she finally answered, though there was something in her voice that made it seem to October like the woman wasn't being entirely truthful. "I do not think it was rabies. Whatever attacked us in that cave, it was..." She shifted in the darkness.

"What?" October urged, looking around, making sure the others weren't listening. "What were you going to say?"

The clouds in the sky shifted, letting faint moonlight seep through. October saw the vague outline of Viorica's face as it turned to stare in her direction. There was a long silence before Viorica answered at a normal volume.

"Come with me, we need some branches." She got up and walked out into the rain, taking her pack with her.

Baffled, October watched the other woman move several yards away from the lean-to before getting up and following.

When October reached her, Viorica asked, "Have you ever heard of something called Enigmata?"

"Enig…mata?" October repeated the strange word. "No, I haven't. Is that a band? And why are we out in the rain?"

"Nu, not a band," Viorica said with an amused snort. She shook her head. "I do not want the others to hear. But how to explain? Well, some are objects or places. Others are living beings. Beings that can do amazing and sometimes terrible things. I'm not good at properly explaining it all in English. These Enigmata, they aren't things that should be played around with by unthinking hands. They can be very dangerous." A pause. The clouds covered the moon once more. "I do not think that Bernadette is alive. That person that attacked us, it might have looked like her. But I don't believe it was her. There are things in this world that you and most people don't know about. Bernadette, even if it was her body in that underground chamber, it wasn't her. I'm sure of it. You saw the eyes. It wasn't her."

"Yeah, I saw her eyes," October said. "But I'm still not understanding what you're trying to get at. And what exactly are these Enigmata and what do they have to do with Bernadette? Can you try to explain it again?"

"Objects, places, entities." Viorica shifted in the dark. "They can do things that most people wouldn't think possible. Some of the most dangerous Enigmata are the living beings that can think and scheme. They probably have the same capacity for good and evil as humans do." Another lengthy pause. "The origins of some Enigmata have been discovered. It's said that many come from a history that we know nothing about. A history before our history." She sighed. "Enigmata are very rare. Worth much more than money. Worth much more than life to some people. And those sorts of people want to control them."

October didn't know what to think of all this. If it hadn't been for Viorica's serious demeanor and the situation they found themselves in, she would have been positive the other woman was goofing around. She was about to ask Viorica again why she even was telling her all this Enigmata stuff and what did this have to do with anything, when she stopped herself. The cold, exhaustion, and fear had made her mind sluggish. But it eventually clicked: Noel opening the stone chest down in the underground chamber and pulling out that strange metal wheel, which he then tossed to Bryan. The memory flashed through her mind. Had *that* been one of these Enigmata things Viorica was talking about? Had they unintentionally unleashed something through their bumbling curiosity?

"The chest," she said. "That metal thing Noel took out. The Wheel of whatever it was called."

"Kurkoth."

"Yeah, that," October went on. "The guy whose skeleton we found was looking for it. So, the dead man wasn't just some archaeologist, was he? The wheel isn't just some artifact he wanted for a museum."

"Da," Viorica answered, nodding her head. "That wheel is most likely an Enigmata. I'm still unsure exactly what the object is capable of, though I'm certain it's the cause of what happened with Bernadette."

A horrifying thought struck October. "Did you know that thing was down there?" she asked, accusation tinging her words.

"The Enigmata?" Viorica replied. "Da. The murderous creature? Nu. I did not, and still do not, know precisely what the object does. Not all Enigmata are dangerous, you see. But it seems that this one is. Or at least, it's connected to something dangerous."

This woman is a liar, the Overshadow said, venom in every word. *She's been misleading you this entire time. What else is she hiding? She obviously wants this Enigmata. Would she kill you for it if you got in her way?*

"So, you're not just some tourist on fucking vacation." October felt suddenly furious at Viorica's almost nonchalant attitude toward all of this. "You knew that thing was down there and that it might be dangerous."

"I knew there was something important here in this region." Viorica shrugged her shoulders, picking at her fingernails again. "I didn't know what or where, exactly. I've been looking around here. I have a sense for this." She hesitated. "I can sometimes feel that an Enigmata is calling to me. Something called to me from here." She exhaled. "This hunt has been a difficult one."

Quietly unzipping her pack, Viorica reached in and removed something. She clicked on her flashlight for a split second before killing the light again. It was all the time October needed to see what Viorica had taken out.

The Wheel of Kurkoth.

"You *took* that thing?" October hissed. The last she had seen of it, Bryan had been fiddling with it down in the ritual chamber. She had assumed he had dropped it in the ensuing chaos. However, here it was. "What if it hurts us or infects you like it did with Bernadette?"

"It does not work that way, I don't think," Viorica said, returning the object to her pack. "Both Bryan and Noel handled it without harm besides a small cut. Bernadette was dead before we found it. I wasn't going to leave it behind, anyway. It's what I came here for." She bowed her head. "I did not intend to lead you people into any danger, though. That was never my intention. I came on this hike to get a sense of the area. I didn't expect all of this. Either way, what happened today would have most likely happened whether I was here or not."

That was true, October knew. And if Viorica hadn't been on the hike with them, they might have fared much worse. Maybe more of them would have died during that bear attack, the trek through the caves, and the ambush by Bernadette. Still, it made her nervous that Viorica was now carrying around the wheel like some cool rock she'd found. She had even admitted she had no idea how it worked.

October rubbed her hands over her arms to warm her soaked self while her mind reviewed everything that had happened that day and especially how Viorica had dealt almost matter-of-factly with unimaginable events. The way she had thrown that knife. The way she had handled that gun like a pro.

"Where did you learn to use weapons like that?" October asked, sort of glad for the pounding rain so that the others couldn't hear this very strange conversation they were having. "Who trained you? Who are you really?"

"I am Viorica Mărculescu," Viorica quietly snapped. "I am nobody else. And I trained me. I learned to defend and take care of myself on my own. I do not need anybody else."

"Then why bother staying with us?" October retorted. She wasn't sure why she felt as hurt as she did by the woman's words.

Nobody needs you, the Overshadow said. *Haven't I always told you that?*

"I didn't mean it like that," Viorica said, half-apologizing. "In truth, I'm glad to have met you. You seem like a good person to be around. You are more friendly with me than many people I have dealt with. If we get out of this crazy forest alive, perhaps we can keep in contact. I can maybe show you how to defend yourself. If you wish."

"Yeah." A faint smile tugged at the corners of October's mouth. As a child and early teens, October had desperately wanted to take up karate at a local dojo nestled in a strip mall by her house, but had felt too self-conscious to ask her parents about classes. "Yeah, sure. I'd like that. I wouldn't mind knowing how to kick some ass like you do."

Viorica chuckled, then strode back over to their shelter. As they settled in again, she grabbed something from just outside of the lean-to's protection. October heard Viorica take a swig in the darkness. Then a canteen was placed in October's hands. She gratefully accepted it.

"Why are you being so nice to me?" October asked after taking a drink and handing back the canteen.

Viorica put the canteen back out into the rain to refill, readjusting the leaves she used as a funnel. "Why not? Like I said before, you're a tough woman and have been good company. Good to have someone like you in difficult situations."

October certainly didn't feel tough, but was touched by the woman's words. "Thank you. I appreciate that."

Bringing her knees up to her chest and wrapping her arms around them, October rested her chin on her forearm, feeling her body giving in to the exhaustion. There was a faint sound a good distance away, further muffled by the loud splattering of the rain. It could've been the cry of some animal. She listened closer, trying to filter out the rain's constant drumming.

Had that been a howl just then? A bark? Did coyotes bark or was that something only dogs did? Wild animals were supposed to leave you alone if you left them alone.

The memories of the day replayed in October's head as she shivered.

It seemed there were much worse things than wild animals out there.

CHAPTER SIXTEEN

I'm pulling into the parking lot right now," Wendig said to the phone laying on the passenger seat next to him. He shut the car off. Hot ticks sounded as the engine died.

"Did you get there in time?" Jordan asked, her voice emanating from the phone's speaker. "Please tell me you did."

"I hope so," Wendig answered, grabbing the pistol that lay next to the phone. "I don't see anything at the moment." His eyes scanned the two-story, red-brick exterior of the Forestleaf Juvenile Behavioral Health Center. There was no movement he could see.

It was almost ten o'clock. Visiting hours were surely over for the day. Even if they weren't, there was no way Wendig would be able to explain to the staff the real reason why he was back here again. If he told them that he was chasing a malevolent monster that could run across the treetops, they might very well lock him up in there.

"Jordan, I'm going to hang up now." Wendig grabbed the phone. "If you don't hear back from me soon, you know what to do."

"I'll kick your butt is what I'll do," Jordan said.

Wendig checked the time. "I'll call or message you in one hour. Just notify the authorities if I fail to do so."

"I will," Jordan replied in all seriousness. "Be careful."

He ended the call, putting the phone in his pocket. He checked the Glock 19's magazine just to be sure. Fifteen rounds. Not legal in California where he resided, but then again, he was in possession of things the government would find more questionable. He secured the magazine back into the pistol and chambered a round before stepping out of the car, closing the door as quietly as possible. He knew he couldn't explain his presence—gun in hand—on the grounds of a children's mental hospital at night. But better to be caught carrying a gun by a security guard than caught unarmed by the Watcher. Those crime scene photos were incontrovertible evidence of what the Watcher could do to a person.

Under his feet, gravel crunched much too loudly for Wendig's liking until he reached the grass that surrounded the building in an expansive lawn. The Center loomed up before him as if daring him to come closer into its embrace. No guards in sight at the moment. Security lights were affixed to the building's walls every dozen feet or so. Most of the windows were dark, although some were lit. In one room he could see a boy staring out at the night sky before retreating from view. In another, he saw two nurses chatting for a moment before going their separate ways.

Which room is Caleb's? Wendig thought, scanning each window. He should have checked it out when he was here before.

Sneaking across the lawn and wishing there was more cover, Wendig made his way around the side of the building to the back, constantly on alert for guards or the Watcher. The rear lawn was about the size of two football fields side by side. A fleeting thought sprinted through his mind: *Rowan would have loved to just run across that field.*

Putting his back against the wall, he peeked around the corner, his eyes traveling from the first to the second floor.

He saw it, outlined by the moonlight and the glow from an illuminated window.

The Watcher was there, clinging to the side of the building on the second floor, tapping on the window fourth from the left corner. Its body was obsidian black, almost scaly, but fleshier than that of a lizard. Wiry limbs corded with muscle angled out from its emaciated-looking torso like a spider's legs. Huge talons sprouted from both its toes and fingers, which it used to grip onto the building's exterior. What disturbed Wendig the most, however, was how humanoid the creature's frame was. It could pass for a person in a dark alley if bundled up in just the right clothing.

Its face, covered with that dried leather mask it wore—the stolen flesh of Evan Brooks—was turned away from him.

Wendig took aim with his Glock, getting the target within his sights. He hesitated. The creature was too far away. Not only that, the shot would alert not just the Watcher to his presence, but everyone inside the building as well. If he missed, the creature would either take the chance to escape, or perhaps attack anyone who came to investigate. Would the Watcher expose itself like that to others? Wendig couldn't take the chance.

Returning the pistol to his shoulder holster, Wendig reached his left hand into a coat pocket and pulled out the small, wooden container that rested there. The ancient container, about five inches long and made from lacquered cypress wood carved into a crescent moon shape, encased the hand bones of an unknown person. Although he had had the object x-rayed, he had never seen the bones with his own eyes, as the container was sealed with a substance he thought must be some sort of sap.

A dread coursed through Wendig and beads of sweat appeared on his forehead as he briefly regarded the item in his hand. He didn't want to have to use this. The wooden container and hand bones inside were an Enigmata he had recovered years ago from a reliquary in a long-abandoned church in the south of Spain: a relic called—according to his research—La Mano de Gaia, or the Hand of Gaia. It had taken him several months of cautious study to figure out what the Enigmata did. When he did discover the hand's power, he knew it could be extremely useful to him at some point in the future. He regretted that he never learned exactly who the hand bones had once belonged to, but that didn't stop him from bringing the Enigmata with him on investigations in case he ever needed to use it.

Would he have the strength to wield the Hand of Gaia again? Relic Enigmata were not objects to be used impulsively. Most demanded a price be paid. The more power an Enigmata granted, the larger a sacrifice required from those who would seek to utilize it. A sacrifice of both body and mind.

Such objects took a massive toll when used. Did Wendig have a choice here, though? He couldn't let this monster escape again.

Wendig gripped the crescent-shaped container in his hand, feeling its lacquered surface become warmer and warmer, though that had nothing to do with the body heat that radiated from his palm. He looked back up to where the creature clung to the window, now hanging upside down. Beyond the glass, Wendig thought he could make out the terrified face of a young boy.

Hang in there, Caleb, he thought.

Suddenly, an all-consuming pain seized Wendig's left arm in a vice, and his fingers clamped down on the Enigmata. An excruciating sensation—as if every vein, nerve, and muscle in his limb were being individually squeezed—nearly overwhelmed him. *This* was why he didn't use the Hand of Gaia indiscriminately.

Though the pain was intense, Wendig stood firm. The molten agony in his arm throbbed in time with his own pulse. He could deal with it for now, but not for long.

He looked up at the window. The Watcher cocked back a talon-tipped hand, ready to shatter the glass that separated it from Caleb.

Wendig raised the arm that held onto the Hand of Gaia, concentrating, letting the Enigmata become an extension of his own body. He extended it toward the creature. With an almost silent gasp, the Watcher was yanked off the building by a giant, ghostly hand that had appeared in midair. At Wendig's command, the giant hand threw the Watcher viciously to the ground where its body smacked against the lawn with a sickening *thud*, a wheezing cry of agony escaping its mouth. Wendig's arm was on fire. His mind was becoming fuzzy, his vision darkening. It was as if the entirety of the cosmos was trying to fit itself into his insignificant human brain to wield this inhuman power.

Before the Watcher could move, Wendig focused again, imagining the monster being pulverized into the ground. At his thought, the ghost hand hovering in the air balled into a fist and came slamming down onto the Watcher, crushing the creature into the soft earth with the impact.

Letting go of the Enigmata, Wendig fell to his knees. That was all he could take. Multi-colored lights danced in front of his eyes. He couldn't do anything else, only wait until his mind cleared enough of the agony before he could stand up without his legs shaking or swaying. Gathering up the wooden container that had fallen to the ground, he slipped it back into his coat pocket.

It was done. He had saved Caleb and taken care of the Watcher.

Regaining enough of his strength, Wendig stumbled over to where the Watcher lay motionless in a large, campervan-size depression in the ground. He had to get rid of the creature's corpse. Better to let the staff of the hospital deal with a mysterious crater in the ground than with a horrific abomination lying dead in their backyard. Seeing such things—things that should not exist in human reality—could easily break a fragile mind. What would happen if any of the patients saw this thing? The boys didn't need any additional catalysts to worsen whatever issues they were dealing with.

God, his arm burned, and his head pounded.

Lowering himself several feet into the crater, Wendig stood over the body that lay before him. With the moonlight and the security lights, he could see that it was even more hideous up close, and its fetid stench surrounded it like a bubble of miasmic perfume. Wendig kicked the creature's leg with his toe. The body made no movement or reaction.

Wendig sighed heavily, still waiting for his breathing and heartbeat to return to normal. This wasn't the first time he had come into physical contact with a disgusting creature of nightmare. Still, the thought of touching it revolted him. He needed to search it for the Enigmata it had stolen.

That face.

Its pale, leathery complexion stood out in such a stark contrast to the thing's coal-black body. Wendig stared at that weathered skin. Studied the ragged edges that surrounded the face.

He heard Caleb's voice in his mind.

He wears pieces of Evan's skin like a costume.

The crime scene photographs that Jordan had showed him raced through his mind as he looked at that dead face.

Revulsion and horror shot through Wendig's veins like ice water as he unwillingly thought of the Watcher visiting Evan that final night, torturing the boy with those metal rods and hooks, and peeling off his skin with sadistic glee.

In his split-second of distraction, a black-clawed hand flew up from the ground, catching Wendig along his left side; a searing dagger slicing through both clothing and flesh. He screamed in agony and fell backward, a monstrous dark shape scurrying past him out of the crater and bounding off into the darkness.

Gasping in pain, Wendig lay in the depression in the ground, trying to catch his breath. He clutched at his left side just below his ribs. Warm blood spilled through his fingers. He couldn't tell how deep the wound was or if anything vital had been damaged.

A sudden dampness hit his face, and he realized the clouds he had seen gathering earlier in the distance had finally decided to wander over and let loose the rain they held. Struggling to his feet and slipping several times, Wendig crawled out of the crater in the grass. Getting shakily to his feet, he stumbled in the direction of the parking lot where his car waited.

Can't pass out here, he thought, his mind becoming more sluggish by the minute. The physical and mental exhaustion from using the Hand of Gaia had not totally abated, and now it was compounded with the pain of having his ribs slashed open. Wendig felt like he was on the brink of death.

Putting a steadying hand on the building for support, Wendig rounded the corner and spotted his car. Heavy raindrops drummed against its roof in a rhythmic tattoo. Hopefully no security guards would come outside to do their rounds. He had to make it to the vehicle and get himself to a hospital emergency room. This was a hospital, but not the one he needed.

Finally reaching his car, Wendig unlocked the door and eased himself inside. He pressed the ignition button, and the car rumbled to life.

Hell, his side stung. His left arm and hand burned. His head throbbed. Everything was agony, and he was bleeding all over the place.

That's going to cost a lot to clean, he thought off-handedly.

He clumsily reversed, then put the car into drive and sped away, nearly hitting a parked white van on his way out. Making it to the road, he turned onto slick asphalt. The black trees on either side of his speeding car seemed to be closing in on him. His eyes drooped, the car starting to stray to the other side of the road. He shook his head, coming back to his senses and bringing the car back into his lane.

"Come on," he rasped. His fumbling fingers managed to get his cell phone out of his coat pocket and turn it on, getting bloody finger-prints all over the screen. He knew he shouldn't be dividing his attention between the phone and the road, most definitely not in his present condition. The rain came down harder as if to screw with him. He knew he needed to get the windshield wipers going. His hand struggled with the lever.

God, the pain. His head was swimming. How much blood had he lost?

"Call Jordan," he croaked as he finally flicked on the windshield wipers.

A voice answered after the first ring.

"Lucas? Did you find the Watcher? Did you get it?"

"Jordan… I need help…" Did he just slur his words, or had it been his imagination? He felt so dizzy.

"Where are you?" Jordan asked, her voice rising in panic. "Lucas, talk to me! Crap! Okay, I'm going to trace your phone."

"The Watch—"

At that moment, the front of the car crumpled as Wendig slammed into a tree.

CHAPTER SEVENTEEN

October

"Did you hear that?" October asked. She peered out from under the lean-to, her eyes trying to scan the lightless forest.

"You mean the howling and barking?" Viorica asked from beside her. "Probably a coyote or dog out there. Nothing to worry about. Coyotes won't come near us."

"Are you sure?" October asked, still thinking about the bear.

October and the bear, the Overshadow said in a sing-song.

October and the bear.

Did you hear the tale of that whole sad affair?

October, the fuck up, she drags down the rest.

She is a total loser, just look at how she's dressed.

Her life is unfulfilled. She's gotten people killed.

Being a disappointment is her only major skill.

She caused Bernadette to get eaten by a bear.

And she has the audacity to complain that life's unfair.

October ignored the Overshadow as best she could. Another howl reached her ears. She'd been hearing this for about an hour or so. It seemed very close now. "You sure a coyote wouldn't come here? They don't just attack people for no reason?"

"Nothing to worry about," Viorica said.

How can she always be so composed and unafraid? October mused. Why couldn't she herself be so calm in the face of danger?

"I thought you were going to sleep," Viorica said. "It has been a long tiring day. You should get some rest. You need it."

"I don't think I'll be able to sleep for a long time." October ran her fingers through her hair and pulled a leaf out. Ugh, her hair felt dirty and greasy. She looked over at where the rest of the group lay, indistinct shapes in the dark. "I don't know how they can sleep knowing what might be creeping through the forest right now. Just the thought that there's something out here that can make a person turn into whatever Bernadette has become terrifies me. Stuff like that isn't supposed to exist in the real world. Like, how do you cope with your reality just being upended like that?"

"It is difficult at first," Viorica answered, rubbing a smudge of dirt off the back of her hand.

October stared at her. "Do you mean you've seen stuff like this before?" she asked.

"Like Bernadette?" Viorica replied, looking up. "Maybe. I have seen Enigmata make people go crazy. I'm unsure that's what this is, though." She paused. "There are many strange situations you encounter when hunting these things is your work."

The two women sat in silence for several moments.

"When did you start looking for these things?" October asked. As dangerous as these Enigmata things seemed, she had to admit that her interest was piqued.

Viorica scooched closer, and October heard an intake of breath as if she were about to say something. But before Viorica got any more words out, shouts erupted from right beside them.

"Argh! Help!" Bryan shrieked and flailed around like a madman from where he lay on the ground. "Get it off me! Help!"

The others who had been sleeping, or had been trying to, were instantly awakened. Viorica and October had sprung to their feet,

Viorica flicking her flashlight on. The beam of light illuminated a large hairy creature looming over Bryan's thrashing form.

"Bryan!"

Without thinking, October made a move toward the animal. The creature's head spun in her direction, and a pair of dark amber eyes regarded her. The yellow Labrador, which had been eagerly licking Bryan's face, stood in the midst of the group, rain falling off in rivulets from its drenched fur. Its tail wagged in circles like a helicopter.

"What's happening?" Arthur croaked. He struggled to sit up.

"What the hell?" Noel held a hand to his heaving chest. "Scared the shit out of me, man. A damn dog? Jesus."

Bryan finally managed to push the yellow lab away from his thoroughly licked face. "I thought it was the bear!" he whimpered. "I-I was sleeping. I didn't know what was happening. I thought I was being eaten!"

Ahahaha! The Overshadow roared with laughter, delighting in Bryan's fear. *Look at him squealing. What an idiot.*

Fuck off, October growled inside her own head. *That wasn't funny. The kid is traumatized already, and he thought he was going to die just now.*

The dog shook the rainwater off itself, spraying everyone in the vicinity. When Bryan made it apparent that he wanted nothing to do with the dog, it glanced around at them all before moving over into Noel's lap.

"Where did you come from, buddy?" Noel scratched the dog behind the ears. "He's wearing a collar." Noel grabbed the tags and angled them into the beam of Viorica's flashlight so he could read. "I mean *she's* wearing a collar. Looks like her name is Maddie."

"Are you okay?" October asked Bryan as the others focused their attention on the dog.

Bryan just nodded without a word, not looking up at her.

"Where did you come from, Maddie?" Samira asked the lab. Maddie just cocked her head and stared at Samira. "What are you doing out here all by yourself, girl?"

"If the dog has collar, then she has an owner, nu?" Viorica said. She and October had sat back down once the threat of potential danger had passed. "Then there must be someone nearby, I think. Maybe someone who can help us get out of this forest."

"Where's your home, Maddie?" Arthur asked in a hoarse voice. "Hmm? Where is home?"

The dog seemed to recognize the word "home" because her ears pricked up and she started to dance about energetically, her tail wagging even faster. Maddie whined, then let out an eager-sounding bark. October realized that Maddie must have been the barker she had heard earlier.

"Maybe we could follow her?" October suggested, staring into the dog's happy eyes. She always felt that she could read animals better than humans, and this dog seemed trustworthy. "She looks like a smart pup. Maybe she'll lead us to her home and better shelter?"

"Are you kidding me?" Bryan said, having regained most of his composure. "You want to follow a random dog through the woods at night in the rain? How stupid are you?"

Yes, how stupid are you, October? The Overshadow asked. *I've seen all the decisions you've made over your whole life, so I'd say you're very stupid.*

"Weren't you the one who wanted to keep going?" October retorted, turning to face him.

Indeed, he did. Tell him how much of an insufferable imbecile he's being. Tell him now!

Get out of my head!

"Well, yeah," Bryan said, unaware of October's internal argument. "But you're talking about following a dog. You want to risk our safety on some animal? This isn't Sassie or Lassie or whatever."

An unfamiliar voice rang out in the night rising above the hard rainfall, halting October and Bryan's argument. "Maddie! Maddie, where did you get to? Maddie!"

Out of the corner of her eye, October saw Viorica remove the gun from her waistband and thumb off the safety. She hoped Viorica was just being overly cautious. *Please let this be someone who can help us out.*

"Who could that possibly be?" Samira asked in a tone half hopeful, half suspicious.

A harsh cone of light speared through the foliage, and seconds later, a tall figure crashed through a thick tangle of brush, stepping into the beam of Viorica's own light. It was an older man, most likely in his fifties, with a weathered face and a large gray mustache. He wore an oversized raincoat, waterproof boots, and a cowboy hat. In one hand, he carried a heavy-duty LED flashlight, and in the other, a double-barrel shotgun.

"Holy cow," the man said in surprise. "I almost didn't see you there."

"Mister, please," Bryan began after overcoming his momentary shock. "We really need help. Please."

"You're in luck, kid," the man said. He then looked around at the others. "Well, looks like I actually found you people! The name's Henry. Henry Kinsey. I live in these here woods, and I've been looking for you."

"You've been looking for us?" Samira asked, voicing everyone's confusion.

"Well, of course," Henry said. "They've been searching for you folks ever since you failed to return from your nature hike. There's been a whole search party looking for you around the vicinity of the hiking trail. Sheriff Simmons up there in Cinter gave me a call a few hours ago, telling me that you folks were missing. I know Adrianna runs these nature hikes, so I immediately went out searching for you. Been out canvassing this area. Thank God I decided to give this spot another look in case you moved over this way. You people sure went far off the trail! Is everyone okay? Where's my nie—" His words were cut off as his eyes widened. He had caught sight of Adrianna's mangled form. "Christ! What happened?"

"Please," October started. "We really need to get to the hospital as soon as possible. We have two people here who need medical attention. Especially Adrianna."

"Adrianna!" Henry repeated. He scrambled over to the girl, kneeling beside her prone form. Tears welled up in his eyes as he surveyed her bloodied and clawed body. "Dear Lord, no."

"You said you know her?" Noel asked, taking a step toward the man.

"Yes!" Henry looked up. "She's my niece! That's why I've been looking for you people for hours out here!" He turned his face back to Adrianna. "Addy, can you hear me? It's Uncle Henry. Addy?"

"She's been unconscious for a long while," October told him. When he looked around at her with wide eyes, she quickly added, "She's still breathing, though! She needs a hospital."

After handing his shotgun to an unexpecting Noel and a small, extra flashlight from his back pocket to Bryan, Henry scooped Adrianna into his arms and began heading back in the direction he had come from. "All of you, follow me. Keep the light ahead of me so I can see. I live not too far away. I got a truck at home. Maddie, come on!" He let out a piercing whistle, and Maddie bounded to his side. "Let's go, people!"

They all scrambled after the man without any protest. Despite their current surroundings, October was beginning to experience a shimmer of hope blossoming in her chest. They were finally going to get out of this damn forest. Finally going to get out of the rain and hopefully into someplace warm and dry and safe.

"Here." Noel handed Viorica the shotgun. "You can handle this thing better than I can. Probably safer in your hands too. I don't want to accidentally set it off."

October knew she would have done the same.

It turned out that Henry lived a little farther away than "not too far away."In about forty-five minutes, the group had reached an old two-story farmhouse-style home. October surveyed the exterior as the group walked up to the covered porch. She wouldn't call the place run-down, but she couldn't say it was kept up very well either. The house looked as if it hadn't seen a fresh coat of paint in decades, and several shingles were missing from the peaked roofs. None of the windows were broken, although they were filthy.

Still, she had to admit, the warm glow emanating through the glass felt very welcoming. If she had come across this house while in the woods by herself, she definitely would have run the other way. But Henry seemed like an honest enough guy. Plus, after the day they had had, any house would seem inviting. Hell, October would have gone into the *Amityville Horror* house if it meant getting out of this rain and darkness.

Samira opened the front door per Henry's request, and they all stumbled inside a large living room decorated with old-fashioned furniture and rustic décor that made October think that a certain chainsaw-wielding maniac was hiding around the corner.

Eh, who cares? She was glad to be someplace that wasn't wet and freezing; someplace that had four walls and a roof surrounding her protecting her from everything out *there*.

"Watch out," Henry puffed as he sidled past everyone and gently lay Adrianna on the green couch that sat in the middle of the room. The front of Henry's jacket was now splotched with blood just like Noel's, though he didn't seem to notice.

"Finally, something over our heads that isn't rocks or trees." Bryan adjusted his dad's arm where it lay draped over his shoulder. "Do you think my dad could lay down somewhere? He's not doing too good."

"Up the stairs and to the left." Henry pointed to the staircase at the back of the living room. "There's a guest room with a good bed that your daddy can lie down in. There are blankets in the closet. Help yourself to whatever you need."

"Hey, where's this truck of yours?" Noel asked, peering out the windows that faced the front of the house. "I don't see any vehicles out there."

"My boy's got it," Henry answered. He pulled an older model cell phone from out of his pocket. "I told him to go look around the road in case you people had gotten yourselves over there. Let me give him a call and tell him to come back." Henry pressed some buttons on the phone. "I hate these things. Can never get them to work right. But when you ain't got no phone lines out here, you gotta make do. Ah, here we go." He put the phone to his ear and waited, then hung up a few moments later. "Ain't going through. Service is shit up here. I think Isaac should be back soon anyhow. Lord, I hope he is."

October watched Bryan and Arthur hobble up the steps for a few seconds before she turned her attention toward the toasty fire that danced in the fireplace. The heat felt so good on October's skin, and even a little painful as her body thawed out. She held her palms out toward the blaze, letting the heat soak down into her muscles and warm her icy bones.

"I'm sorry I don't have any extra clothes for you folks," Henry said as he tended to Adrianna's wounds with some fresh bandages he had acquired from a nearby bathroom. October couldn't tell if the tapestry of gashes that covered the girl's flesh were just wet from the rain, or if they still oozed their sanguine fluids. "I don't think my clothing would fit any of you. You're welcome to sit around the fire and warm your-selves. I'll get you all some towels in a sec."

Bryan came back down the stairs moments later, a haunted look in his dark-circled eyes.

"How's your dad?" October asked the boy as he came to warm himself by the hearth with everyone else.

"I don't know," he answered, a hollow quality in his voice. "His breathing hasn't been normal for a while now. I just have to get him to a hospital. I'm all he's got now. I can't let anything else happen to him."

Like what happened to his poor mother, the Overshadow said inside October's head. *Remember that, October? Down in the cave?*

"Christ." Henry stood before Adrianna for a long moment, his jaw clenching and unclenching, before he strode out of the room and returned with a stack of towels for everyone. As he handed them out to the group, he asked, "Now is someone going to tell me how the hell my niece got into this state?" His tone was sharp and suspicious, although October heard no accusation in his words.

"Something attacked us." Samira stared into the fire with a towel draped over her head. "It attacked Adrianna."

"What attacked you?" Henry asked, looking from face to face. "You mean like an animal?"

"It...it was..." Samira stuttered.

"It was my mom," Bryan interjected, his face wretched. "My mom did that to her." He didn't meet anyone's eyes.

"Your mom?" Henry asked, confusion showing plainly on his face. "Your mom have some sort of psychotic breakdown? Hell!"

"Nu." Viorica rose from where she had been kneeling by the fire.

The only thing worse than being dead, the Overshadow said, slithering through her mind, *would be having to live with you.*

If you don't shut the hell up, I'll take Henry's shotgun and blow my head off, taking you with me.

The Overshadow simply laughed. She was able to will the awful sound out of her head for a moment and focused back on the scene before her.

Viorica just stood before the old man, holding the wheel in her palm, an indifferent look on her face.

"Listen—" Viorica started to say when there was a lull in Henry's shouting.

October cut her off. "Look, we're sorry." She stepped between Henry and Viorica. "We had no idea what the object was. We got trapped in a cave and had to find another way out. We stumbled across that weird chamber. It's all a long, exhausting story. I'm sorry we took whatever this artifact is. Either way, we have more important things to worry about at the moment, don't you think?"

"Bad!" Henry shouted. He snatched his hat off the ground and placed it back on top of his head. He began pacing around the living room. "This is all very bad."

"It seems like you know what this thing is then." Noel indicated the wheel Viorica still held. "What exactly is it? And what does it do? Can it turn people into monsters?"

Viorica exchanged a look with October. *Does this Henry guy know about the Enigmata things Viorica was telling me about?* If they had been under different circumstances, October would have liked to discuss these mysterious objects in more detail while sitting around the warm fire and perhaps sipping hot chocolate.

"Where is Isaac with the damn truck?" Henry growled, pushing aside a curtain to look outside. "Boy shoulda been back by now."

"Hey, are you going to answer Noel's questions?" Samira demanded, grabbing Henry's arm and pulling him away from the window. "Explain to us what this metal disc did to Bernadette."

Henry looked at her with wide, frightened eyes that flicked around the room as if he were expecting something. "Who's Bernadette?" he asked in a wavering voice.

"My mom," Bryan answered. "Something got to my mom. Something made her crazy. It turned her into a demon."

"No, son," Henry said with a long sigh. Calming himself, he walked over to the kid. "That thing may have looked like your mom, but trust me, it wasn't. It's not a person. It wants you to think it is. It wants to torment you."

"What do you mean?" Noel asked. "There was definitely something wrong with her, but that was Bernadette."

"No, it wasn't!" Henry shouted. He shook his head. "You don't understand. My gran told me stories about it. It loves to watch people suffer. It loves," he gulped, "to wear people's skin."

A hush fell over them all as Henry's words hung in the air. The only sound October could hear was the thrumming of the rain against the roof and windows. The words sank slowly into her brain. This creature Henry spoke of—it wore people's skin? The image of a crazed Bernadette standing over Adrianna back in that cavern flashed in her mind. That one sulfur-yellow, evil eye. The other ruined eye. The black talons that had ripped through the tips of her fingers and toes. The partial bear head she had been wearing like a hat. October had instinctively known that the person standing before them in that moment wasn't Bernadette. She just didn't know how right she had been.

"It wears people's skin?" October asked in hushed tones, as if speaking of the creature could summon it to them.

"It was wearing my mom," Bryan said. It wasn't a question. His face contorted with rage and revulsion. "It was wearing her skin like some sort of suit." His fingers balled up so tightly, as if he were trying to crush his own hands.

"That's sick." Samira had one hand over her chest, the other pressed against her stomach. Her eyes were fixated on the ground. "Utterly sick. What kind of living creature would find pleasure in such a thing?"

"Tell me, old man," Viorica finally piped up, leaning against the wall just beside the hearth. She had returned the wheel to her pack. "How do you know so much about this creature? You said someone told you about it. Have you seen it before?"

"Seen it?" Henry asked, turning a hollow gaze on the woman. "No, no. I ain't never seen the abomination myself." He lowered himself back onto the couch where Adrianna lay. He regarded her sorrowfully for a moment before continuing. "Ain't never seen the monster. My gran did, though. She was the one who told me about it. She and her family came from Wyoming. Settled here in Fulgent County 'round 1893. Course, it wasn't called Fulgent County back then. Not 'til 1901, when Cinter got neighbors with the founding of Black Ashes and Shadow's Path. My gran was a young girl when her family came here to live. She grew up hearing stories about evil things in the woods that would come out at night. Course, what community that lives by a forest don't have those types of stories, right?" He laughed without mirth.

Getting up from the couch, Henry walked over to a wooden cabinet on the far wall. Fishing a key out from the mouth of a small, porcelain frog on a neighboring shelf, he unlocked the cabinet and extracted a thick red binder, returning to the couch to resume his seat.

"What's that?" Samira asked, craning her neck to get a better look.

"These are pages from the journal of Edith Goodner, my grandmother," he answered. He patted the binder before opening it and flipping through several yellowed pages that had been laminated and secured on big metal rings. "She left them to me when she passed. She hoped I could keep her work going after she was gone." He stopped when he found the page he had been looking for. "Here, this is it. I think she was about fifteen when she wrote this part. Alright, listen." He cleared his throat and began to read aloud. "'Grandad told one of his wicked tales to Barnabas and me after supper last evening. It was a frightful tale and made my arms prickle in gooseflesh. He said up in the mountain caves were some sort of monsters. Awful things that ain't of our sane world. These monsters can steal one's skin and live inside, pretending to be you! Momma told me and Barnabas that

Grandad is an old fool full of foolish stories. But I swear I heard something crawling on the side of the house a fortnight past, before I even heard the tale.'" Henry flipped forward a few entries before stopping and reading more. "'Before he left for his trip to-day, Grandad told me about a special object with a funny name. A Wheel of Cercot? Kerrcoth? It's supposed to be hidden somewhere in those mountain caves. I believe that may be the reason he really left; to go look for this wheel. Grandad said that it helps control the creatures, keeping them tied to this land and unable to move too far away. It contains part of their essence, like their soul, Grandad said. If the wheel is disturbed, then little by little, the creatures will be able to freely roam the world beyond their prison.'" He flipped forward a few more pages. "'Last evening, after I wished Momma and Barnabas a good night, I went to bed. I was unable to sleep, though, for I kept hearing a sound: a light, peculiar tapping.'" He skipped ahead a bit. "'I saw Grandad's face outside my window, smiling. But it couldn't have been him. I swear it was not him! I have known my Grandad since I was born. The person I saw outside was wrong in some way that I cannot explain. It was as if something was wearing his face.'"

Henry closed the binder and sat immobile, his eyes closed. No one said a word as they all stood around, processing his grandmother's words. Even the Overshadow was strangely silent. A shudder slithered through October's body, icy fingers running their frigid nails down her spine. Goosebumps sprang up on her skin, and she crossed her arms to hug herself.

Before anyone could think of anything to say, the front door burst open, and a figure ran inside. They all jumped about a foot into the air, Bryan letting out a terrified squeak. October aimed Henry's shotgun straight at the figure.

"Whoo! It's storming bad out there." The person froze as he saw everyone standing there, one person with a shotgun pointed at him. A young man in jeans and a raincoat, water dripping from his curly brown hair, eyed them warily in deep confusion. "Uh, Dad?"

"Damn, Isaac," Henry said. "I didn't even hear you pull up." He walked over to October. "Give me that before you kill someone." He eased the shotgun out of her grip. "It's just my boy."

Isaac smiled sheepishly until he noticed Adrianna lying on the couch. "Oh hell! Dad, what happened?"

"These are the folks Adrianna was with that was lost out in the forest," Henry answered. "I found them wandering around out in the rain."

"Yeah, I got that," Isaac said. "I mean what happened to her?" His eyes widened further as if in recognition and he ran to kneel beside the couch. "Oh my God, *Adrianna*! What happened?"

Henry headed toward the door. "We'll talk on the way. We got to get Addy to a doctor, now."

At that very moment every light in the house winked out. Darkness enveloped them in a suffocating embrace. Henry tried flicking a nearby light switch off and on. Nothing happened.

"It's fine," he said to the others. "Happens all the time when it's storming bad. The wiring ain't the best in this place."

Before anyone could respond, there was a loud crash, like a window shattering, then a heavy thump as if something large had fallen over, up on the second floor.

Maddie began to whine, tucking her tail between her legs.

"Is there someone upstairs?" Isaac asked, bringing out a flashlight from inside his coat and turning it on.

"My dad," Bryan whispered.

CHAPTER NINETEEN

Jordan

Oh, come on!" Jordan yelled as she threw her phone onto her bed after her twentieth attempt.

Nathan shuffled around nervously on her desk, his scaly tail twitching.

"I'm sorry for yelling," she told the lizard, petting his head. She bit her bottom lip, leaving the skin red. "I just can't get through to Lucas. What if something terrible actually happened to him this time? What do I do?"

The bedroom door suddenly burst open, making Jordan squeak in surprise. Nathan scrambled behind the computer monitors.

Her brother flew into the room, his eyes wide.

"What the hell, Gabe!" Jordan shouted. "Don't you knock?"

"I heard you yelling!" Gabe shouted back. "I thought something had happened!"

"Well, nothing happened!"

"If I hear my sister shrieking, I'm going to come running!"

"I could've been naked in here!"

"Ew, gross!"

"Don't just barge into my room!"

"Okay!" Gabe replied, matching her volume. He stared at her, then said in a normal voice, "Can we stop yelling now?"

Jordan took a deep breath before replying. "Yeah, sorry. I'm just frustrated. I was…playing a game and got killed by a boss."

Gabe flicked his eyes first toward her TV, then over to her computer monitors—Nathan still hiding behind them. He had to have noticed that neither device showed any video games being played.

"Are you sure everything's okay?" Gabe asked, stepping toward her. His voice and expression held none of the jocularity they usually did.

Oh, how she wanted to just tell her brother about everything. Lucas, the Enigmata, their work. But she couldn't. Jordan knew she was terrible at lying. And she knew that Gabe knew she was terrible at lying. It was obvious she was withholding something from him. She just couldn't bring herself to tell him. Lucas had sworn her to secrecy. Gabe couldn't be involved in any of this work. Enigmata were too dangerous. Not only that, she didn't want Gabe to have any connection to what she did if she was ever caught doing the—sometimes illegal—things she did to obtain the information needed to solve these cases. Plausible deniability.

Generous Cyber-Criminal Jordan, heh.

Or if she broke down and told him the whole story, Gabe would just disbelieve everything about Enigmata and tell her to stop getting so invested in whatever video game she was currently playing.

"I'm sorry for scaring you." Jordan rose from her desk chair. "I'll be fine. It's just something personal. I can't tell you what. Yet. Maybe later, okay?"

Gabe nodded. "Okay. But listen. You can always talk to me, alright? I'm not trying to get mushy or anything, I just want you to know that I'm here for you. You may be my weird little sister, but you're *my* weird little sister. I want you to be okay. Got it?"

Stepping over to her brother, Jordan opened her arms and embraced him. She was never one for physical contact with other humans, much less physical affection. However, the urge had over-whelmed her at that moment.

"What is this?" Gabe said, caught off-guard. His whole body went rigid. "This is both uncomfortable and bizarre, you know. Ugh, feels like I'm being hugged by a praying mantis with your bony twig arms." He tried to pull away.

"Stop making it awkward." Jordan gave him one last squeeze before letting him escape. "Thanks for checking on me."

"No problem." Gabe patted her on the head like she was a puppy, then headed for the door. "Like I said, I'm always here to talk. And if you ever want to grab some pizza and watch a movie or play a game, just hit me up. You know where I live."

He walked out of her bedroom and closed the door behind him, then immediately popped his head back in. "Oh, and take a shower. You smell like an anime convention."

"I do not. I took a shower this morning, butt-breath." She flipped him off, but smiled. "It's just your upper lip."

Gabe winked and shut the door once more. His muffled laughter could be heard coming from the other side as he walked away.

As soon as she was alone again, Jordan's mind snapped back to her predicament. She resumed her frantic pacing around the room, anxiously chewing on her fingernails and spitting out flakes of blue nail polish. She felt frustrated tears begging to be set loose so that they could race down her cheeks. Nathan watched her for a long moment before emerging from behind the monitors. He crawled over to the chopped-up zucchini in his little metal bowl.

"What do I do? I don't know what to do."

If only Lucas would take her out into the field, this wouldn't happen. Even if she just sat in the hotel room of whatever town the current case led them to, she'd still be able to help more than she could now, halfway across the country.

She had to find some way to show Lucas how valuable it would be for him to have her nearby. If she just jumped on a plane to California someday and showed up on his doorstep, he wouldn't really send her back to Nebraska, would he?

"Argh, concentrate," Jordan growled at herself under her breath. She pulled on her own hair. "Present situation. Present danger. Focus!"

Picking up a mesh squeeze ball that she kept on her nightstand, Jordan squished the hell out of it, the sensation helping her focus and calm down. Finally tossing the ball aside, she scooped up her phone again from the bed. Tapping it awake, she squinted at the screen; a picture of Nathan wearing tiny wizard's robes served as her background image. She pressed on the phone icon, going to call history, then called Lucas again.

Still no answer.

She groaned, barely noticing that the tears had decided on their own to free themselves from her eyes.

There was no doubt that something bad had happened to Lucas. Jordan was certain of that. She sat back down in front of her computer and pulled up the Cinter, Washington emergency services phone numbers. Her thumb pressed the phone icon again on her phone's screen and dialed the number but didn't hit the call button.

She stared at it, gears turning.

"He told me never to speak to anyone," she said aloud. Nathan scuttled closer to her on the desk. "Although he did say to call the authorities if I didn't hear from him." She stared at Nathan. "So I have to call. Right?"

Nathan blinked slowly, never averting his gaze from her.

"You're right," she said.

Turning back to her computer screen, Jordan looked at the dot on her map that indicated Wendig's GPS signal. He hadn't moved in some time. A worrying amount of time. His last call with her had ended so abruptly after hearing an earsplitting screech blast through the speaker. Endless scenarios danced through Jordan's mind, each worse than the last.

"Screw it." She tapped the call button.

After two rings, the call was picked up, and a woman's voice came on. "Cinter Sheriff's Office. Is this an emergency?"

CHAPTER TWENTY

October

All eyes were on the stairs that led up to the second story of Henry's house. The lights still hadn't come back on. October didn't expect them to. The only illumination came from their flashlights and the orange glow from the fireplace, neither of which was strong enough to dispel the hungry darkness from more than the bottom four stairs.

"My dad is up there," Bryan hissed. He tried to make his way toward the stairs. Noel held the boy back by the shoulders. "Get off of me, man!"

Noel didn't let go.

There were more loud thumps from upstairs, then a strangled gasp. An unnerving silence followed. October strained her ears to listen for any more sounds. The firewood popped behind them, causing October to jump. No one else moved, not even Bryan. There was another gasp, then a muffled choke.

No, no, no, October repeated inside her head. Those were bad sounds. Sounds she had heard before, when something had ambushed them down in that ritual chamber, just before Bernadette had appeared before them, standing over the blood-soaked Adrianna. *Be brave. Be brave.*

Everyone tensed as they heard the shuffling footsteps coming from the second story. Henry cocked his shotgun while Viorica readied her pistol, both aiming up the stairs. The flashlights shone up the staircase as well, though they saw no one.

"Arthur?" Samira called out in a forcedly calm voice. "Are you okay up there?"

"Dad!" Bryan shouted without waiting for an answer.

A rasping noise floated down the stairs as if a frigid breeze were sweeping dead leaves down each step.

October suddenly realized what the sound was: soft, malicious laughter.

And it was coming from the direction of the guest room where Arthur was supposed to be lying down and resting.

"I'm not the only one who hears that, right?" Noel whispered, his voice shaking.

There was a sudden flash of gray and red that billowed out at the top of the landing before hurling down the stairs, like a fluttering bedsheet with weighted edges. October heard something rubbery smack the floor in front of her, and she felt wet droplets hit her face. She winced at their touch.

"What the hell?" Noel said.

Isaac immediately pointed his flashlight to his right where the thing had landed. The beam illuminated Bryan, standing immobile as a statue with something draped over him like a flabby, greasy blanket.

"Oh God!" Samira's hands flew up to cover her mouth as she gagged and averted her eyes.

"What is that?" Isaac shouted. He stumbled backward, his light never leaving Bryan.

Bryan began to peel the material off himself with hands that were shaking so badly he had trouble gripping it. October watched in dawning horror, now recognizing what exactly had landed on him. She stifled a gasp and a retch as the boy managed to finally throw the whole thing off himself. It landed on the floor with a sickeningly moist splat.

"It's skin!" Isaac blurted. "It's like someone skinned a person!"

Bryan looked down and took in the bloody, ragged flesh. Connected by thin, fraying strips of neck tissue was an empty, deflated head, staring grotesquely up at him like a discarded latex Halloween mask.

"Mom?"

That single word that had carved its way out of Bryan's mouth overflowed with disbelief, heartbreak, repugnance, and utter tragedy.

October didn't know whether she wanted to vomit, cry, or run away. Probably all three. Just seeing Bernadette like that, when the woman had been alive and happy just that morning, caused a primal horror to envelope her, terror and mind-twisting revulsion at the nightmare object heaped on the ground before all of them. October felt as if her sanity were slowly edging toward a precipice, off of which it wished to fling itself and never return so that she could escape this madness.

Maddie growled deep in her throat.

"Stay right where you are!" Henry bellowed.

October's eyes flicked upward, away from the wet pile of flesh on the floor, following the beams of Isaac's flashlight as it trained back on the staircase. At the top of the landing stood a figure smiling at them. If October's nerves hadn't already been stretched beyond belief, she surely would have fainted at what she now saw.

Arthur stood there, smiling at them—a smile far too wide and sadistic to belong to the kind man she had met that morning. His clothes had been torn to shreds and his exposed skin was coated in slick blood. His baggy, loose flesh hung off his bones in folds like some twisted clown costume. Then, to October's horrified disgust, the skin began to swell and fill out into the proper proportions and shape Arthur had been. It was like watching an inflating meat balloon.

The process was accompanied by a soggy, gristly, stomach-churning stretching sound. Arthur stuck two black-clawed fingers into the corners of his mouth and tore the skin all the way up his cheeks to his ears, giving himself the same sort of grotesque smile the imposter Bernadette had made on her face.

What had Arthur become?

Then the creature spoke, a whispering deep voice as dry as sand baking in the desert heat. It spoke its hideous words at Bryan in a mocking, almost gleeful voice that seemed to be a composite of different accents that October couldn't even begin to identify.

"Say good…bye to Mommy…and Daddy," Arthur said. Its one yellow eye filled with manic delight, while the other, damaged eye—scabbed over now, though still weeping with viscous pus—attempted to mimic its neighbor.

That's when Henry and Viorica simultaneously shot at the Arthur-thing, and the creature escaped with an agile leap into the over-whelming gloom of the second floor.

"Futu-i!" Viorica shouted.

"We're getting out of here now!" Henry roared. "Get to the truck!"

There were no arguments as everyone, even Maddie, ran outside into the pouring rain to the weathered red Ford truck that sat in Henry's unpaved driveway. Henry ordered Isaac into the driver's seat while he himself got into the passenger side. Samira and Bryan crawled into the back seat, Noel climbing in after them and placing Adrianna across their laps as best he could.

"No room for us in there," Viorica shouted over the torrential rain to October as the truck roared to life. "Get in the back."

"Oh hell," October said as they both climbed into the truck's bed and hunkered down among various toolboxes and gardening imple-ments covered with green tarps. Maddie leapt up to sit with them. October hugged the dog and wished she could crawl under the plastic tarps to get out of the rain.

My eyeshadow must look awful from all this rain, she mused, making herself snort at the utter triviality of such a thought. Viorica gave her a curious look as Isaac brought the engine to life and hit the gas. The Ford sped off into the unrelenting rain.

As the truck made its way away from the house, October saw a dark mass burst from an upstairs window out into the surrounding blackness. That creature couldn't possibly keep up with a speeding vehicle, could it?

Pretty soon, the house was out of sight, obscured by the thick enveloping trees all around them. At that moment, October couldn't decide what frightened her the most. The monster she had just witnessed? Or the fact that Isaac was tearing madly across a winding dirt road that cut through the dense forest during a nighttime rainstorm when he probably couldn't see anything outside the cones of light from the truck's headlights? She just had to hold on to the hope that the guy knew the ins and outs of this road like the back of his hand. If they crashed at the speed they were going, it wouldn't be pretty.

There was movement among the trees all around them. *The storm's picking up*, she thought. The winds were getting worse.

There was no way that October could tell where they were going, even if she had been facing forward. Tree after shadowed tree whipped past on either side of the barreling vehicle. Some branches and tree trunks passed by so close, if she had allowed even so much as a finger to hang over the walls of the truck bed, it would have been a goner. She clutched onto Maddie as if the dog were a giant teddy bear protecting a small child from the terrors of a bad dream.

A lifetime later, the dirt road ended, and the wheels grabbed hold of a paved highway. Never in her life could October have guessed a day would come when asphalt looked so beautiful. The highway indicated civilization was close at hand. She didn't know where they were exactly, but she felt they would get to safety soon. Streetlights began to appear, standing guard on both sides of the road, casting dim, rain-soaked illumination and guiding them into town.

Without warning, something slammed onto the hood of the truck, causing Isaac to swerve all over the road. October held onto Maddie's collar with an iron grip to keep the dog from flying out of the truck bed, her other hand grabbing one of the straps that secured all the cargo into the bed's floor. Isaac finally regained control, and the vehicle came to an abrupt, screeching halt.

"What the hell was that?" someone's muffled voice shouted from inside the cab.

After her momentary daze passed, October knocked on the little rear window of the cab. Samira opened it for her and October stuck her face in.

"What happened?" she asked the people inside. "Did we hit something?"

"A tree branch fell and slammed into us," Henry said. "Put a big-ass dent in the hood!"

"Uh, guys." Noel turned toward the window as lightning flashed. "I don't think a branch 'just fell' on us." He pointed, his fingertip pressing against the glass.

October followed Noel's finger to the spot he was pointing to up in the treetops. "I don't see anything."

A brilliant flash of lightning illuminated the sky above them. In that split second moment, October clearly saw the monster dressed in Arthur's skin gazing down at the truck. It grasped onto the very pinnacle of a tree. A figure of death, its stolen features standing out in stark contrast with the shadows the lightning created. It was a jarring image—the once-jolly Arthur perched up in the pouring sky like a vicious bird of prey on its arboreal throne.

The lightning subsided. The sky went dark once more, only the streetlamps providing their weak orange glow. Thunder rumbled, shaking the very air itself.

"Screw this!" Isaac shouted and slammed on the gas, knocking everyone backward into their seat. Unfortunately for those in the bed, there were no seats, and October was almost thrown from the truck. She saw Viorica gracefully keep her balance, although Maddie went sliding a couple of feet. *Good thing I was holding her collar*, October told herself, dragging the dog back into her arms.

Chancing a look back up into the tops of the trees, October could just make out the barely defined shadow that was the Arthur-creature jumping from treetop to treetop in powerful leaps, an oversized frog moving through the rain. He was somehow keeping pace with the car, even though Isaac must have had the truck going about eighty miles per hour.

"How is it doing that?" October shouted at Viorica over the roar of the engine and the deluge of rain.

"I don't know," Viorica responded. She patted the handgun in the waist of her pants. "It's not fast enough to dodge a bullet, though. That I know."

That was true enough. October nodded. She had seen Viorica shoot that thing a couple of times now.

How many bullets has the creature already taken? the Overshadow asked, breaking its silence. *Yet it's still coming after you. Barely slowed down.*

The glint of hope died in October's chest.

Maddie began barking like a maniac, her ears flat against her skull. A ferocious look came over the dog's face just as something slammed into the truck again, this time hitting the rear bumper. The vehicle went swerving again. Isaac was able to straighten the truck out and didn't stop. Viorica made to move, gun in hand, to look down over the tailgate.

An obsidian-black hand shot up, gripping the edge of the tailgate, claws digging into metal with an ear-splitting nail-on chalkboard screech.

"Morţii şi răniţii măsii!" Viorica cursed.

October screamed, gathering Maddie up into her arms in a protective death-grip. She heard muffled cries coming from those inside the cab.

A figure pulled itself into the truck bed just as several forks of lightning streaked across the sky and momentarily lit up the night in front of October's eyes. The Arthur-thing narrowly evaded Viorica's gunshot before swiping its knife-like claws at her. Viorica threw herself backward to avoid being disemboweled. The talons grazed her stomach, leaving four ragged slits in her sweater.

Viorica squeezed off another round, hitting the Arthur-thing almost point-blank in the shoulder. It stumbled backward with a piercing shriek and went head-over-heels over the tailgate, falling out of the speeding truck.

"Are you okay?" October asked in a hoarse voice.

Viorica ran gentle fingers over the cuts on her stomach. Not only had her sweater been sliced, but her shirt and skin as well. Three thin red lines now wept blood. "I'll be fine. I can get some bandages when we get to the hospital."

"Did you get it?" October heard Noel shout through the small rear window of the cab.

Viorica looked at him then turned her eyes back on the tailgate. She carefully crawled closer with the gun still in her right hand. October was about to tell her not to look when a pitch-black shape leapt up and landed on Viorica. The gun went off, shooting into the air with another deafening crack. The Arthur-thing's body was torn and ragged from the chest down, revealing the coal-black skin underneath. The creature must have been holding onto the bumper, being dragged along the road. Arthur's flesh still covered it from the shoulders up.

The creature had Viorica by both wrists, preventing her from aiming her weapon. October knew she had to help. What could she do?

With a furious growl, Maddie lunged at Viorica's attacker, biting the Arthur-thing on its right forearm, latching on with tenacious force. The creature shrieked again, letting go of Viorica's left wrist, attempting to shake the dog off. Maddie held fast.

Taking the opportunity, Viorica began punching the monster in its Arthur-face. Even over the truck's screaming engine and the torrential downpour, October could hear the sickening sound of flesh smacking flesh as Viorica punched the thing with all her might.

"Bag pula-n gatu tau!" Viorica bellowed at her opponent. "Stati-ar flocii ma-tii-n gat!"

Reaching under a tarp for one of the strapped-down toolboxes in the truck bed at random, October fumbled the lid open and extracted the first thing her hand grabbed: a rusty pipe wrench. *Perfect*, she thought, gripping the heavy thing. It was difficult to aim while bouncing along in the back of a pickup truck, and she struggled to get proper leverage while scrambling around on her knees.

October swung that pipe wrench with every ounce of strength she could muster, making brutal contact with the Arthur-thing's jaw, and hearing the most satisfying crunch.

The creature bellowed in a way that only a mouthful of blood and broken teeth allowed. The Arthur-thing went toppling over the edge once more. Viorica's quick reflexes kicked in, and her hand shot out to grab Maddie—still latched onto the creature's arm—by the collar and prevented the dog from going over as well.

In the road behind the truck, October saw the shadowy figure tumbling on the asphalt, growing smaller by the second as it disappeared into the distance.

Dropping the pipe wrench with a clunk, October let her body plop down in the truck bed. She didn't think it was possible after the day she'd experienced, but her heart was beating more quickly than it ever had before. She had been face-to-face with that creature and had attacked it. Had hit it out of the back of a truck.

"Mersi, thank you." Viorica lay on her back, breathing heavily. She gave a weary smile. "For a little second, I was worried."

October couldn't seem to form coherent sentences at that moment. "That thing…"

"Almost killed me," Viorica said, sitting up. Her stomach was still bleeding, and it seemed the gashes had opened more during her struggle. "If you hadn't been here, I would have most likely died. Thank you. Surely, I owe you my life."

"Don't," October started to say as she pulled Maddie back into her arms, not caring about the wet dog smell or the scent of rank blood on the lab's breath. "Don't call me Shirley." She then burst out laughing hysterically.

Viorica gave her a confused look, then started laughing herself.

October laughed and laughed. What the hell was she laughing at? Was she losing her mind?

Were those tears streaming down her face, or was it just the rain?

Excerpt from the Logbook of Hasegawa Naritsura, Traveling Scholar
  Date: Approx. 1287 CE
  Translated from Japanese by Professor Sato Hisayo

[PAGE TORN] —*have arrived at the village as the sun sets in the cradle of the horizon. I have been travelling with my companion, Urakami Teruhisa, for two weeks now. A quiet, yet fascinating man, he is without equal when it comes to the art of the fist and of the sword. Urakami is a ronin,* [note: a ronin is a masterless samurai]. *He has dedicated his life, for what purpose, I do not know, to wandering the land and providing aid to those who require it. He does so not for wealth, but only asks for lodging and a meal.*

I met Urakami several days ago while staying at an inn. After asking him several times, he allowed me to venture with him. It is always ideal to travel with someone capable of handling the bandits and scoundrels that frequent the roads. His destination was a squalid village without a name in the north. I would not have chosen such a place— [HALF PAGE MISSING]

The people here in this village are a superstitious lot; however their simple-mindedness has a certain degree of charm to it, and I am determined to experience everything this beautiful land has to offer. For in my life— [TEXT ON REST OF PAGE ILLEGIBLE]

Urakami and I had our evening meal at the home of one Gohei, a local millet farmer. His ugly, yet hilarious wife cooked us a delicious meal the equal of which I would have never guessed these plain folk to be capable of. We feasted upon—[MOST OF PAGE MISSING]

—told us of a yokai [note: yokai are supernatural beings and spirits] *that has supposedly been seen at night in recent weeks, stalking through the*

village. Gohei called this particular spirit the Black Shadow Who Desires Misfortune. I have never heard of such a being. It is curious that—[SEVERAL PAGES MISSING]

I have now witnessed the work of this horrid monstrosity with my own eyes. By all that is divine, I have seen the gruesome aftermath of whatever lurks around this village when the sun sets. Urakami discovered the body of Gohei the previous night. The unfortunate man was dead; but this was no ordinary death. It is hard for my mind to believe what I saw. That dead farmer was missing the entirety of his skin. He had been expertly flayed like an animal, and protruding from his corpse were many strange metal implements.

Urakami called on the Shinto priest of a neighboring village for consultation this morning. They allowed me to be present at the discussion. The priest instructed Urakami to obtain a talisman of some sort held within a shrine located in the nearby hills. He called the talisman the Blood-Disc of Kurukosu's Judgment. What—[SEVERAL SENTENCES ILLEGIBLE]

Urakami and the priest have gone out this evening, presumably to look for the evil spirit that preys upon this village. Whether it is truly a yokai, I cannot begin to guess. What I do know, after seeing what it did to Gohei, is that this foul creature is dangerous, sadistic, and mad. Whatever happens, I believe—[PAGE TORN]

—has been many hours already. Urakami and the Shinto priest have not returned yet. I cannot manage sleep. Each time I shut my eyes, a noise from outside awakens me, though I cannot decide if I am simply imagining it. I thought I briefly saw Urakami outside the window of the room I am resting in. However, this was probably the product of dreaming while being half-awake. I have decided to forego sleep for the moment. My only comfort is writing down—[A DARK SPLATTER ACROSS THE PAGE RENDERS THE REST OF THE TEXT ILLEGIBLE]

CHAPTER TWENTY-ONE

October

W elcome to Cinter," the broad, wooden sign declared as they drove into town; the same sign October had driven by when she had first arrived here. It was hard to believe that had only been the previous day. It seemed like weeks ago. Perhaps it had been *years* ago. Perhaps she was just in some sort of coma and THIS was an endlessly repeating dream. What a nightmare.

Perhaps you are in the deepest bowels of hell, the Overshadow said.

Shut up.

No. They had made it to town. Cold, wet, and bloodied, they had reached Cinter. Though all the shops were closed, and she couldn't see anyone out and about on the quiet streets, October still felt much safer surrounded by buildings, street signs, and parked cars. A relieved sigh escaped her lips as they passed the darkened building of Melba's 24-Hour Diner.

So much for being open twenty-four hours, she thought wryly.

"Where is everyone?" Noel asked from inside the truck's cab.

Henry turned around in the passenger seat to face him. "Son, this isn't the big city. People here eat dinner at five and are in bed reading a book by nine."

The rain had let up some, but it was still falling in low, heavy drops that landed on October's exposed arms and face like falling ice pebbles. She didn't care about that anymore, though. She didn't care about the iciness that had seeped into her very marrow, didn't care about her exhaustion, she didn't even care about Maddie's stinky breath as the lab licked her.

Turning away from the dog, October glanced inside through the cab's rear window at the dashboard clock. It read 11:37 PM in bright green numbers. A strong sense of unreality settled over her. It hadn't even been twelve hours since the group had set out on their fateful hike through the wilderness, led by Adrianna.

"How's she doing?" October asked Samira, sticking her face in the window. She indicated the girl lying across Samira, Noel, and Bryan's laps. *Damn, she looks terrible.* It was like that monster had put the girl through a meat grinder back in the darkness of that cave. October didn't know how someone could be that messed up and yet still be alive. Adrianna would most likely need lots of hospital care, surgery, pain meds, and therapy. Definitely lots of therapy. Hell, they would all need it.

"She's still breathing," Samira answered, stroking Adrianna's filth-caked hair. "She's a tough girl. She's held on this long." Samira leaned down, her face close to Adrianna's, and whispered, "Just hang in there a little longer. We're almost there."

"Dad," Isaac said in a croak like he had just regained his voice. "What the hell was that?

"The Skin Stealer," Henry answered in a breathy whisper. "It's out."

"What are you talking about? Those stories you used to tell me? Dad, come on!"

"They ain't just stories!" Henry snapped at his son. "I told you them things were real! I've been expecting this day, hoping it would never actually come. But it has, Isaac. Just ask these folks. They've seen the damn thing!"

Isaac kept his eyes on the road.

"This is all my fault." Henry rubbed at his jaw. "We need to get to the museum in town."

"The museum?" Noel asked. "What for?"

Henry turned to look at him, taking a deep breath. "It's all in my gran's journal. She was determined to figure out what exactly took her grandad and wore his face. It kept tormenting her. She spent years traveling around the state of Washington and even up into Canada, gathering up whatever tiny scraps of folklore and rumor she could about these things. She talked to Indigenous folks, people at universities, hermits who lived out in the middle of nowhere, you name it."

"What did she learn?" October leaned as far into the window as she could.

"That these skin-stealing creatures could be contained," Henry answered. "Devices called Wheels of Kurkoth can bind those monsters somehow. Before she disappeared, she had told me about everything she knew. My parents didn't believe in any of it. She said she couldn't fully work the wheels. Needed something called 'The Cinter' to actually stop the monsters. Her eye was always on the Cinter Stone that's on display at the museum."

"Adrianna told us about that Cinter Stone." October recalled Adrianna's speech on the bus ride to the start of the hiking trail. "She said the stone has inscriptions on it. Like about Black Ashes, Shadow's Path, and something about Cinter helping protect your body and soul. It's what they named the towns after."

"Right," Henry grunted. "The translated inscriptions are: 'Cloaked in ashes of utmost black, thy path lies in shadow. For only the Cinter shall protect flesh and soul.' My grandmother really tried to learn how the stone worked so she could activate the wheels' full potential."

"Your grandmother sounds like a tough woman," Samira said.

"You said 'wheels' several times," Noel interrupted. "That's wheels as in plural?"

Henry nodded. "Yep. Edith wrote about two Wheels of Kurkoth that she knew of."

"Wait," Bryan said. "You've figured out how to use the Cinter Stone by now, though. Right?"

Henry shook his head, looking ashamed.

"After all this time, you haven't learned?" Bryan said in a deadpan tone.

"I delved into it when I was younger. I know I was wrong to stop. Before she left, my gran told me to destroy the monsters if she failed. But when Isaac was born, I quit. I was scared. Scared I might draw the attention of those things. Scared that I might lose my family to them like I lost my gran."

"Jesus, Dad!" Isaac bellowed. "Those were just ghost stories and fairy tales. Folklore your grandma believed in! That doesn't mean any of it was real."

"Listen here, pulete," Viorica interjected. "Did you not see the creature?"

"Exactly!" Henry nodded.

October looked around at the others. Isaac drove in silence, Henry talking to him in a hushed voice while gripping his shotgun like a life preserver. Noel just stared out of the window, his face turned away. Bryan looked terrible. If he hadn't given October a brief glance, she would have sworn he had gone catatonic.

Yes, let's not forget the monster flinging Bernadette's skin at Bryan so that it fell on top of him like some fucked-up Snuggie.

October's gorge rose at the memory of that horrible scene. Her own mind and spirit were reeling from all of the day's experiences. She couldn't fathom how much worse it had been for Bryan. October resolved to call her own parents when she was next able. Screw it, she would go visit them and Uncle Shane as soon as possible. At that moment, she missed them all more than she could have thought possible.

Looking over at Bryan once more, October felt tears threatening again. Despite how annoying and confrontational Bryan had been at the beginning of the day, he was still a human being. One that was close to breaking, if he hadn't done so already. She wanted to lay a hand on his shoulder and tell him something comforting. But October was not the kind of person who could easily do that, and it saddened her. Besides, what words could she possibly offer that would cheer the boy up even an iota? What could any person say to him that would make anything okay?

No, she had to say something. She had to let Bryan know that even with his parents gone, he wasn't alone. Any minute now, she would tell him.

"We're here," Henry called out from the passenger seat.

October looked up as a hospital came into view. Except it wasn't a hospital, exactly. The building was a squat, two-story, concrete and timber structure painted a moss green. Rainwater cascaded off the peaked roof in mini waterfalls. They drove past a lighted sign that said "Pemberton Medical Clinic" written in white letters with a red arrow instructing them to follow the driveway and pulled up to the drop-off zone, which was covered by a wooden canopy. The passageway beneath led to a set of double-doors of frosted glass.

The lights were on inside the clinic. *Small town*, October reminded herself as the truck came to a stop. She hoped the doctor was in.

As soon as the engine cut off, October leapt out of the back, along with Viorica and Maddie. She and Viorica helped extract Adrianna, so that the passengers in the back seat could get out. Noel then took Adrianna in his arms and carried her to the doors, everyone else following.

"Dr. Warren!" Henry shouted. He pounded on the doors with a fist.

"Don't tell me there's only one doctor in this whole town," Samira asked, echoing October's own thoughts.

"No, there isn't only one doctor in town," Henry replied, surveying the night around them. "There's two. Dr. Miller is away visiting her family in Arizona, if I recall. Dr. Warren! You here?" He pounded on the doors again. "Warren!"

They all saw an indistinct blob materialize beyond the frosted glass before the doors swung open to reveal an older blond man wearing a white coat, and a young brunette woman in green scrubs.

"I'm right here!" the man puffed loudly. His eyes landed on Adrianna in Noel's arms. "Oh my Lord, what happened? Come in!"

"Doc, help us," Henry said.

"Michelle, get a gurney. Quick!" Dr. Warren ordered.

The nurse, Michelle, ran off and disappeared around a corner, returning almost immediately with a gurney. Noel laid Adrianna's still form down on it.

"Henry, what's going on here?" Warren asked, eyeing Henry's shotgun. He checked Adrianna's breathing, then placed fingers on her wrist to check for a pulse. "It's faint, but steady. And her breathing sounds unobstructed."

"Adrianna," Henry started to say. His voice was heavy, exhausted. "She was attacked."

"Attacked?" Michelle asked as she checked Adrianna's neurological responses. She looked at all the wounds with a worried look. "By an animal?"

"Yes," Henry answered. His brow furrowed, and he didn't elaborate further. "Can you help her?"

"We'll do our best to stabilize her here. She's going to need to be transported to Sacred Light over in Black Ashes, though." Dr. Warren glanced at Henry with a grim, determined expression. He turned to the nurse. "Okay, Michelle, we need to get Sacred Light on the phone, let them know the situation. If they can't send their chopper, I'll have Jesse drive Adrianna there himself in the ambulance. He should be at home, but you know Jesse. Anyway, let's get her to the exam room. Henry, we're going to hook her up to monitors and get an IV going, take care of these lacerations, and prep blood. Okay?"

"God, these bite wounds, claw marks," Michelle said as she pushed the gurney through a swinging door. "I've never seen anything like this before."

Everyone followed the doctor and nurse. October was at the back of the group, Maddie running beside her. October didn't want to let Adrianna out of her sight, and it seemed like no one else in the group did either.

The group pushed farther inside into a warmth that eased away the cold air from outside, its frigid fingers melting away and losing their grip. Even Maddie seemed glad to be inside out of the rain and shook herself, splattering the floor and everything around her with water.

As they made their way down a hallway, October saw a handful of other rooms. They were all empty save for one. She caught a brief glimpse of a man lying unconscious in a bed, scrapes and bruises all over his face and arms. It looked like he had been in some sort of a car accident.

"You can't take care of her here?" Henry asked.

"Not if she needs surgery," Dr. Warren said. "We're not equipped for that, Henry. Don't worry, we can stabilize her. And you know Black Ashes isn't far."

The doctor and nurse pushed the gurney into a cramped room with baby-blue tiles and began tending to Adrianna's plethora of grisly wounds. Dr. Warren ordered everyone to stay outside while he and Michelle worked. There was a window they could watch the proceedings through from outside in the hallway, and thankfully the blinds hadn't been drawn. October wouldn't have normally watched such a thing, but she was desperate to make sure Adrianna pulled through.

They had done it. They had gotten Adrianna to safety, to a doctor that could help her, that could save her life. Or at least stabilize her enough to be transferred to an actual hospital. *Would I have been able to hang on for so long after an attack like that?* October asked herself.

Of course not, the Overshadow said. October could feel cold, snake-like coils slithering through her head.

I hope I could be that strong.

You're not.

You're in good hands now, Adrianna.

She's going to die after having suffered so much. Have you thought about how long she's been in her current state? Her wounds must be all infected by now. And have you seen how much blood she's lost?

They can give her a blood transfusion.

What if they don't have her blood type? She isn't long for this world of yours. You should have put her out of her misery a while ago.

Adrianna has a chance. She has to, after all we've been through. After all she's survived so far. It wouldn't be fair.

Fair? You know the universe doesn't work that way. There's no good and evil on the cosmic scale. The universe is indifferent. It doesn't care about you.

Without warning, Samira burst into tears, pulling October out of her mental argument.

"Dara," the woman sobbed into her hands. Noel put an arm around Samira's shoulders. "I wish he was here. I wish he was here so much."

"He was brave," Noel said to her. "He gave his life for all of us. Your husband's a hero. Always remember that."

Bryan began to weep as well, crouching down and hiding his face in his hands. He didn't say anything, just cried, tears dripping onto the floor. Samira knelt beside the boy and embraced him, bringing his head under her chin, and closing her eyes, tears still spilling down her own cheeks. Maddie padded over to the crying pair, whining and nudging them with her nose.

October turned to look back through the window into the room where Michelle and Dr. Warren had carefully removed Adrianna's damp, ragged, blood-stained clothes, and now set about gingerly cleaning her injuries and applying fresh bandages. Warren paused for a minute, midway through his examination of one of the larger gashes on Adrianna's right thigh. The doctor's eyes widened, and his expression sent a shiver down October's spine.

Setting down the gauze to step out of the room, Dr. Warren approached Henry.

"Tell me again," he said. "When did this happen to Adrianna?"

"This afternoon," Henry replied.

"And what kind of animal did you say did this?"

Henry looked around at the others, who all exchanged similar glances of uncertainty.

"I didn't say," Henry finally answered.

"Dr. Warren!" Michelle shouted from inside the room, and the doctor hurried back in. "She's regaining consciousness." Michelle indicated Adrianna's twitching eyelids.

Adrianna gave a wet, hoarse cough, her hands spasming.

"Adrianna, can you hear me?" Dr. Warren asked. He took a penlight from out of his breast pocket, switched it on and opened

Adrianna's right eye. He immediately stumbled backward with a yelp of surprise. "What in the hell?"

The girl continued to cough as she lay on the table. The coughing turned into raspy wheezing, which then morphed into something even worse.

"No," Noel said as everyone heard it. "No way. No, no, no."

"Fuck me," Bryan whispered, standing back up and starting to hyperventilate.

October's throat constricted so tightly she began to have trouble getting air into her lungs, and she was absolutely certain her eyeballs were going to pop right out of her head like some cartoon. She couldn't believe what was happening.

"I was carrying her this whole time." Noel's words were enveloped in disbelief. "This whole time. This whole time, I've been *carrying* it."

"Futu-ti dumnezeii matii!" Viorica hissed.

"No," Samira whispered harshly. "It's not possible."

Adrianna sat up on the table with ease, laughing that hideous, hoarse laugh that cut at October like corroded razor blades. Dr. Warren and Michelle backed away, crashing into tables and a cart full of medical tools, spilling metal instruments onto the floor.

"Yes...doctor," the creature posing as Adrianna rasped out in a voice that in no way belonged to the sweet, kind, real Adrianna October remembered. With a lithe maneuver, Adrianna flipped her legs up and crouched on the gurney like a vulture. "Yes... I hear...you." The words were in that unidentifiable mixture of dozens of different accents. She perched on that table, half-naked, bloody bandages hanging off her limbs. Patches of damaged skin sloughed off, revealing wet, coal-black flesh underneath.

"W-What's wrong with h-her?" Michelle stammered out, cringing away. "What in God's name is wrong with her?"

As quick as a bullet, Adrianna's hand shot forward toward Michelle's face. A brief sickening scream erupted from the nurse's mouth as her blood splattered across the wall and ceiling. She stumbled for a few steps around the room, then fell against the window the group had been watching through, all of them rooted to the spot in overwhelming shock. Michelle's face was gone. The flesh had been torn from the bone, one eye clawed out, nose hanging by a thread of cartilage, lips completely ripped free. Her brutalized visage left a crimson imprint on the window before sliding down, leaving behind a trail of gore.

The Adrianna-thing bellowed a guttural laugh full of gleeful mirth. Red spittle flew from its lips. She glared at the group through the window, yellow eyes full of murderous intelligence.

"No!" October found herself shrieking while her fist pounded on the glass that separated her from the monster. "Fuck you! Why are you doing this to us?"

The creature locked eyes with October at that moment. Its yellow eyes burned into hers.

It smiled and said in that scratchy croak, "Because…it …is fun."

The Adrianna-thing then turned its evil gaze upon Dr. Warren, who had fallen to the floor in paralyzed terror. October was certain it would attack him as well, but the creature just laughed again before jumping onto the ceiling and clinging to it like an overgrown spider. It tore through one of the overhead panels. Viorica ran in and blasted three shots at the thing as it disappeared into the ceiling. Whether Viorica had hit her target, October couldn't tell. There was so much blood everywhere already.

Through the open door, Dr. Warren crawled out on his hands and knees. October could smell the fact that the man had wet his pants.

Viorica kept the gun trained on the hole in the ceiling. "Sugi pula, curva!"

Dr. Warren had tears and snot running down his face. "Oh, merciful Christ! What was that? Michelle. It killed Michelle. Why did it kill her? Why? Why did it just laugh at me?"

No one responded. Viorica looked down at the still form of Michelle, shook her head, and came back out of the room.

She seemed as calm as she always did, her face a mask of stoicism and determination. However, October saw that Viorica's white-knuckled hand, gripping the gun, was trembling.

CHAPTER TWENTY-TWO

Wendig

Wendig ran as fast as he could.

Where was he running to? Through the mist and shadow, darkness and fog. There were no walls, no floor, only a ceiling of stars splayed out into an endless tapestry of night that was the infinite cosmic ocean.

"Hey." A voice drifted out of the ether. He couldn't tell which direction it had come from. He looked around, eyes desperately searching for something. But what? What was he looking for?

A dirt road appeared beneath his feet, no, it was a field of grass that tickled his ankles; no, it was a wooden floor that creaked with each step; no, it was a bridge that swayed dangerously in the wind. An iron door materialized before him like a ghost stepping out from the shadows. A hand grasped the large iron ring. His hand. He pulled with all his strength, and the door swung inward. Inward? A gale pushed him forward into the doorway, yet he fell backward away from the threshold, though somehow through it.

He fell.

And fell.

Upward into a dizzying vortex of nothingness.

"Hey," the voice said once more. He knew that voice. How he had longed to hear that voice again, so sweet and comforting to his ears.

He looked around. All was blackness. He was inside a room, a room filled with knee-deep water. He waded forward, oblivious to where he was headed. His foot caught on something, and he tripped face-first into the icy embrace of the water. He fell again, sinking, sinking, ever lower into the frigid depths of an ocean for an eternity.

A blue light appeared in the distance, growing ever larger as it slowly neared. The light was attached to a face, a face made of murk and memory. Such a beautiful face. Two hands gently grasped the sides of his head and pulled him closer.

The eyes in the beautiful face began to bleed with dark blood that drifted around him, clouding the water, obscuring his vision.

"Dad," the face said to him in a tone of utmost sorrow.

"Rowan," he answered. He reached out to touch the face of his daughter. There was nothing there. Despair crept into his heart.

BANG

BANG

BA—

—NG

Wendig opened his eyes as a loud explosion tore him from the fever dream his subconscious had been subjecting him to. He tried to sit up, immediately collapsing back down with a groan, his head pounding. He waited for his vision to focus on his surroundings. Glancing around, he saw he was in a hospital room, in a hospital bed, and wearing a hospital gown. A monitor beeped, slowing down to match his decelerating pulse as he calmed himself.

What had happened?

He attempted to sit up again, managing to right himself. His head wasn't so foggy now. There was a burning pain in his left side. Lifting up his hospital gown, Wendig saw bandages dotted with specks of blood. He peeked under them to find fresh stitches holding together his torn flesh.

It all came back to him. The Watcher, his injury, trying to drive away, needing to get to a doctor. He had made it, somehow, although he had no memory of actually driving all the way back to town. What town was he in anyway?

He heard a commotion somewhere nearby.

Wendig leapt out of his bed—those explosions he'd heard, his mind now realized, had been gunshots; he was sure of it. He groaned, realizing he shouldn't have moved so quickly, but he was up and awake now. He didn't have his gun or his clothes. It didn't matter. Some instinct told him to go find out what was happening.

Voices were shouting from around a bend in the hall, and as Wendig rounded the corner, several pairs of eyes fastened onto him. One woman with sharp features, holding a pistol, swung the firearm in his direction. Her eyes widened for a fraction of a second, then she lowered the gun. An older man with a mustache stood holding a shotgun but seemed too stunned to have noticed his arrival.

The rest of the motley crew of people wearing dirty, blood-stained clothing and weary faces looked at him without a word. There was even a yellow lab with them, wagging its tail.

"What's going on here?" Wendig asked in a dry voice that scratched his throat. He saw a man in a white coat, a doctor presumably, quivering on the floor. He looked like he had been crying. That was when Wendig noticed the large smear of blood on the glass that allowed a view into another room. He took a step toward the room's door.

"Don't go in there," one of the women warned. She was quite pale, and wore all black, with dark makeup that had run down her cheeks; arm tattoos and nose and lip piercings completed the goth attire. Her black hair was a mess with a twig in it. She looked absolutely exhausted, as did they all.

"Why?" Wendig asked.

When the woman didn't respond, he crept closer and looked

through the glass. Lying on the floor was a woman in formerly green scrubs. Her face was nothing but a mangled mess of torn flesh.

"Oh." It was all Wendig could say before stepping away from the window. What the hell was going on in this place? Maybe he hadn't woken up after all and was still trapped in that dream.

"Mr. Wendig, you shouldn't be up," the doctor on the floor said in a flat, robotic tone, not looking up at him. The haggard man looked frightened beyond belief. "You should be resting. The wound in your side was shallow, but you have a mild concussion." He tapped his own head three times in a slow rhythm.

"Can you tell me where my things are?" Wendig asked, kneeling beside the doctor.

"Your personal effects are secured in my office," came the whispered answer. "The sheriff was notified. He's been busy today. He'll be by when he can. I hope you have a permit for the gun the paramedic found."

"Can we go somewhere else?" the youngest member of this strange group asked. It was a teenage boy, tall, athletic, with a haunted look in his eyes that reminded Wendig of photos he had seen of war refugees.

Two members of the group helped the doctor up off the ground as everyone moved farther down the hallway, away from the bloody scene.

"We have to get out of here," the goth woman said. Everyone else nodded and mumbled agreement.

"Why?" Wendig asked. "What's going on here? Who did that to the nurse back there?"

Except for the boy and the woman with the handgun, who looked vaguely familiar to Wendig for some reason, everyone started talking at once. The jumble of voices hurt his head.

"Slow down." He rubbed his temple. "One person at a time, please."

The woman with the pistol began explaining in a calm, accented voice.

"A creature stalking us," she said. "Well, two creatures now. We've been attacked many times."

"They wear a person's skin!" the muscular man shouted. "Like a fucking suit. They killed the nurse, and they killed Bryan's parents!"

"Damn," Wendig growled, running a hand down his face. That wasn't what he had wanted to hear. "This can't be happening. There's more than one, you said?"

"Have you seen them too?" the goth woman asked.

"Yes," Wendig answered. There was no point in hiding the truth from these people. They had already seen the creature. And now there was more than just one Watcher apparently. Had the one he encountered found a buddy? This wasn't good. "I fought one. It attacked me. Gave me a clawing. I remember I was driving."

"You were in a car accident," the doctor, his nametag identifying him as Dr. Warren, said in a monotone. "You were found on the side of a road after someone called the police. You smashed into a tree. They brought you in an hour or so ago."

A car accident? Wendig looked down at all the scrapes and bruises on his arms. The fuzzy memories replayed in his head again. A car crash made sense. He remembered bleeding. His side being on fire. The rain pouring down on the windshield and the wipers struggling against the downpour.

"We need to get out of here," the goth woman said again with more urgency. "We need to find help. We should call the cops or something."

"I don't know how much help they'll be in this situation, but we can try," Wendig said. The police—though most of the time just doing their jobs—had almost always hindered him during his Enigmata hunting. However, this situation was quickly spiraling out of control. Wendig hated involving anyone else in the danger. Unfortunately, he didn't think he could defend this group of people alone. Not against *two* Watchers. He massaged his temples, trying to think.

"Why do you say that?" the goth woman asked, breaking into his thoughts. "Who are you anyway? What do you know about these monsters?"

Wendig gazed at her for a moment before answering. "My name is Lucas Wendig. And you are?"

"October. October Night," the woman answered, then started

pointing to the other haggard members of her group. "Samira, Noel, Bryan, Henry, Isaac, and Viorica."

As October Night pointed, Wendig noticed the tattoo on the back of her right hand. It was the Sigil of Deep. An odd thing to have popped up. Did it have anything to do with what was going on? And did this woman know the meaning of the mark? Maybe she had come across the symbol on some obscure occult website and just thought it looked cool. He thought he'd better keep an eye on her. The places he'd come across the sigil before were not good ones. It signified being blessed, touched, or cursed (depending on the interpretation) by something that lurked in the darkness between the stars.

"What exactly do you know about the creatures?" Viorica asked him.

Instead of answering, Wendig stared at the woman named Viorica. He had seen her twitch when October had named her. She really did seem familiar. Why?

"Have we met before?" he asked Viorica. "I swear we have."

"Nu," Viorica replied almost too quickly. "I am on vacation."

Wendig looked around. "Does anyone have a cell phone? Or has anyone tried the landlines here?"

Jordan would be worried sick.

There was a loud crash from somewhere far off. It sounded like something banging against the air ducts in the ceiling.

"That thing is still up there somewhere!" Dr. Warren blurted out. He wrapped his arms around himself.

"We need to move to a safer area." Viorica gestured down the hall.

Wendig didn't think there really was a safer area here in this building with the Watcher potentially anywhere. Maybe Viorica just meant somewhere less gruesome.

The others nodded and followed her, the dog loping after them. They gathered in the quiet lobby. All Wendig could make out through the frosted glass of the entrance was nighttime darkness.

"Our truck's just outside," the young man named Isaac said to Wendig.

"We can't leave yet," Dr. Warren started to blubber. "We can't leave Michelle behind. We have to help her!" He refused to keep going.

"Michelle is dead," Viorica told the doctor. "We can't help her." After a pause, she added, "I'm sorry."

"Go start the truck," Henry—the older gentleman with the mustache—said to Isaac. Then he turned to face Warren. "Doc, Michelle's gone. There ain't a thing we can do for her now. We gotta go."

"No, we have to help her!" Dr. Warren cried out. He attempted to loosen the grip Samira and Noel had on his wrists as they prevented him from returning to the grisly scene of the nurse's death. "I-I can't leave her there! What am I going to tell her parents? I was Michelle's godfather!" The doctor had tears streaming down his cheeks.

The dog began to bark furiously.

"Dad!"

The muffled yell came from outside the hospital entrance. All eyes turned away from the doctor and toward the open glass doors. Dr. Warren took advantage of this momentary distraction to break out of Noel's and Samira's hands and run back down the corridor. Wendig barely noticed. His gaze was locked on the scene quickly unfolding outside.

The Watcher had followed him here.

Wait. No, that was *not* the same creature. This new horror was not wearing Evan's dried and weathered face. Instead, a middle-aged man gazed at them with one yellow eye, one grayish, milky eye, and a far too-wide smile.

The Watcher had Isaac pinned against the truck.

"No!" Henry yelled from beside Wendig and aimed his shotgun at the abhorrent beast.

"Don't shoot!" Wendig shouted. "You'll hit both of them!"

Henry hesitated. And in that brief moment, the Watcher jammed a black-clawed hand into Isaac's mouth and forcefully pulled his jaw downward. With the sickening noise of bone and gristle ripping and snapping, Isaac's jaw detached from his face in a cascade of blood and torn muscle. He then fell to the ground, spasming, blood coating the driveway.

"Noooo!" Henry bellowed and fired two shots from his shotgun as the creature bounded away into the darkness, laughing.

Henry made to run outside. Wendig caught the man's arm.

"What the fuck are you doing?" Henry yelled, tears now streaming down his weathered face. "Let go of me! That's my son!"

"You can't risk going outside!" Wendig shouted, trying to keep hold of Henry's arm.

Henry managed to pull his arm out of Wendig's hand, then just sank to his knees, the shotgun clattering onto the floor beside him. The old man pulled off his cowboy hat, then began to weep. Outside, the now-still body continued to ooze blood. Henry continued to sob bitter tears on the floor.

Wendig's jaw tightened, teeth grinding together.

He'd end these things. These Watchers.

He didn't yet know how, but he *would* end the unholy lives of these goddammed monsters.

CHAPTER TWENTY-THREE

October

The real-life sound of a fist punching someone's face is not the sound heard in movies—that almost cartoonish *whap* noise everyone is so used to. No, the actual sound is far more subdued, yet sickening and visceral. October once again heard that sound, this time in crisp detail, when Henry got up and swung at the man named Lucas Wendig.

"Son of a bitch!" Henry shouted, eyes blazing, as his knuckles cracked against the side of the other man's jaw. "I could've saved him if you hadn't stopped me!"

Yes! the Overshadow roared. *Let them fight. Let them attack each other. Fight. Batter. Tear. Mangle. Kill! Kill! Kill! As much as I'd love to see those creatures murder every one of you, turning on each other might be even better to watch.*

To October's surprise, Wendig didn't go down, but he did stumble backward, then wiped blood from his split lip.

"You said you encountered two of those creatures." Wendig massaged his jaw. There was no anger in his voice. He acted as if the punch had never happened, only sparing Henry a single glance. "If the one I encountered is a separate entity, then we should assume there are three of them. It's hard enough to fight against one. You would have been killed if you went out there."

"Then I would've died with my son!" Henry yelled. The fury was gone, and only heartsick grief remained in his words. "I could be with him and his mother right now if you hadn't stopped me." His body sagged to the floor.

"Let's move away from these doors for now." Viorica gave a quick look outside and closed them. She then checked how many rounds were left in her handgun.

Samira and Noel helped Henry back to his feet. October heard Wendig tell them all to come along as he followed the signs leading to the clinic's eating area. October stepped over to Viorica as the others followed the man.

"How many bullets do you have left in that thing?" October asked, her eyes continuously darting back and forth between Viorica's gun and the glass doors. She hoped Isaac had died quickly and had not suffered. How long did it take for someone to die from having his jaw ripped off? That image, and the sound of his mouth being torn open, made her shudder.

"Not many," Viorica replied. "Three rounds left. Though they're proving ineffective. If only we had something else to use against them."

"Something like what?" October asked. Viorica's tone had infused the word with a strange emphasis. "You mean like those Enigmata things you told me about?"

"Let us catch up with the others." Viorica ignored October's questions. "It's not safe here." She slipped the gun back into her pocket then walked over to the front desk and picked up the phone, holding it to her ear for a few seconds. "Dead, of course. They're trapping us here. I didn't think the power loss back in Henry's home was because of the storm." She replaced the handset. "October, bring that with you, please." She indicated the shotgun Henry had dropped and turned down the hallway to follow the others.

October grabbed the weapon from the floor and hurried after her.

It felt awkward and clumsy in her hands. The only time she'd even touched a firearm before was earlier at Henry's house, and before that, the gun Viorica now wielded. October remembered taking the pistol from the dead man's bag in the ritual chamber. That seemed like forever ago.

I sure hope the safety is on, October thought as she carried the shotgun in both hands like a spear, pointing it upward away from anything, and keeping her fingers away from the trigger. Did shotguns even have safeties? They had to, right? She didn't know how to tell if it was loaded. How many rounds—shells, she thought they were called—could this thing hold? Henry had shot twice already.

The group assembled in the clinic's eating area, which consisted of a tiny (and currently empty) buffet table with two spots for warming trays, a microwave in the corner, and two vending machines that hummed along the far wall, one offering soda, the other with candy bars and packets of chips in colorful, enticing packaging.

October handed the shotgun back to Henry who took it with a solemn nod. She sat down at one of the round tables that were crammed together in the small space. Despite the danger all around them, she needed a minute to sit and gather herself.

Viorica checked the phone mounted on the wall. October saw her shake her head and hang it back up. Henry stood like a sentry by the room's entrance—Maddie panting by his side—his finger just above the shotgun's trigger guard, ready to blast anything and everything that came at them. Bryan sat by himself a short distance from the others. Noel and Samira kept eyeing the ceiling then exchanging nervous glances with one another. October hoped that if the Adrianna-thing came toward them through the air ducts or whatever was up there, everyone would hear it first.

"What are we doing here?" October asked the group, rubbing the back of her neck. She was going to be sore tomorrow, that's for sure. If they survived the night. "Should we be looking for Dr. Warren? Or trying to call the cops?" She pulled out her cell phone. A deep crack now marred the black screen, probably a result from the wild ride in the back of the truck. Holding the power button did nothing.

"I don't know how much more of this I can take!" Noel shouted, causing Bryan to nearly jump out of his seat. "I've been trying to be as calm as I can, trying to think of all of this as logically as possible. But I can't anymore. I'm so fucking tired of all this." Suddenly, Noel began to cry. October had never expected to see this from him. After Viorica, October felt like Noel was the strongest of the group. If *he* was going to lose it, she would certainly break down altogether. "I just want to see my home again, man," Noel went on, dropping into a chair. "I want to see my parents and my sister again. I want to see my dog."

As if understanding his words, Maddie nudged his lap. Noel petted her, then bent down to put his forehead on the lab's.

Samira shuffled around in agitation, an unsettling look dawning on her face. "We should hunt those things down and kill them. Slaughter them like they've been slaughtering us."

There was a new menacing fire in the woman's eyes.

"They're too strong," Bryan whispered, picking at a hole in his shirt. "They can tear us to shreds super easy. We're like ants to them. Viorica threw a freaking knife in its eye this morning. It's been shot how many times? That didn't stop it at all. How do you kill something that can take all that? Bullets and knives barely slow it down."

"I need to think. Let me eat something first," Wendig said.

With all that had been happening, October hadn't realized just how hungry she herself was. If she tuned out all the horrible thoughts that were dancing through her head—which she desperately wanted to, especially what Bryan had just been saying—she could feel, and now hear, her stomach crying out for sustenance.

"Does anyone have a dollar twenty-five?" Wendig turned away from the vending machine he was examining to look at the group. "I don't have my wallet. Or my pants."

Getting to her feet and striding over to the vending machine, October pulled some wrinkled bills from her back pocket and handed them over. "Get what you want," she said. "Get me a water, then those chips and that Twix." She pointed to her desired items through the machine's window then sat back down at the table, putting her feet up on a chair. *When I get home, I'm going to go to sleep for like a month*, she promised herself, rubbing her eyes.

Don't you mean if *you get home? Those creatures have been picking you off one by one. Do you really think you're going to make it out of here alive? You're not going to even get out in one piece. Don't get too comfy during your little break here. Your killer might be around any corner.*

After buying the snacks, Wendig strode over and sat down at October's table. He handed over her change and food, then started eating his own purchase. Noel got up, wiped his tears, and headed over to the vending machine as well, saying something to Bryan and Samira. October looked back at Wendig who was munching on a granola bar, Maddie now watching him with intense interest. Wendig gave the dog a piece, and she swallowed it with gusto, barely bothering to chew.

"You said you fought one of these creatures?" October asked. "It attacked you, but you got away? How?"

Swallowing a mouthful of granola, Wendig stared at the table for a moment before answering. "I fought back against it." He opened his own bottle of water and took a long gulp.

"And you actually managed to fend it off?" October asked, astonished. "Our guns haven't been able to deter it—or 'them' now, I guess —for long. They just keep coming back."

Wendig looked up at her, then back down at the table. "I have my methods." He picked up a Sacagawea one dollar coin from the change, examining it like he'd never seen one before.

"Christ," October said. "You're not going to be some 'mysterious stranger,' are you? I've had enough mystery for one day. Don't make me get Viorica over here to get the info out of you." She jammed her thumb in Viorica's direction. The woman sat by herself on the floor, cross-legged with her eyes closed. She appeared to be meditating, although she held her gun in her lap.

"Viorica," Wendig said, rolling the syllables around in his mouth. "She seems familiar. Does she live in this town?"

"I have no idea where she lives," October replied. "She likes to say she's 'on vacation' though." She made air quotes with her fingers.

Wendig rubbed his chin, then finished off his granola bar. "I swear I've met her before." He gave the final piece of his granola bar to Maddie.

"You're trying to change the subject." October crossed her arms. "Just—"

"We gotta get to the Cinter Museum," Henry announced. "We gotta get to that stone."

"What stone?" Wendig asked.

"The Cinter Stone." October recounted everything Henry had told them at his house: the monsters, his grandmother's work, the theory about the Cinter Stone. All the while, Wendig had an expression on his face as if he knew something.

"Going to the museum and getting the stone is our best chance," Henry replied. The muscles in his face were slack, and his skin had a grayish tint. His eyes were lifeless. It was the haunted look of a man with nothing else to lose. "We're going to use it to kill these mother-fuckers."

Noel shook his head. "No, man, we need to go to the police. They'll have more guns."

"I want to go to the museum," Viorica said. She stood up from the floor. "I agree with Henry."

The police sounded like the better option to October. She knew why Viorica wanted to go to the museum, though: the Cinter Stone could be an Enigmata. What was the inscription on the stone again? She couldn't remember. And what was a "cinter" anyway? October didn't know the word. It probably wasn't English.

Wendig looked as if he was about to speak when the overhead lights died, plunging them all into complete darkness. October realized she couldn't hear the humming of the vending machines any longer.

"Not again," Noel whispered.

"Did the storm knock out the power?" Samira asked from the darkness.

"The phone lines here were dead before the power went out," Viorica said. October could tell that the woman was somewhere to her right. "I don't think the weather had anything to do with that or the power."

"Shit," Noel replied.

A few sets of lights kicked back on. They seemed to be emergency lighting; dimmer, but bright enough to see almost normally. Their small break from the horror was over. Time to return to the nightmare.

"This place must have an emergency generator," Wendig said.

"Correct, it does," a voice answered.

They all turned to look at the doorway. October was surprised to see Dr. Warren there, a sorrowful expression on his twitching face. He held a gun, flicking it back and forth between everyone.

"What are you doing?" Noel hissed as he took a step backward.

"That's my pistol." Wendig frowned at the doctor. "Please put it down, Dr. Warren. Look, if you went through my belongings, you must have seen my cell phone. If it survived the car accident, we can call—"

"No one's calling anybody!" Dr. Warren shrieked. His hands shook as they gripped the gun. "Those things. They found me. They...spoke to me. Whispered to me. They said if I killed one of you, th-they would bring Michelle back! A life for a life. Fair, right? You brought them here! They said..."

"Who said?" Henry asked. He had his shotgun aimed at the doctor. "Those demonic bastards?"

"I have to do as they say!" Warren cried out. "For Michelle."

October heard a thumping sound, like the beating of a taiko drum, so loud that she could feel it in her bones. She realized the sound was her own blood pounding in her ears.

"Listen, just give me the gun." Wendig took a slow, cautious step forward. October could tell he was trying to sound soothing, but she could hear the strain in the man's voice. "Just give it to me and we can figure this out."

Dr. Warren looked at each of them, his eyes locking briefly with everyone who stood before him. A pained grimace stretched across his face. Maddie growled.

This can't really be happening, October thought. *We survived those creatures, and now one of us might get killed by a doctor losing his mind.*

"Hand it over," Wendig kept saying. "Do you even know how to use that? You don't want to accidentally hurt someone, do you?"

"Michelle," Dr. Warren squeaked.

"The nurse is dead," Viorica said firmly. She took several steps toward the doctor. "Are you that stupid? You think those creatures will do anything to help you? They're the ones that killed her."

"Sh-sh-shut up!" the doctor stammered out. He stomped up to Viorica and shoved the gun into her impassive face. "I have to do this!"

It was at that moment that October realized that Samira had slunk alongside the far wall where Warren couldn't see her. She managed to get within feet of him before he finally caught sight of her and she jumped at him, a wild look on her face.

"Stay back!" Dr. Warren screamed.

"Fuck you!" Samira screeched as she attempted to wrench the gun from Warren's hand.

"Get off me!" the doctor bellowed, flailing his arms, trying to aim the pistol.

The gun went off, deafening in the small room, and October immediately threw herself to the floor on instinct. Had she been shot? She would have surely felt if she had, right? There was no pain, no hot blood spilling out of her. Then again, adrenaline was pumping through her body like electricity. It would dull pain, right?

October opened eyes she hadn't even realized she had shut and looked up from the floor.

She saw a stunned Bryan stumble backward, his face uncomprehending, before collapsing, his neck pouring a crimson river.

"No!" October yelled. No one seemed to notice. They were all busy surrounding the tangled forms of Samira and Dr. Warren as they wrestled for control of the weapon. She crawled over to where Bryan lay. There was a gaping wound on the side of his neck where blood gushed out like undammed waters set loose. She placed her hands on Bryan's neck, trying to staunch the blood, but it just flowed under her palms and through her fingers, warm and wet.

Bryan looked up at her and their eyes locked. A profound sadness blossomed in October's chest, for in those haunted eyes, she saw the spark of Bryan's life escaping him. He squirmed weakly on the floor.

He doesn't deserve to go out like this, she thought.

"I…" Bryan sputtered through all the blood that must be filling his throat. "I don't…want to die…"

The Overshadow cackled inside her head.

"Bryan," October said, her hands still pressed uselessly against the cascade of blood from his neck. "We're going to get you help. Just hang in there. Bryan!"

Her words fell upon deaf ears. As she stared into Bryan's eyes again, October realized that they were empty and dull. He was gone.

A loud grunt of pain erupted in the room, tearing October's gaze away from Bryan's corpse. She saw Maddie biting Warren's leg as Samira repeatedly kneed the doctor in the stomach and groin until he collapsed to the floor in a heap, writhing in pain. Samira stood over him, hands clenched in iron fists, ready to smash the doctor's face in.

A second shot rang out. Then another.

Samira fell backward and slammed into a wall where two bullet holes had appeared, one high, near the ceiling, and the other lower, with splatters of red around it. Samira slowly slid down before flumping to the floor. A small puddle of blood began pooling underneath her left outer thigh, which now had a fresh bullet wound glistening darkly in the dim light.

The gun clattered to the floor out of Dr. Warren's hand as he stared at the woman now sprawled on the ground, grimacing in pain and clutching her thigh.

"Oh," was all the doctor said, his face paling at the realization of what he'd just done.

"Asshole!" Henry bellowed, keeping his shotgun trained on the doctor. Dr. Warren leapt to his feet, leaving the pistol on the ground, and dashed out the door. Henry took aim at the fleeing man's backside, but then swiveled to point the barrels at the ceiling. He unleashed a bestial howl and fired upward.

Warren threw himself face-first onto the ground, hands covering his head, screaming in terror. When he realized he hadn't been shot, he stumbled to his feet and fled as fast as he could. Maddie barked and chased after him. October called out to the dog. Maddie didn't listen, though.

"Shit, shit," Noel was saying as he took his t-shirt off and pressed it against Samira's wound. Henry crouched beside them and helped keep the shirt pressed to her thigh, though it was quickly saturated with blood. "Bandages!" Noel looked around at the room. "Someone get some fucking bandages! It's a health clinic! There should be bandages in like every room!"

October watched Wendig retrieve his gun from the floor and sprint from the cafeteria.

"Hurry, man!" Noel shouted after him.

"Dumnezeii măsii!" Viorica growled. "I will kill that doctor!"

"Just focus on Samira for now!" Noel yelled, keeping pressure on Samira's wound. The woman, to her credit, hadn't yet cried out in pain once.

"Guys," October said softly. No one seemed to have heard her.

"Noel." Samira put a hand on the man's arm. "I hope you get to meet my son one day."

"Oh, don't start with that crap," Noel said with forced joviality. "You just got shot in the leg. Nothing major. You got this."

"Yeah, just a scratch," Samira said. A sheen of sweat had appeared on her face and neck, soaking her shirt. "Just a scratch that hurts like hell."

"Guys," October repeated louder this time. She didn't realize that she was crying and that her hands were still held against the wound in Bryan's neck.

They all looked over at her. Their collective gaze dropped to Bryan's waxy, lifeless face and dead eyes that no longer peered upon the mortal world.

There was silence in the room, though October could hear the faint sobbing of Dr. Warren from somewhere down the hall.

"Aw fuck, man!" Noel shouted, his hands still on Samira's bloody leg. "He was just a fucking kid!"

Finally removing her blood-covered hands from the torn flesh of his neck, October sat back, unable to look away from Bryan's pale, still face. She wanted to cry for the boy who had lost everything in one day, but she didn't think her body had enough energy to produce any tears. *Bryan had his whole life ahead of him*, October thought. *He might've not even graduated high school yet. What dreams did he have? What aspirations? It doesn't matter now. He's as dead as his parents. God dammit.* "God dammit!" she yelled. She hid her face in her hands, realizing too late that she had just smeared blood all over herself, then realized she didn't have the strength to care.

"Să-i fie ţărâna uşoară," Viorica said softly. "Rest in peace."

"He's with his parents now." Noel wiped tears from his face. "Bryan is with Bernadette and Arthur, wherever they may be. They're together."

Suddenly, Wendig burst back into the cafeteria, carrying an armful of gauze. His eyes fell upon the still form of Bryan. He almost let everything he carried fall to the ground. October couldn't decipher the man's expression.

"Here." Wendig handed all the rolls of bandages to Noel and Henry. "I'll be right back. I need to get some things." He turned around and left once more.

For a while the only sound in the room was Noel and Henry wrapping the gauze around Samira's leg, and Samira's hisses of pain every now and then. No one spoke, as if they were all silently paying respects to those they had lost throughout the horrid day; Dara, Bernadette, Arthur, Adrianna, Isaac, Michelle, and now Bryan.

"What do we do now?" Noel asked after a while. He then seemed to realize he had blood all over his hands and grabbed another roll of gauze to clean the red off himself.

"I still say we hunt those bastards down," Samira said. "I don't care how hurt I get."

"I'm with you," Henry said. He wore an expression of hellfire. "I'm going to put this here buckshot through those creatures' goddamned heads." He spat on the ground as if he were spitting out acid. "They killed this young man. They killed Adrianna. They killed my son. And I'm gonna kill them and send them to rot in hell."

"You think we can figure out how the stone works?" October asked, rising to her feet.

"Yes," Henry replied, his fists clenched, his jaw set. "Nothing's invincible. Nothing. I'm going to use that stone to kill these monsters even if I have to bash them over the heads with it."

It was at that moment that Wendig walked back into the eating area. He had traded his hospital gown for jeans, a blue shirt, and a light jacket—all of which were covered in dried blood, the shirt and jacket sporting ragged slashes on one side.

"My clothes," he said. "Better than walking around in that flimsy hospital gown with my ass hanging out."

Normally, October would have chuckled at that. Normally.

But then again, normally she wouldn't be in some strange town, far from home, battling skin-stealing monsters from the pits of nightmare and watching people get brutally slaughtered around her.

Wendig put his gun into a shoulder holster underneath his jacket. October glanced over at Viorica. *I need to learn how to shoot*, she thought.

"So, you found your things?" October asked, turning back toward Wendig. "You said you had a cell phone. Was it there? Does it work?"

Wendig shook his head. "I'm afraid not," he answered. He took the phone out of his pocket, displaying its busted screen to everyone. "I assume it was broken during my car accident. Or maybe the good doctor smashed it while he was looking for my weapon." He swallowed loudly, then muttered to himself, "I'll contact you when I can, Jordan."

"Piece of garbage doctor," Viorica growled. "I wasn't fond of Bryan, but he didn't deserve to die." She shook her head.

"No one that's died today deserved it." Noel was still trying to get the blood off his hands. "This whole shit day has been a trip through nightmare crazy town."

"I'm heading to the museum," Henry said, though he seemed to be talking more to himself. He looked over at Viorica. "You still got the wheel with you?"

Nodding, Viorica unshouldered her pack and removed the object within.

Eyes wide, Wendig moved toward Viorica. "That thing," he whispered, October barely catching his words.

"A Wheel of Kurkoth," Henry's eyes were transfixed on the smooth object.

"Yes, I've seen one just like it earlier," Wendig said, staring at the Enigmata in Viorica's hand. "Before the car crash."

"You what now?" October asked, completely thrown for a loop. "You've seen another wheel?"

"Where is it?" Viorica said, her voice eager.

"You shouldn't be handling it so casually," Wendig said, as if the spell hypnotizing him had suddenly broken. Out of his back pocket, he pulled out a pair of gloves. "Give it to me."

"I know what I'm doing," Viorica replied.

Without warning, the Wheel of Kurkoth slipped out of Viorica's grasp and fell onto the floor. No, that wasn't right. The thing had jumped out of Viorica's hand.

"Did you see that?" October asked, pointing at the artifact. Of course everyone had seen it. They'd all been staring at it.

The wheel moved of its own volition, rolling like a car's tire into the lake of blood next to Bryan's head and neck. Whatever October was expecting to happen, it wasn't what occurred next. The thin grooves between the three concentric rings lit up with a red luminescence. The almost imperceptible glyphs etched onto the face of the wheel came to life with the red glow as well. The circles began rotating, each independently turning and twisting like a mechanized contraption, and making only a whisper of a grinding sound. Something, a small panel or an aperture, October couldn't tell, opened up right in the center of the Enigmata's polished surface. A thick, sharp-tipped tube, like a crooked needle or a proboscis, much too long to have logically fit inside the wheel, extended out from the hole and stuck its tip into the blood. The dark pool on the floor began to disappear as if the wheel were sucking it all up through a straw. It was drinking it.

"What the devil?" Henry pointed his shotgun at it.

"The fuck is that?" Noel asked. Disgust was written all over his face.

From her seat on the floor, Samira said, "What is it doing?"

At a loss for words, October just stared at the wheel as it vacuumed up all the blood around it. It made a sickening, wet sucking sound as the blood ran dry, leaving a red stain on the linoleum. October really had no idea what had just happened. The wheel had moved all on its own, reconfiguring itself for what? To drink up blood?

The proboscis retracted itself back inside the circular object. The little center aperture closed, and the glow faded. The wheel then sat still, and October felt as if the thing were staring at her, wanting more blood to drink.

"How many more disturbing things do I have to see today?" Noel asked, grabbing the sides of his head. "I'm sick of it! I'm done! We need to get out of here right now! I'm done with all this!"

When Noel finished, there was a prolonged silence, everyone staring at the wheel, as if they all were all expecting it to move again. October noticed that even Viorica's eyes were fixed on it, an expression of uncertainty on her face.

The object remained sitting there, unmoving.

Wendig then crouched down and carefully picked up the wheel with his gloved hands. October cringed, waiting for something bad to happen. Nothing did.

I wonder if this guy knows more about these Enigmata things than Viorica does? October mused. He gave the impression of being experienced with them.

"How much ammunition do we have left?" Wendig asked, checking the magazine in his gun after placing the wheel into his coat pocket. "I have thirteen rounds."

"Trei," Viorica told him. "Three."

Henry reloaded his shotgun. "I got two loaded, two shells left." He patted his breast pocket.

"We have to find out exactly what this thing does," Wendig said after the ammo check. He slipped the gun back into his holster, then took the wheel out of his pocket again. "If only we knew, we might have a chance against those Watchers." He studied the artifact, turning it this way and that, tracing faint lines with a gloved finger. "It drank that blood. Maybe that's how it's fueled? Perhaps that's how it gets its power?"

"This is all kinds of messed up." Noel shook his head. "Don't start with that kind of talk now, okay? Drinking blood for power? Are you trying to say that metal disc thing is some sort of Satanic witchcraft magic artifact? Don't we have enough to worry about without adding that mumbo-jumbo bullshit to the mix?"

"Have you *not* seen everything we've seen?" October asked him, incredulous. "Haven't you been paying attention? There are monsters straight out of a horror movie. You think they're natural? You can accept their existence, but you don't think there's something to this wheel that just drank blood?"

Noel shook his head, turning away from the group to sit down next to Samira on the floor in silence.

"Where did you say you got the wheel from again?" Wendig asked, still examining the Enigmata.

"It's a long story," October said, not really wanting to recount any of it. "We ended up in a cave, some sort of ritual chamber. The wheel was in a chest on an altar."

"Jesus," Henry interjected, staring at her. "That didn't seem weird enough to you? That didn't scream 'stay away from me' enough? You people make a habit of taking things out of weird places not knowing what they do?"

October ignored Henry's comments. "The chamber was deep within the mountain. There were strange cutting implements all over the walls. And a body..." Her words drifted off as a thought struck her. "The body. All those bones." She turned to look at Viorica. "We thought it was some sort of place where they sacrificed people. And maybe it was. If the wheel needs blood."

"I see." Viorica chewed her lip in thought.

"Interesting," Wendig said. Ensuring he had a firm grip on the wheel, he stepped over to where Samira and Noel sat. Kneeling, Wendig held the Enigmata out toward the blood splatter from Samira's wounded leg.

"No, man." Noel objected, but he didn't make any move. "What are you doing? Come on."

The wheel began to vibrate in Wendig's hands, as if it were eager to lap up the crimson fluid in front of it. Could it sense the blood somehow? Could it see it? Could it *smell* it?

Wendig pulled it away with a jerk. October could tell that his thoughts were going a mile a minute.

Before October could inquire, Wendig pulled out a small pocketknife, rolled up his sleeve, and made a small nick on the inside of his forearm that slowly bled.

"The hell are you doing?" Henry asked, his expression reflecting everyone else's confusion.

Wendig said nothing as he pressed the Wheel of Kurkoth against his cut.

CHAPTER TWENTY-FOUR

Wendig

What had started as a grunt of discomfort quickly turned into a howl of pain.

Wendig felt what he could only describe as ice-cold tendrils slithering into the cut he had made on his arm, crawling deep into his muscles and veins. It let off its red light, glowing brighter and brighter. The wheel was drinking from him. And it drank greedily.

"We have to get it off of him!" he heard October shout from what seemed a far-off distance. At least he thought it was her voice. His head was swimming. Blood was being siphoned from his body, from his brain. October didn't understand. She didn't know that the power of an Enigmata required a sacrifice. Excruciating sacrifice, sometimes, in one form or another.

Fingers gripped the object that was latched onto his arm, and he felt a painful tug on his skin. The wheel didn't let go, however. It didn't want to let go. It wanted more. It wanted everything.

Through blurry eyes, Wendig saw another hand grip the object. Its circles and glyphs burned red hot now. With a heaving, stinging yank, his limb was free. All the way up to the shoulder, his arm felt empty, drained. He collapsed to his knees.

"Are you crazy?" someone shouted at him, and when his vision came back into focus, he saw that it was October.

"Now that was damn stupid," the old man, Henry, said. "The hell, son? There ain't been enough death? You trying to kill yourself?"

"Maybe that wasn't the best idea," Wendig answered, somewhat sheepishly. He had already lost an unknown quantity of blood earlier that night. His mouth felt dry, desperately in need of a drink of water. "Still, I needed to test something." He struggled to his feet with the help of Noel and October, then held out his hand. "Give it to me."

Viorica stood in front of him, holding the wheel. Its proboscis was pointed at him, and she seemed to be struggling to hold onto the object. It was straining in her hands, trying to get back to the blood. With an air of reluctance, Viorica handed the wheel back to him.

Wendig held the Enigmata firmly in one gloved hand, fighting to keep it from leaping to his arm like trying to hold back two strong magnets. He forced his thoughts to focus on the object, trying to connect his energy, his mind, to the Enigmata in the same way he did when using the Hand of Gaia. If only he had the hand now. It hadn't been with his belongings. Had he dropped it when the Watcher had clawed him? Had it been destroyed in the crash? Or had someone taken it?

It was troubling, but he couldn't worry about it now. There were more pressing matters at the moment. He placed his attention back on the Enigmata before him.

The wheel quivered in his grip then went still, its proboscis retracting with a sharp whir.

The Enigmata's red glow dimmed to a soft pulse, its concentric circles and glyphs spinning by themselves once more. The others all watched in mute wonder and bewilderment as the wheel's illuminated surface rotated and turned in seemingly irrelevant and meaningless ways.

"I think..." Wendig began, not taking his eyes off the thing.

"You think what?" Viorica demanded.

With one last movement, the pieces of the wheel clicked into place and the device emitted a frenzied animalistic shriek, as if the object itself had just experienced a great deal of agony.

No. That wasn't right.

The shriek of pain hadn't come from the wheel, but from somewhere else in the hospital. Wendig pressed his fingertips to the wheel's center, where the sucking tube had come out. This time, the piece popped upward, and Wendig was able to slowly rotate it like a dial. He had experienced this sort of sudden intuition before while using other Enigmata. It was like the wheel was beaming instructions right into his consciousness. The center piece rotated clockwise with a metallic rasping. Wendig heard the Watchers wailing in pain from some distant part of the building. So they were both inside now.

The center piece of the wheel stopped and wouldn't rotate further. Wendig could have sworn he felt the thing become instantly cold in his hands. It was as if the blood it had used as its fuel had run out and the object refused to move until it drank more.

"Did you hear that?" October asked, her eyes transfixed on the Enigmata. "It sounded like those things were in pain."

"We can hurt them," Viorica said from beside Wendig, a hint of triumph in her voice. It sounded like something she had believed had just been confirmed.

"Yes, I believe so," Wendig answered, finally lowering the wheel, and looking at them all. "We need to go further than just hurting, though. We need to eradicate them."

CHAPTER TWENTY-FIVE

October

They all stepped out into the corridor. Noel and Wendig supported Samira as she limped along. October felt guilty for leaving Bryan's body behind, just lying there on the floor.

We won't leave you here forever, she thought. *We'll come back for you when this is all over.*

This will only be over once you lie dead on the ground in a puddle of your own viscera as your body turns cold and begins to putrefy.

Why don't you leave me the hell alone? October growled inside her head at the Overshadow. *Don't you have anything better to do?*

The group crept down the hallway, staying as close to each other as possible. The emergency lights provided sufficient illumination to see, but the details at the farthest ends of the corridors were hard to make out. When they reached the hospital's lobby, back where they had first come in, October saw that the entrance doors stood wide open again, Henry's truck visible just outside.

Isaac's corpse was gone, only a dark stain marking where his body had lain. This didn't surprise October, in fact, she'd expected it. Still, she shivered at the implications, then heard Henry gulp loudly. He must have looked as well.

"They took him," Henry whispered.

There was no immediate sign of the creatures. What had Wendig called them minutes ago? Watchers? She had far more apt names for them: monsters, skin-stealers, motherfucking-pieces-of-utter-shit-that-deserved-nothing-less-than-the-most-agonizing-death.

"I hear something," Viorica quietly announced. She pointed down another corridor. "From that way."

No one said anything when Viorica moved to investigate. When Wendig went after her, the rest followed suit. It took a few seconds for October to realize that this hallway led to the small exam room where Adrianna had been taken when they had first arrived.

It hadn't been Adrianna, October reminded herself. That thing, that Watcher, had been hiding inside Adrianna's skin.

Idiot, the Overshadow said, its slimy voice dripping through her brain. *All of you are such idiots. Haha! The monster was wearing her flesh the entire time. You were too stupid, too frightened, too blind to see how it tricked you. Wow, I'm living inside the head of an absolute moron.*

October tried to ignore the Overshadow's taunting, refusing to admit how it got to her. When the blood-stained window came into view, a pitiful crying reached her ears. They stopped in front of the glass to peer within. October's hand went to her mouth as she saw Dr. Warren inside, sitting on the floor against the far wall, weeping. In his arms he cradled Michelle's corpse, the woman's mangled face drenching Warren's pants with gore.

Dr. Warren finally noticed them staring at him through the glass, and he hugged the corpse to his chest. "They'll never bring her back!" he wailed. "They said they would bring her back. You didn't let me do what I had to. Now she'll stay dead! Look what that monster did to her face. What am I going to tell her parents? I can't... I can't bring her back...Goddamned monsters! Why did this happen?"

October was almost certain Warren didn't know he had shot and killed Bryan, but she wasn't going to tell him, and she hoped no one else would either. At least, not until all this was over with.

"Where's my dog?" Henry growled at the man, tears beading in the corners of his eyes. There was no sign of Maddie anywhere.

Sensing swift movement right next to her, October looked over at Viorica. The woman had her gun pointed at the doctor, her hand trembling slightly, and a shadowed expression on her face.

More death, yes. Let Viorica do it. Let her send bullets flying through this fool. Let the gun tear him apart and splatter his brains on the wall so that he can join the dead woman he so wishes to be with. Kill him! Kill him now! He doesn't deserve to live after what he did. Slaughter him like a pig!

The words burned like a flash of napalm inside October's skull. So much so that she almost cried out in physical pain. Oh, how she just wanted to scream and tear her hair out. No! She wouldn't give the Overshadow the satisfaction. A fresh sheen of sweat sprouted on her forehead from her internal struggle.

"Don't," October said to Viorica, having used an enormous amount of willpower to push the Overshadow's tendrils away. "Just leave him. Don't waste the bullets. Just leave him here." She placed a hand on Viorica's arm.

Turning her head toward October, Viorica glared, but her expression softened at once, and she allowed October to push her arm down to her side.

"Fine," Viorica said. "Let's go."

As the others turned away, October took a second to regard the doctor holding the dead nurse in his arms, all the while struggling to keep the Overshadow's voice muted, an almost impossible task. It was as if someone had taken a sledgehammer to her mind since all this craziness had first started and destroyed all the supports and fortifications she had built up over the years. Had the Overshadow become stronger? She feared she might shatter at any moment, millions of fragments of October falling to the floor. What would happen if she lost control? Would her mind plunge into the depths of unfathomable madness? Or would she welcome the sweet bliss of uncaring insanity?

How could someone come to question their entire reality in the span of just one day? She listened to Dr. Warren wailing, and she shuddered. Her mostly empty stomach roiled and churned, as if the repercussions of everything that had happened that day were frantically dancing inside of her, ready to burst from her mouth to spatter the world with her own madness.

A revolving slideshow of faces flashed before her; people she had met less than twenty-four hours ago. Faces that were once alive and happy. Now they were dead, mangled, murdered by abhorrent creatures from the deepest nightmare; monsters that saw humans as nothing more than toys to play with and dress up as so they could get off on all the misery they caused.

What *were* these things, really? How could they exist?

October didn't realize she had fallen until she was already on the floor, staring up at the ceiling. She felt the dark pit in her mind open, the dark recess where her depression lived and festered like a parasite.

Why bother to go on? the Overshadow asked, its voice curiously calm and reasonable. *If there are things like this living in the world, then how can you possibly go on? Imagine what other awful secrets this world is hiding, each more maddening than the last. If beings like these Watchers exist, doesn't that open the gates to all sorts of possibilities? Possibilities that can kill you or those you love at any moment. They can hunt you down and play with you. You're basically nothing but a pawn to them. You are cattle to them. Just imagine what horrifying things are lurking in the darkest corners of this planet. Makes you shiver, doesn't it? If things like this exist, well, fuck everything, right? There's no point in going on when you realize humans are not the top dog. Just lie here and die. Let them find you and kill you. Maybe they'll even make it painless if you don't struggle too much.*

"October!" a muffled voice rang out beside her.

No one on this tainted, festering planet will miss you, October.

"Viorica..." October mumbled.

Viorica? The Overshadow sighed. *You think she's your friend? She is obviously just using you for something. Viorica won't miss you when you die. She's a much tougher woman than you are, and she certainly knows it— everyone does. She doesn't really want you around anyway. You slow her down. She's only helped you so far because she feels sorry for you and your pathetic existence.*

October could still hear Dr. Warren crying in the next room.

The doctor has the right idea. He's given up, October. He's going to sit there on the floor like a frightened child and wait for the monsters to come for him. You should have let Viorica shoot him. Actually, no. That would have been too good for the bastard. He murdered Bryan. So let him suffer. Suffering is what he deserves. Let the Watchers come and play with him. Fuck him, right? Fuck all of them. Fuck the world. Who gives a shit? Everyone's going to die anyway. Just let them have you. No one cares about you. How stupid do you have to be to think someone would care about a worthless nobody like you?

"No," October whispered. A flame sprouted in her chest. A flame that rapidly became a furnace of hot anger. Why had she ever listened to that stupid voice in her head for all these years? October had had enough. Not of life. No, not that. She was sick of the bastard in her head.

What did you say? the Overshadow demanded.

You heard me, she mentally answered. Her eyes closed and she focused inward. *I said no. I'm tired. I'm tired of listening to you. I'm tired of you making my life hell. If anyone is worthless, it's you. You can try to stop me right now, but I'm not going to allow that. You don't control my life. I'm going to push through this. I'm going to push on for Bryan, for Bernadette and Arthur, for Dara and Michelle. I'm going to make it home. And I don't care how many hours of therapy I'll have to go to or how many different brands of antidepressants I'll have to try, I'm not going to let you infect me anymore. I know I may have to live with you all my life. I know depression and anxiety and all that crap is something I'll have to always deal with. But I'm done with you. I know I can't just force myself to be happy. Fortunately, there's still something I can do: Not give in. And the idea of that actually makes* me *happy. Why? Because I bet it pisses you off. Well, too bad. I'm going to make you* my *little bitch.*

October opened her eyes and grasped Viorica's waiting hand, getting back to her feet.

The Overshadow was silent for a long, blessed moment before its hissing words squirmed in her head.

You still haven't figured things out? You still have no clue about anything. You still think I'm actually some chemical imbalance in your—

"Are you okay?" Viorica asked, her arm on October's shoulders.

October ignored the other woman's words and spoke to the Overshadow.

What are you saying?

Silence.

Say what you were going to say!

The Overshadow didn't respond.

"Oh shit!" Noel screamed, grabbing October's attention.

Behind Viorica, October saw two figures crawling on all fours like giant spiders, one on the ground, one on the ceiling. They were close enough that she could smell the coppery blood dripping from their ragged skin suits. The Adrianna-thing and the Arthur-thing advanced toward them, though the creatures seemed sluggish. The ever-present smiles on their stolen faces had been replaced with dreadful grimaces. The wheel must have done something to them when Wendig did whatever he did.

A shotgun blast, then another. Bright flashes illuminated the hallway like lightning for a split-second.

Ringing and muffled shouts filled October's ears.

"Back to the truck!" Henry shouted, reloading his shotgun. "We're going to that damn museum if it kills me!"

The blasts had knocked the Watchers down, though they struggled back to their hands and feet. Whatever effect the wheel had had on them seemed to be wearing off more and more as the moments ticked by.

"Let's go!" Viorica yelled, propelling October forward.

The group raced back to the lobby and out through the front entrance. They saw no sign of Maddie anywhere. Wherever the dog had gotten to, October hoped she was alive and safe and sound and getting treats and—

As October ran to the truck, her boot kicked something. Looking down, she saw Isaac's disarticulated lower jaw, half grinning up at her. October snapped her gaze away before her body could decide to vomit. Her lungs momentarily forgot how to take in breath as the dreadful image stained her mind.

Henry jumped in behind the steering wheel. October could tell from the set of his shoulders that the old man was trying to ignore his son's blood all over the truck's hood. Viorica and Wendig got into the back seat, while October and Noel helped Samira into the passenger seat—so she could have more room for her injured leg—before squeezing themselves into the back as well. It was utterly cramped, and October was practically sitting in Viorica's lap.

"Can't we please go to the police station?" Noel uttered, giving up trying to buckle his seat belt when he couldn't get the buckle to the socket underneath everyone's posteriors. "I'm sure this town has one, right?"

"My grandmother left me a job, son," Henry said, a seething anger just below the strangely calm surface of his voice. "To destroy the Skin-Takers. I should have done this decades ago. I was a coward. I didn't continue my gran's work because I feared for Isaac. Now he's dead because of me." The truck started up with a roar and pulled away from the clinic. "By God, I'm going to finish this job. If you people want to drive over to the station, by all means. But first I'm going to the museum. I'm doing this. For my grandmother. For my son."

"Dammit," Noel muttered through gritted teeth.

As the clinic disappeared from view behind them, October realized she should have checked for any medication that would have silenced the Overshadow.

"So, if we discover out how to activate the wheel's true potential with the Cinter," Viorica said, "we can deal with these Watchers, as you called them."

"And how are we going to figure it out?" Noel asked. "Maybe we should just go. To. The. Police. Station."

Viorica didn't respond to him. She was looking over at Wendig. "You look like you are thinking hard about something."

Wendig had taken the object out and was staring at it in his hand. "These Wheels of Kurkoth. There are at least two, maybe more. I'm thinking that maybe certain Watchers are bound to certain wheels. If we manage to activate *this* wheel's 'true potential,' as you put it, will it destroy all of the Watchers? Or just some of them?"

"Let's hope it kills every single one," October said.

Wendig nodded before returning the wheel to his pocket.

"We have to kill them," October went on. Many thoughts, worries, ideas, and emotions swirled through her head like a twister. She tried to focus on their goal: kill the skin-stealing bastards. "I have to believe that we can stop them somehow." She finally remembered some of the inscription Adrianna had told them was written on the stone. "'For only the Cinter shall protect flesh and soul.' That rock has to be the Cinter. I mean, what else could 'the Cinter' be?"

"The Cinter," Wendig repeated as they sped down the road, Henry driving with abandon through the empty, wet streets. The whole town seemed to be sleeping.

Wendig muttered something else to himself that October didn't quite catch, though she thought it sounded like, "More Enigmata."

As they sped away, she realized the rain had finally let up.

But the nightmare wasn't over.

CHAPTER TWENTY-SIX

October

Cinter wasn't a big town by any means, and they arrived at the Cinter Museum of Local History, Folklore, and the Occult, situated right off the main street on Courtney Avenue, less than five minutes after leaving the clinic. For whatever reason, October had expected something grander than the building she looked at now. The museum was a wooden two-story affair that looked like it had once been an oversized cottage. It was flanked by a candy shop on one side and an antiques store on the other.

Everyone, save Samira, leapt out of the truck as soon as Henry came to a halt in front of the museum.

"I assume it's closed." October peered at the lightless front window. "How are we going to get inside?"

"I don't know, just hurry up," Noel urged, looking over his shoulder and down the street. "Henry, can I get the keys, please?"

Henry threw him the keys to the truck. "Police station is down two blocks, turn left onto South Wade," the old man said.

Noel turned back to the truck with Samira still inside and paused. He was obviously debating something with himself. October could

240

almost see the gears turning in his head. After a moment, he sighed as if irritated with something.

"Samira, do you think you can drive?" Noel asked her.

"Uh, yeah," Samira said through the truck's window. "My right leg is fine. I can work the pedals. Why? Aren't you coming to the police station with me?"

Noel was silent, his hand gripping the keys tightly. "No," he finally said. "We need to stop these things. I can be of more help here. Hopefully. You go and tell the cops everything. Get to safety and get your leg taken care of."

"Are you sure?" Samira asked.

"Nope." Noel chuckled weakly. "Not at all. Just go before I change my mind. Be safe."

"You too," Samira said. She carefully scooched from the passenger side over to the driver's seat. "All of you. Please. And everyone get to the police station as soon as you can so they don't think I'm some lunatic."

Once she got settled, got the engine going again, and wished everyone the best of luck, Samira drove off in the direction Henry had indicated.

Noel shook his head as he turned back to the others. "Staying behind, heh. I'm an idiot."

"Friends." A voice drifted over to them like dead leaves.

October's head snapped up, as did everyone else's. Her heart skipped a beat when her eyes settled on the Adrianna-thing, standing half in the glow of a sodium light across the street.

"Friends... I have...found you."

"Get inside now!" Henry shouted at them.

With a purposeful stride, Viorica ran up to the museum's front entrance and kicked the door in like it was made of popsicle sticks.

The group fled into the building, October the last one to cross the threshold. She helped Wendig and Viorica grab a nearby cabinet and move the heavy piece in front of the door.

"Dammit," Noel muttered, then louder, "Dammit, I *am* an idiot."

Someone flicked on the lights, and October surveyed the studio apartment-sized room. Immediately in front of the main entrance sat a little information desk, while the rest of the area was crowded with six long tables covered in glass cases protecting the items displayed within. There appeared to be pieces of old-timey clothing, rusted tools and utensils, books with yellowing pages and cracked spines, and various other odds and ends. There was not an inch of wall space that wasn't covered in shelving, displaying more curious items: tomes covered in aging leather, crystals in a myriad of colors, statuettes of all sizes and shapes that depicted what looked like gods and goddesses from various ancient religions, handmade dolls, memento mori, and oddities preserved in jars that October couldn't even begin to identify. In the far corner, two mannequins—a man and a woman—were dressed as pioneers, their blank, expressionless faces indifferent to what was unfolding before them.

"At least the windows are reinforced." She pointed out the iron bars she noticed beyond the glass.

"You really think that's going to keep them out for long?" Henry asked in a flat voice. He shook his head.

"The stone is this way." Viorica headed through a doorway, flicking on more lights that illuminated a hallway

"Have you been here before?" October asked, following. Viorica must not have heard the question since she didn't answer.

The short hallway was lined with paintings depicting scenes of occult rituals and black masses that October would have found inter-esting under much different circumstances. The hallway led to a smaller, less cluttered room than the previous area. Locating the switches on the wall, October turned on the overhead lights.

More light, fewer shadows for things to hide in.

Here there were only two long glass-covered tables containing more artifacts: effigies made of twigs, metal plates etched with runes and glyphs—which reminded her too much of what they'd seen down in that ritual room underground—vials of dark substances, skulls with strange holes punched into their heads, and daggers of all sorts. One highlighted display presented the dried-out fish-like corpse of some animal. October couldn't really tell what the thing could be, but the exhibit informed her it was the remains of an unknown creature discovered on the shores of Devil's Eyes Lake in the nearby town of Black Ashes. She suspected it was actually just a dead fish and a dead monkey or something sewn together. Fulgent County's own "Fiji Mermaid."

"Going to pay for what you did," Henry muttered to himself. He checked that his shotgun was loaded with his last two shells.

In the middle of the room, atop a white cloth-covered plinth, in a square display case, sat the item they were looking for.

"The Cinter Stone," she whispered, stepping forward and reading the name on the display's plaque that told of the artifact's history. The octagonal stone, about two feet high and a foot across, was a stunning deep blue color that reminded her of magic and royalty. The top came to a jagged point that looked like it had been chipped at some time in the past. Its eight sides hadn't been polished to a smooth finish as October had expected. Instead, they were still rough, as if the stone had formed into this shape naturally somehow.

She felt drawn to the stone. Or perhaps that was just the last kernel of hope barely hanging on inside of her, urging her on. It had to work. Work how, though? How to use the thing? What secret did the Cinter Stone hold that would allow them to finally be rid of the monsters picking them off one by one?

Walking around the display case, October could see the inscriptions carved into the stone. She couldn't read the different languages, though she now remembered what Adrianna had told them the inscriptions said:

Cloaked in ashes of utmost black, thy path lies in shadow. For only the Cinter shall protect flesh and soul.

"Do you think it's just one monster out there?" Noel asked, breaking October's fixation on the stone. He kept looking over his shoulder. "Or did the other one follow us here too?"

"No doubt it did," Henry said, patrolling the room.

October had to agree. If the Adrianna-Watcher was here, the Arthur-Watcher was likely skulking around as well.

Wendig studied the Cinter Stone. "I think the Watchers can sense the wheel they're bonded with." He didn't elaborate further.

"Okay, man," Noel said, stepping next to Wendig. "What now?" His gaze swept from Wendig to Viorica to Henry. "Everyone wanted to come here and use this rock to help us survive. Well, now what?"

Wendig rubbed his chin for a moment before answering. "Maybe we do what the inscription says." He carefully lifted the glass case that surrounded the stone, setting it on the floor.

"Not great on security here," Noel said. "No alarms when we broke in or you picking that up."

"What do you mean?" October asked Wendig.

"'Cloaked in ashes of utmost black, thy path lies in shadow. For only the Cinter shall protect flesh and soul,'" Wendig read from the information plaque.

"Yes, maybe," Viorica said before hurrying from the room and returning with a handful of pamphlets and flyers from the museum's front desk. She handed them to Wendig.

"What are those for?" Noel asked. Nervousness suffused his voice.

Understanding dawned on October. "We need some black ashes." She stared at the stone. Would it work? Would it do anything?

"Come on, people!" Noel burst out. "What are you going to do? Cast a spell?"

"You can say that," Viorica said.

The sound of a window shattering somewhere else in the building drew everyone's attention. It was quickly followed by a sound October realized were iron bars being wrenched apart.

"Oh no," October whispered. *They're here. God, maybe Noel's right. What are we doing?*

That rasping laugh that grated like hot needles against October's ears floated out from beyond the doorway—a frigid wind that froze muscle and chilled bone.

Henry gripped his shotgun. "Come on, you abominations." The old man stepped closer to the room's exit, his weapon at the ready. "I got something you can wear."

"Whatever we're going to do, we have to do it now," October said.

The blood in her veins froze more by the second as the hideous laughing grew closer. She could now hear two voices giggling.

Viorica produced a lighter from her pants pocket and flicked it on.

"Hurry," she said to Wendig, pushing the flame toward him.

Wendig held out the papers for her to set alight. "Let's hope this does something."

"Man, don't say it like that!" Noel exclaimed.

The lighter's flame touched the stack of papers, and they caught fire. Curling in on themselves as the flames fed, the pamphlets and flyers disintegrated. Wendig let the ashes from the burning offering fall over the top of the Cinter Stone, sooty flakes covering the stone and its pedestal. They were more gray than black.

"Nothing's happening," Noel whispered as they all stared at the stone. He backed away, his eyes flicking between the doorway to the other room and the nearby barred windows.

"Come on, come on!" Wendig entreated. He brought out the Wheel of Kurkoth and held it close to the stone.

Still, nothing happened.

Close. Not quite, the Overshadow said in October's mind.

The inner voice startled her. She'd been wondering where the pest had gotten to. The Overshadow had been unusually quiet for some time. She had been hoping it had gone back into dormancy. Desperately hoping.

Not now, October told it. *Go away.*

Take the ashes, the Overshadow said, ignoring her demand. There was none of the usual mocking in its voice. *Smear the ashes on your palms and then take the wheel.*

What? October had no idea what was happening. The voice in her head was speaking to her in a calm and non-aggressive tone. This was something that had never happened before. It disturbed her, more than insults would have.

The Cinter Stone is just a stone. Just a rock, the Overshadow answered. *Unless you want to try bashing the creatures over the head with it, the stone can't do anything. Unlike you.*

What was this mind game the Overshadow was attempting?

"Daddy... Papaaaaa..." the coarse voice of one of the Watchers gurgled.

From out of the hallway, the two monstrosities appeared through the doorway, crawling along the walls like giant insects into the room. The Adrianna-thing scuttled up to the low ceiling, grinning at them. The other Watcher, the one that had been wearing Arthur's flesh, had changed costumes.

"Oh God," Noel breathed out.

Are you listening?

Every muscle in October's throat squeezed painfully as she saw the creature drop to the floor in front of Henry. It now wore Isaac's bloody skin, the flesh on its lower jaw torn and ragged, revealing the wet obsidian chin underneath. Through the eyeholes of the stolen face, October saw one bright yellow eye, and one faded yellow, only a shade duller than the other. She realized the eye that Viorica had thrown the knife into when the creature had been the bear was mostly healed now.

"Shoot it!" Noel yelled at Henry.

I asked you a question.

The old man just stood there, staring at the distorted face of his son. The shotgun went limp in his hands, the barrel dropping to point at the floor.

Viorica growled, her pistol raised, as she tried to get a bead on the Adrianna-thing that scuttled around on the ceiling in disturbing, jerky movements.

"Lord," Henry breathed, his voice quavering, "deliver me."

"Papaaaa," the Isaac-Watcher said with a laugh. "Father...joins ... son."

In a lightning-quick flash, the creature thrust its deadly black talons into Henry's gut.

"Joins son...in death."

Do you want everyone to die?

"No!" October shrieked, watching in horror as the sharp claws slid deep into Henry's abdomen. She felt as if she had received the blow herself, an empathetic pain shooting through her own body.

Viorica snapped her head around to see what had happened to Henry. The Adrianna-Watcher took that split-second distraction to attack, leaping from the ceiling at her and October. Wendig had still been trying to get the Cinter Stone to do whatever it was supposed to do, but he quickly abandoned it and drew his pistol to fire at the monster. Viorica managed to shove October out of the way before diving to the side and shooting as well.

A cacophony of gunfire, shouting, screeching, and glass shattering erupted all around October as she landed painfully on the floor. Looking up again, she saw that the Isaac-Watcher still had a dying Henry skewered with its talons.

"You…motherfuckers are going…going to be sent to the deepest pits…of hell," Henry snarled. He coughed up blood as he spoke, his every word drenched in pure hatred and boiling fury.

The shotgun, which October realized had been pointed down at the creature's foot, went off in an ear-pounding blast, blowing the Isaac-Watcher's left leg off in an explosion of buckshot and gore.

October cringed at the scream the Isaac-Watcher loosed as it, and Henry, fell to the floor. It flailed for a moment, then bounded away, blood trailing behind it.

Henry's body lay still on the ground, a slowly expanding pool of crimson forming around him.

Picked off, one by one.

"God dammit!" Noel bellowed. He scooped up the shotgun that lay next to Henry. "I've *had* it! Let's go, you face-stealing assholes! I'm going to shove this double-barrel down your fucking throat!"

Catching her breath, October picked herself off the floor.

"Where's the other one?" she asked, tearing her eyes away from the dead man on the ground.

"It ran away," Wendig said. "I think we managed to hit it."

Viorica stepped over and knelt beside Henry's body. "Rest now." She closed his eyes.

At that moment, something snapped in October's brain. Her hands squeezed into shaking fists, and her jaw clenched like a vice. How much horror could one person take in a single day? She had seen so much blood. So much death. How much could she endure before she completely lost it?

Okay, October. Fuck it then.

No. Enough of those kinds of thoughts. Life had thrown enough horrifying obstacles her way. Too many people had died already today. There was no way she was going to give up now. She would fight until she couldn't fight anymore. Death had claimed enough. It had gorged itself on the innocent. A veritable feast of suffering.

She would give death its just deserts. Two more lives. Two disgusting, monstrous, inhuman lives.

Wait. Tell me why I should listen to you? October demanded inside her head.

Ah, are you finally ready to do something helpful? the Overshadow asked. *Are you ready to stop being an observer and finally be a participant? Are you finally ready to be useful?*

October ground her teeth. *Yes,* she hissed internally. *You have to give me some extraordinary reason why I should trust you, though.*

The Overshadow was silent.

Well?

I'm stuck with you as much as you are stuck with me. I didn't choose to be here inside you. I was forced inside your mind.

What are you talking about?

You've never been in control of your own life, October. You felt the urge to come visit this town when your work offered you a transfer. More than an urge, a compulsion to come visit. I know how your mind works, and the majority of this particular desire came from an outside force. I could've said something. However, I was curious to see where it would lead us. You see, things like that have been happening since you were born. You've been manipulated ever since you could think. Your biological parents had you, not because they wanted a child. They wanted a vessel.

October was having a hard time digesting all this information, so much conflicting with what professionals had told her all her life. Could this be the truth?

A vessel for what? she managed to ask.

For me.

For you? Why?

The man and woman who are your blood, they wanted what so many people do. Power. They knew of the things your new friends call 'Enigmata.' And they discovered there was a certain being who could harness an Enigmata's true power. That being is you, the Cinter. You have been forced into this role because of other people's desires.

I never asked for this!

That doesn't really matter at the moment, does it?

If you really are some being living in my head and not just my own thoughts, how come you've never said any of this before? Why torment me my whole life?

Because I don't like you.

That's really your answer?

We can talk about this more later. For now, I'll say we've never been in a situation like this. Oh, you've been in some dicey places before, but nothing like being hunted by supernatural creatures for sport. I've become... concerned. Now, before you doubt my intentions, I want you to tell me, where do I live?

What?

Answer the question. Where do I live?

In my head. In my stupid brain. Right? What about it?

Yes. I'm bonded to you. If you die, if you actually get torn to shreds by those beasts, what do you think will happen to me?

October considered that for a moment. If she died, then so did the Overshadow? It made sense. And the Overshadow wanted to save its own life. Self-preservation. Well, that was a good reason for it to help her survive. If it was telling the truth. Did she have another option, though?

Time is ticking, October. Are you ready to begin taking control of your own life for once?

Fine! But if this is some sort of trick, by fuck, you're going to regret it. Now tell me what to do.

Spread the ashes on your palms, the Overshadow directed.

Without a word to the others, October went over to the Cinter Stone. She gathered the gray ashes that had accumulated on the plinth into her cupped hand, then rubbed her palms together, covering up Bryan's blood that still stained her hands red with a sooty gray.

"What are you doing?" Wendig asked.

Take the Wheel of Kurkoth, the Overshadow instructed.

October turned to Wendig; the only emotions coursing through her now were hate and determination.

"Give me the wheel." She held out an ash-covered hand, amazed at how calm she sounded.

"Why?"

"Give it to me."

"Give it to her," Viorica said. There was no hesitation or uncertainty in her voice that October could detect. It was as if Viorica had been expecting this.

Without another word, Wendig handed the object over.

The wheel rested in October's palm, and, by some instinct, she covered the Enigmata with her other hand and closed her eyes.

Brace yourself, the Overshadow whispered. *This isn't going to be fun. Power requires sacrifice.*

Pain like heated knives stabbed into October's palms. The last thought that ran through her mind before the agony encapsulated her was, *The fucker tricked me.*

A scream of pure torture burst from October's mouth as the wheel's proboscis plunged deeper and deeper into her hand to drink. The lights overhead flickered once then shattered as if in response to October's wailing.

"Holy shit!" she barely heard Noel scream.

The very ground beneath her feet shook, and the entire building groaned. A high pitched, mechanical whining sound pierced the air. The windows blew inward into millions of pieces as the forceful winds of a gale rushed into the building.

Was the pain causing her to hallucinate?

"Get it away from her!" Wendig shouted above the noise.

"No, leave her!" Viorica yelled back, stepping in front of October.

Through tear-filled eyes, October looked down at the hands holding the wheel. The hands she was unable to pull away. With a new kind of terror, she witnessed the gray ash she had spread across her red-stained palms turn a deep, sludgy black. It spread over her skin like it was alive. Was her tattoo on the back of her hand emitting a faint blue glow? Yes, it was. It definitely was, and it was growing brighter. The pain caused by the wheel traveled up her limbs as did the blackening ash, coating her with a second skin.

Don't let go, the Overshadow said, its whispering voice cutting through the whirlwind of noise. *Whatever you do, don't…let …go …*

The Overshadow, too, then began to scream.

Now, however, the Overshadow's voice wasn't in her head anymore. Its pained shrieking issued out of October's mouth along with her own scream, their voices twining and threading together into a long string of agony.

"What's wrong with her face?" Noel shouted in a shrill voice. "Look at her eyes, man! Look at that shit coming out of her mouth! Get that thing away from her!"

"Leave her!" Viorica yelled.

October felt that her jaw could unhinge at any moment with her mouth wrenching open to accommodate the anguished cry that escaped her throat. Something thick and viscous poured across her lips. Blurry circles of colors burst before her eyes. Her ears felt on the verge of bleeding from her own shrieking, the ferocious winds, and the mechanical whining. It was a chaotic symphony.

She knew she couldn't let go of the wheel. Not yet. Some alien instincts were being injected into her.

"It's going to kill her!" Wendig shouted. He reached for October.

October's eyes snapped to him. "Don't touch me!" she shrieked in animalistic fury. Had that been her own voice that had just come out of her?

"Guys, guys!" Noel's words cut through the tumult.

Out of the corner of her eye, October saw two shapes charge into the room.

A thunderous blast—Noel firing the shotgun's last shell—followed immediately by Viorica and Wendig discharging their remaining rounds, all added to the aural maelstrom. Yelling, both human and inhuman, joined the monumental din.

The tattoo on October's hand glowed like a lamp now. The wheel added its own growing red luminescence. Both glows pulsed to the rhythm of October's beating heart.

Suddenly, all the noise ceased. October managed to swivel her eyes to take in the scene around her. She saw her companions' mouths moving with no words issuing forth; the wind tossing things around, but no loud crashing; the rings in the wheel spinning, but no metallic screeching. All sound had abandoned reality. There was nothing to hear except the empty void.

So cold, the Overshadow whispered. *It feels so cold.*

Yes, she felt it too. A serpent of pure ice slithered under her skin, entering where the wheel had pierced her palm. It followed the trail of the ash, creeping up through her arm and into her chest.

Is this what death felt like?

She knew she shouldn't have trusted the Overshadow.

The spinning concentric rings in the wheel came to a sudden stop. October had no time to react as something inside the Wheel of Kurkoth gave a final click. That she heard clearly. A wave of—what? Energy? Magic?—burst forth and knocked her hard to the floor, all of the breath in her lungs expelled with the impact.

A world of sound exploded around her. The horrible animal wailing reached her, and she realized it was the Watchers shrieking in pain. She caught a glimpse of one of the monsters, the Adrianna-thing. It came crashing onto the hardwood floor near her. Its costume of skin began splitting all over as the entity inside was forcefully pulled out by something invisible.

A gunshot ripped through the air. No, it hadn't been a gunshot. October looked upward from where she lay on her back on the floor and realized the ceiling and walls around her were now riddled with ever-widening cracks and fissures. The blast from the wheel had damaged the building. A support beam right above her hung precariously.

SNAP

The wooden beam splintered and plunged downward. Before her head could be turned to mush, October's body was yanked by her ankles across the floor. She looked down to her feet to see that Noel had just saved her from being pancaked.

"It's coming down!" Wendig shouted from somewhere to her left.

More of the structure clattered to the floor around October. The entire museum grumbled and groaned, then gave a bone-rattling shudder.

"Get under the tables!" Viorica ordered.

That was the last thing October heard before the museum's second story collapsed onto them all.

CHAPTER TWENTY-SEVEN

Wendig

There was Rowan, opening that sarcophagus. Why had he let her come? Stupid, stupid, stupid. People were shouting. People who wanted the Enigmata for themselves.

There had been a woman hiding in the shadows. Yes, he remembered now. Was she on her own? A third party? Her face was partially hidden by the darkness. But he now recognized her somewhat. She had put her finger to her lips and whispered something to him before everything had gone to hell. Yes, he remembered.

What had her accent been? The memory of those brief words swirled around. European. Eastern European. Perhaps Romanian?

Thoughts clouded his consciousness, muddling his brain, blurring images as—

———

—Wendig woke up.

The world was still enveloped in complete darkness. But there was noise. He was not dead, it seemed.

A cough escaped his lips, and he tried to move but found he couldn't. Had he actually survived? Survived what, exactly? What had happened? Blackness. Blackness all around. He blinked his eyes just to make sure they weren't closed. No, they were open. Why couldn't he move? And he hurt. God damn, he hurt all over. The pain was probably good, though. It meant his body was still working to some extent.

He heard an insistent barking, then voices. Everything was muffled, like his ears were stuffed with cotton, but they worked. Suddenly a blinding light appeared. Daylight? He found that he could now move his head.

"Here's another one!" came a triumphant shout.

Something was whining and licking his face. He heard a lot of movement. Weight that he hadn't realized was pressing down on his body was lifted, piece by piece, until he was finally free. Gentle hands helped lift him up and laid him onto something softer. A stretcher. A yellow labrador ran by.

He looked around as best he could while his eyes adjusted to the brilliant sunlight. The museum was now a ruin. The second story had collapsed in on itself. Was this the Enigmata's doing? From what he could tell, the building had come down right on top of him and the others.

The others? Where were they?

From somewhere behind him, he thought he heard a familiar voice say, "I'm just on vacation."

"Are there other survivors?" he croaked out. His throat felt like it was coated in dust.

"Don't move your neck, buddy," someone he didn't recognize said as a brace was strapped around his neck. "We'll get you to the hospital soon." He was then loaded into the back of an ambulance.

"The others?" he managed to cough out, but no one answered.

As soon as the stretcher he lay on was locked in place, an unfamiliar woman wearing a casual black business suit—and, oddly, black-and-white checkered Vans—strode confidently into the ambulance, closed the doors behind her, and took a seat next to him in the cramped space, leaning over him. The woman studied him for a long moment with slate-gray eyes. She appeared to be in her late twenties, if Wendig had to guess. Her shaggy blonde hair framed her lightly freckled face and reached past her sharp jawline to rest on her shoulders.

"The others?" Wendig asked again, wishing he had a glass of water to moisten his throat.

"There were three other survivors of the building collapse," the woman finally answered. "There is also an injured woman who was taken to the hospital from the police station. Oh, and a dog." The woman examined her manicured nails for a minute before continuing, her eyes now locked on his. "You're lucky to be alive, Mr. Wendig. There was a bad explosion. A major gas leak in this museum."

Wendig frowned, then relaxed as comprehension dawned that that's what the story was. He knew the truth, the awful truth. But if that's what they said had happened, he was not going to try to convince them otherwise.

"At least that's what we've let the authorities believe," the woman said with a smirk.

His jaw tightened.

"Relax, Mr. Wendig." A slight smile curled the corners of the mystery woman's mouth. "Oh, I almost forgot." She pulled a familiar object out of a pocket. "I believe this belongs to you. I didn't want the emergency responders handling it when they found you on the side of the road last night."

The woman placed the Hand of Gaia onto Wendig's chest.

"Who are you?" Wendig asked in a low voice, grabbing the Enigmata, his eyes narrowing. Did he know this woman? No, he was pretty certain he didn't. How did she know him?

Reaching inside her coat to another pocket, the woman pulled out a little metal case. Opening it, she produced a business card and held it out to Wendig between two long fingers for him to take.

Tentatively, Wendig took the card and examined it. It was plain white with a logo he'd seen plenty of times in his life. Her name was printed right underneath.

"Valravn?" Wendig muttered. He looked back up at her. "What does a tech company have to do with all this?" He looked down at the name again. "Kierkegaard. Are you related to Valravn's CEO, Villads Kierkegaard?"

Her close-lipped smile only widened, giving Wendig the impression of a cunning predator.

"Expect me to be in contact soon, Mr. Wendig. We're going to have a lot of things to discuss about your work with Enigmata. I'm sure you'll find everything quite interesting. And even though I know you operate on the downlow, you might want to also urge your new friends to not get too chatty about things."

With that, Freja Kierkegaard opened the ambulance's rear doors, stepped out, and gave him a wink before walking away.

Wendig's brain whirred. He couldn't discern what all that had been about. Why would a tech company be interested in Enigmata? Why would they *know* about Enigmata?

He guessed he'd find out sooner or later.

A commotion sounded just outside. A voice, both surprising and familiar, shouted, "That's my uncle in there!"

A frazzled EMT appeared in front of the ambulance's open doors accompanied by a young woman.

"Jordan?" Wendig sputtered. "What are you doing here?"

"This is your uncle?" the EMT asked with a skeptical look.

"Oh, what?" Jordan rounded on the guy. "I can't be his niece because he's Black and I'm not?"

"No, I just—"

Jordan didn't let him finish before hopping into the back of the ambulance and seating herself in the same spot Freja Kierkegaard had just vacated.

"I'm so glad you're okay," she said. Her eyes were puffy, and her nose was red.

"I'm sorry," Wendig said. "I was in an accident, and my phone got broken."

"It's okay." Jordan patted his arm. "I knew something had to have happened. I called the cops out here when I couldn't get a hold of you after that scary call. Then I jumped on the next flight I could get." She then turned to the EMT who was still standing outside. "Are we going to get to the hospital or what?"

"Yeah, of course," he stammered, flinching. He slammed the doors shut, and soon the vehicle began to move.

Wendig handed her the Hand of Gaia. "Hold on to this for now."

"Oooh." Jordan's eyes widened as she took the Enigmata. She turned it over before looking back at Wendig. "I wonder if I can use this to reach things on high shelves? I kid, I kid. Anyway, I want to hear everything that happened since we last spoke." She reached a hand into her jacket to caress the bearded dragon that rested within an inner pocket. Her eyes then flicked to the business card in his hand. "What's that?"

"Something we're going to have to look into," Wendig answered.

He studied the name on the card once more before flipping it over. On the back he saw what seemed like another logo, though this one had been hand-stamped onto the card, not mechanically printed.

V.O.I.D.

CHAPTER TWENTY-EIGHT

October

October's eyes opened to a white ceiling and bright sunlight streaming in through the windows. She wore a thin blue gown and heard machines beeping next to her. Hospital machines.

"No!" she screamed, sitting straight up. Had the Watchers taken her back to the clinic? "No! No! No!"

"October," a voice said, and a gentle hand pushed her back down. "Shhh, it's okay. We're okay. Everything's fine. We're in a hospital in a town called Black Ashes."

"We're safe now," a different voice added.

Viorica stood next to her wearing a similar hospital gown. There were a multitude of scrapes, cuts, and bruises on her arms and face, but the woman wore a faint smile. Sitting in a chair across from her bed was Noel, also in a gown, smiling at her.

"We're okay?" October repeated. Her brain felt muddled, out of tune.

A nurse ran into the room, summoned by October's shouts. "Miss Night?"

"She's alright," Viorica assured the nurse. "Just a nightmare." The woman hesitated for a second, then nodded and left.

"What happened?" October asked once the nurse was gone.

"The Wheel of Kurkoth took the creatures," Viorica said, turning back to look at her.

"Yeah," Noel said. "It like sucked them inside of it or something, like a vacuum. Really weird. Really gross. Pulled them out of their skin suits, then ripped the monsters apart piece by piece."

"We made it. We're alive." Viorica patted October's hand.

"And the others?" October asked as frantic memories raced through her mind at lightspeed.

"Samira and that man, Wendig, are here and both okay," Viorica answered. "The dog made it too." She chuckled, then quickly stopped. She must have been thinking about those who hadn't been so lucky,

"And you're positive those things are dead?" October whispered. She hadn't realized she was gripping Viorica's hand. Viorica made no effort to remove it.

"Da," the woman answered. "We watched them get torn apart. We watched them become…nothingness."

"Yep, it's a sight I will never forget," Noel said. "Rest assured, I'm going to have nightmares about it for the rest of my life."

Nodding, October closed her eyes for a moment, and Viorica sat on the edge of her bed in silence. Noel eventually said he was going back to his own room to rest.

October couldn't help thinking of the people who had lost their lives during this hellish journey. She opened her eyes as she felt a single hot tear roll down her cheek and knew the dam was breaking. She couldn't stop it. She couldn't hold it back. She broke down, pulling her knees to her chest, sobbing uncontrollably.

"Why?" she sobbed. "Why, Viorica?"

Strong arms wrapped around her curled form—Viorica's arms. The woman didn't say anything, she simply let October cry until no more tears were left.

Noel, Viorica, and Wendig had been discharged already. Samira's gunshot wound, in addition to the depression she had succumbed to once the danger was past, kept her on the patient roster a bit longer. The hospital also wanted to keep October a few more days for observation due to "strange readings" on her vitals, though—despite a few million scratches and bruises and aching feet—she felt physically fine. She didn't contact her parents. They'd freak out. If she was going to talk with them after such a long period of silence, she wanted to wait until she was back at one hundred percent before letting them know what had happened.

Once she was good, she would call them immediately. No. She would just drive to their house and have them get Uncle Shane over there too. She wanted to see them, talk to them, hug them, tell them how sorry she was that she had withdrawn from their lives. She knew they would say it wasn't her fault, but it was hard not to think it was.

What would she tell them about her experience, though? Could she really tell them the truth of everything that had gone down during her little nightmare adventure? Wendig had told her of his encounter with Freja Kierkegaard. October, as a Valravn employee, knew the woman was the granddaughter of the company's CEO. Why and how was her employer involved in this whole situation? Until they learned more, Wendig advised them all to keep certain aspects of their odyssey to themselves. Something strange was going on here. Something involving powerful people. And when powerful people wanted you to keep quiet about something, well, it could be dangerous not to do as they asked.

For the time being.

It was about midnight, and October hadn't been able to fall asleep. The doctor had given her the option to take something to help knock her out, though she had declined. Against hospital regulations, the nurses had been cool and had snuck in Maddie to stay in October's room. The dog was currently snoring softly on the hospital bed with her.

October wasn't exactly sure why she had refused the sedatives.

Maybe she was afraid of the nightmares to come. So she just stared out of her hospital room window, out into the clear night sky.

Leaning over to scratch Maddie's ear, she said, "Never thought I'd have a building fall on me."

The lab opened one eye to glance at October, her tail wagging once.

October lay back down against her pillows. Her eyes felt heavy but sleep still refused to come. That was fine. Whatever.

It was then that she realized she hadn't heard that detestable voice in her head since she had woken up in the hospital. Was the Overshadow still there? Why wasn't it taunting her at that moment? And the Overshadow's sudden about-face? It still weirded her out.

There was too much to think about. Too much to consider. It could all wait for now, though. She knew she should give Dr. Iddrisu a call in the morning and set up an appointment for some time soon.

Yes, she was going to definitely need some extensive therapy. Very extensive.

CHAPTER TWENTY-NINE

Wendig

It's pretty scary," Jordan said. She typed away at her laptop as she sat cross-legged on the hotel room bed. The bed's comforter lay heaped in a discarded pile on the floor. When Wendig had asked about it and heard Jordan's explanation of how often those things were washed in most hotels, he had done the same in his own room.

He gazed over at the bearded dragon dozing in a ridiculous little hammock Jordan had slung across her chest, looking as comfortable as if it were sleeping on a cloud.

"How did you even get the airline to let you bring that lizard onboard with you?" Wendig asked.

"Nathan's registered as an emotional support animal," Jordan said. "And he's reasonably sized and has his own little travel carrier. It's not like I'm asking them to let me bring on a freaking turkey or a minia-ture horse."

Wendig wasn't sure what to think about that sort of thing, but he couldn't deny the comfort the lizard gave Jordan. She had praised the little reptile for how he had helped her anxiety as she soared across the sky in a huge metal tube. It had only been her second time ever on an airplane.

Jordan, Jordan, Jordan, Wendig mused. She had confessed to him that she'd been expecting Wendig to be furious with her. Flying here was in direct violation of the rule he had enforced since the very beginning. How could he be mad, though? Jordan had flown halfway across the country by herself, despite her anxieties, because she had feared for his life. That was an action done out of love.

Wendig leaned back in the armchair he occupied next to the hotel room's little desk. There were too many heavy thoughts swirling in his head at the moment. He was exhausted and hurting all over.

He needed a vacation. Maybe somewhere with a beach and warm sun. And no forests anywhere nearby.

"How about we forget about looking into Valravn and Enigmata for the rest of the evening?" he said. "I saw a pizza place down on the corner. Let's order some to be delivered and watch whatever movie we can find on TV. What do you say to that plan?"

Jordan looked up from her work, pondered for a second, then shut her laptop. "Sounds good! Can't ever say no to pizza. Oh, can my half just be plain cheese? With extra cheese, please. Well, actually throw some pepperoni on there too. I'm feeling adventurous. And be glad we have separate rooms because I am lactose intoleraaaaaaant. Phew."

"TMI, Jordan." Wendig chuckled as he looked up the pizzeria's number on his new phone. "Okay, half pepperoni with…" he sighed, "extra cheese for you, and half Hawaiian for me."

"Ewww, keep your nasty pineapple away from my slices." Jordan grimaced. Then in a pedantic tone, she said, "Did you know that a pineapple is a berry?"

Wendig grunted, holding the phone to his ear.

After making sure Nathan was still comfortable in his hammock sling, Jordan grabbed the remote to the hotel TV and turned it on. After flipping through several channels, she finally stopped on one. "Oooh, *Sharknado 5: Global Swarming*. Nathan and I haven't seen this one!"

"Great," Wendig muttered.

CHAPTER THIRTY

October

October opened the door to her apartment in West Covina, California. Maddie sprinted inside, eager to scavenge whatever crumb particles she could find on the floors. It had been two weeks since October had made it back home from Washington—bringing Maddie with her as the deaths of Henry and Isaac had orphaned the lab. She should have checked her lease to see if the building allowed dogs or pets of any kind, but it was easier to ask forgiveness than permission. Besides, no one had said anything so far.

Snuffling continued to fill the apartment as Maddie went around to every room, smelling this stain, licking that spot, her tail going a mile a minute. October flumped herself down onto her couch, kicked off her boots, then pulled her phone out of her coat pocket. Her mom had texted her about coming over for dinner this coming Sunday. October replied that she would definitely be there.

It had been easier than she thought to talk to her parents after returning home from her ordeal. She had been so desperate to hear their voices after nearly dying, any awkwardness or embarrassment she had anticipated was practically nonexistent. Unable to wait any longer, she had called them the instant she had gotten home, then visited them the next day. Her mom and dad swept her into their arms as soon as she walked through the door. From there, the conversation comfortably flowed, as if they had never stopped communicating. October never brought up the fact that she had even gone on a weekend trip, let alone mentioned all the craziness that had ensued. All her injuries, she explained to them, had resulted from falling down the stairs of her apartment building. She wasn't sure if her parents bought it, but they didn't question her. The truth wasn't something her mom and dad needed to deal with. At least not yet. She did plan on eventually asking them about her adoption, to see if they knew anything about her biological mother and father. Not that she cared about those strangers, per se. She just needed the answer to a question or two hundred.

October studied the tattoo on the back of her hand. Viorica had called it the Sigil of Deep. Why had her birth parents tattooed this on her when she was just a little kid? That had to have been a big part of why October had been taken away from them. Or were there worse things done to her? She just couldn't remember.

Zooming out of the bedroom for no apparent reason, Maddie made a beeline for the couch and leapt into October's lap, her paws finding every remaining bruise they could reach.

"Oof! You're not some little Pomeranian, you know."

Some cooking show was on when October flipped on the television. The host and his guest chef were making sushi rolls. It looked delicious, and October's stomach growled loud enough for Maddie's ears to perk up.

One online order and thirty minutes later, two boxes of salmon, tuna, eel, and yellowtail sushi magically appeared at her door. October tipped the delivery guy and took the food back to the couch. She had also ordered some plain chicken for Maddie.

"Don't think you're getting that every day," she told the dog through a mouthful of rice and fish. "I'm not made of money." Maddie looked up at her with solemn amber eyes, then went back to wolfing down the chicken.

October finished her whole order and stretched out on the couch, Maddie curled up next to her, soft fur like a warm blanket. There was a sci-fi movie from the 80s playing on the TV, although October wasn't really watching. The faces of everyone she had watched die ran through her head, her mind playing its own movie. This one horror.

Hot tears began to drip down her cheeks, but a sudden knock at the door brought her back to reality. She hadn't been expecting anyone.

Wiping the streaks of tears from her face, October got up from the couch and padded over to the door. She had to stand on her tiptoes to look through the peephole.

"What the hell?"

She unlocked the door and flung it open to face the person standing there.

"Bună," Viorica said from over the threshold with a small smile.

"Uh, hi, nice to see you," October replied. "Um, one question before I let you in. How do you know where I live?"

"We have a lot to talk about," Viorica said.

Confusion dancing in her mind, October invited the woman inside. Maddie jumped from the couch to greet their new guest, Viorica giving her lots of pets. October led her guest to the couch where they both sat and turned to face each other. Maddie demanded more attention by nudging Viorica's hand with her nose.

"How have you been?" Viorica asked, scratching behind the dog's ear.

"I'm doing okay," October replied. She let out a deep sigh. "I'm really happy to see you."

"And I'm happy to see you." Viorica wore a genuine smile, which faded after a moment. "How's your little friend?"

October looked down at Maddie. "She's fine?"

"No." Viorica tapped her temple. "Your passenger. I believe you refer to it as 'the Overshadow.'"

October sat there, stunned. She couldn't think of an appropriate response. Her brain had short-circuited.

"Sorry." Viorica shifted her position and scooched closer. "I don't mean to always be so blunt."

October pressed herself into the arm of the couch, her body trying to lean away from Viorica's closeness. The conversation she and the Overshadow had had that night in the museum sprang from her memory.

"How do you know about that?" October asked in a thin, cracking voice that sounded too childish to her own ears. "How could you possibly know?"

"Like I said, we have much to talk about." A contemplative shimmer covered Viorica's eye, and she fiddled with a ring on her index finger, as if still contemplating whether to spill whatever it was she had come here to say. It was the only time October could recall her looking uncertain. Viorica finally seemed to come to a decision. "I work for Valravn."

October wasn't sure what she had expected Viorica to say, but it hadn't been that. "What? I mean, I guess that's a bit surprising, since I work there too, as you know. And you never mentioned it when I told you. Anyway, what does that have to do with anything?"

"Valravn is not only a technology company," Viorica replied. "Valravn was founded as a—what's that phrase? A means to an end. The tech products it is known for are a lucrative source for funding."

"For funding what?"

Viorica locked eyes with October. "Tracking down, retrieving, and studying Enigmata. That was the real reason the company was formed. Though some goals may have changed over the years."

Her answer hung in the air as a heavy silence descended upon the room.

When October said nothing, Viorica spoke again. "Does it still talk to you?"

"Huh?" October was caught off guard by the apparent change of subject.

"The Overshadow."

"No." October shook her head. She fidgeted with her nose ring. "I went back on my meds as soon as I could. I haven't heard anything since the museum."

"I guessed so," Viorica said. "Listen, I have to tell you something. I know you may get angry, but I have to tell you."

"Okay…"

"Before you learned of Cinter, you had maybe a dream about it? Maybe after you got your transfer offer, you felt some strong desire to go visit?"

October tried to swallow her shock, though her throat had gone dry. This unexpected conversation was not only weird and confusing, it was also disturbing. How did Viorica know all these things? Unable to speak for the moment, October nodded.

"I…" For the first time, Viorica looked away, her brows furrowing. She fiddled with her ring again before returning her gaze to October. "I did that. I made that happen. I implanted suggestions in your mind."

"What?" The word came out of October's mouth in a deep, disbelieving monotone. There was an uncomfortable straining in her chest surrounding her heart as she recalled the Overshadow's words.

…this desire came from an outside force.

"Valravn wanted you to go to Cinter," Viorica explained, speaking faster now. "They know you have carried the Overshadow with you since you were a child. They want to study it. They have requested you come with me so they can examine you. They also had me implant suggestions into Mr. Wendig's mind too. They wanted—"

"You mind-controlled me?" October interrupted. She felt a throbbing in her forehead.

"Nu, nu, nu." Viorica blurted out the words in rapid succession. "Merely influenced your decision to go there. You see, Valravn has acquired many Enigmata over the years. Sometimes, when they send me out into the field, they allow me to utilize…" She shook her head. "Never mind. That doesn't matter right now. There is more I need to tell you." Her voice shook with a clearly audible waver.

Viorica's hand disappeared inside her jacket. She couldn't meet October's eyes when she pulled out a tiny, green plastic box. The pill case October thought she had lost during their fateful hike.

"Valravn directed me to take these from you."

Viorica's words were abruptly cut off as October's hand flew up and slapped her so hard across the face that Viorica's neck audibly cracked as her head whipped to one side. The stinging in October's palm only added fuel to the furious inferno that burned inside of her. Maddie slunk away to go hide in the bedroom as the sound echoed throughout the apartment.

"Wow," Viorica whispered. She raised her fingers to her cheek where the hot, red imprint of October's hand was beginning to appear. "That hurt."

"I'm so sorry!" October exclaimed as sudden guilt washed over her. She shot to her feet and was about to run to the fridge for some ice when reason and sense shot back into her like a bullet. "Wait, no. What am I apologizing for? Get the fuck out of my apartment!"

Viorica slowly rose to her feet as well. She stood a head taller and looked down at October. "I deserved that. During my time working at Valravn, I've seen them do some questionable things. They've had *me* do some questionable things. But I do what they ask because I think it's important. Or at least, that's what I have always believed."

A profound sense of betrayal and fury blazed in October. She was so tired of negative emotions, though. She took several deep, clearing breaths. The fire died enough for her to ask, "What do you mean?" She couldn't help wanting to know.

"Valravn wants to study you and the Overshadow," Viorica said. "And not just study. They want to bring you on board too." She touched her reddened cheek again. "Well, I'm not sure I want to do what they tell me anymore. I've seen people die. I've killed people myself."

October gulped.

"I've never had as many innocents injured and killed on a mission as I did in Cinter." Viorica flumped back down on the couch and looked up at her. "And you are right to be angry, October. The way I influenced you with an Enigmata, it was not right. I've done such things before, but as I got to know you, I felt bad for doing it. I don't know if it's because everything I've seen or done is getting to me, or maybe because I'm getting older. Or maybe I've grown a conscience." She snorted. "Who knows? You should have seen me fifteen years ago. When I was in my early twenties, freshly recruited, I could be ruthless."

October wrung her hands together before sitting down on the couch once more. She said nothing.

"I'm sorry you had to get involved in all of this," Viorica went on, playing with her ring. "It's not your fault you have the Overshadow." She shook her head and muttered something to herself in Romanian. "Valravn wants you, since you're the Cinter. I'm not sure exactly what that all means for you. I do know that you can use Enigmata in ways that other people can't, like what you did in the museum. You are special. Not because you were born special, but because it was forced upon you."

October gazed down at the tattoo on the back of her hand. The Sigil of Deep.

Viorica nodded. "Yes, that was your biological parents' doing. I think it has something to do with the Overshadow. The people at Valravn can explain things to you better than I can. Listen, I'm having doubts, you could say. My mind is in a strange place. I'm uncertain what I want to do now."

Finally, October spoke. "Really?"

"I don't know what they truly plan to do with you." A pause. "But if you want to go to them, I will go with you. I won't want to send you in there alone. There are good people who work there. There are not-so-good people too. I don't know everything I wish I did, and I don't know how much they will explain to you. Either way, if you want to go to the V.O.I.D, then we'll go."

"The void?" October asked.

Viorica gave another soft snort. "The V-O-I-D, yes. It's what is known to a few of us as the 'real' Valravn. You know those corporate types like their little, what is the word...acronyms? It means Valravn Otherworldly Interests Department."

"This is a lot to take in," October said the words softly, despite the maelstrom of confusion, anxiety, and astonishment inside her. This company she worked for didn't just make cell phones and computers? They were actually founded as some secret society who searched for monsters and magic artifacts? If October hadn't already seen and experienced everything she had in Washington, her brain would have dismissed all of this as outright lunacy. But Cinter, the Watchers, the Overshadow—that was all real. Unless, of course, she had gone bonkers at some point.

She didn't believe that, though.

She knew it had all actually happened.

Her mind racing, October stood up from the couch and strode over to the kitchenette. She could feel Viorica's eyes following her. Could she trust Valravn? For some reason she trusted Viorica, despite the "influencing" she had admitted to. Either way, October had just reconnected with her family. Plus, she had Maddie to take care of now. Could she risk giving all that up if Valravn decided to dissect her or something? On the other hand, could she risk not learning everything she could about herself?

Everything Viorica had said buzzed in her skull. Perhaps she could learn something about her birth parents as well. Who were they? Did they have a connection to Valravn? Did they really know what the Overshadow was and what it would do to her? These were burning questions. Would the answers she received quench the flames or stoke them into an inferno?

Grabbing some ice from the freezer and wrapping it in a tea towel, she came back and handed it to Viorica.

"Mersi," she said, raising the ice to her hand-printed cheek.

Sitting back on the couch, October stared down at the floor, thinking.

Thinking. Thinking.

October looked over at Viorica.

"Okay, let's go."

Excerpt Taken from the Diary of Edith Goodner (age 63) - 15 October, 1965

This is the first time I've written in my diary in a long, long while. I can't even recall how many years it has been. Not since Barnabas passed.

Well, I've led a good life I'd say. I decided to visit my grandparents' home here in Wyoming and stay for a while. Perhaps a month or two. Eliza wasn't too happy when we came here, but she's got over that. She grew up to be a fine woman and a fine daughter. She even thinks she might have a little one on the way. I've been helping her pick out names. Mary if it's a girl. Henry if it's a boy.

I've been doing a lot of research. I've managed to collect many obscure texts that the average person couldn't possibly—[TEXT SCRATCHED OUT]

Never mind all that. I tried to distract myself by writing my trivial things in this diary, but it's not working. I know what I really have to write.

May God help me, I haven't seen him in forty-eight years.

Why?

Why did he come back? Have I done something? Have I committed some sin that God is punishing me for? What [TEAR STAINS] *this day?*

It was last night. I awoke late. At first, I didn't know why. Then I heard a tapping on the window, even though my bedroom is on the second floor.

[TEAR STAINS] *at my window. The skin is old and ragged and weathered.*

However, I recognized the face.

God help and preserve me and my family. He followed me here. How can that be?

Why won't Granddad leave me alone?

Well, whatever that monster is, it's going to figure out that I've learned a thing or two these past many years.

Selected Case Notes from the Valravn Otherworldly Interests Department

Case: The Fulgent County Watcher Killings

    File#: NA-US-42-[REDACTED]

    Incident Location(s): Cinter, Washington, USA (& Immediate Surrounding Area)

    Enigmata Types: 6

    -Relic Types: (4) Wheel of Kurkoth; Hand of Gaia; Scorched Banpo Ding; Heset's Compass

    -Entity Types: (2) Watcher; Overshadow

    -Domain Types: (0)

Relics: (4)

  --

    ID#: ERA-[REDACTED] / "The Wheel of Kurkoth"

    Status: Intact/In Repository

    Designation: Arcane

    Bonded: EER-IP-[REDACTED] / "The Watchers"

Physical Description: A perfectly round metal disc constructed of some as yet unknown dark-blue metal, with a 10 1/3-inch circumference. Faint markings such as glyphs and concentric circles are etched into the highly polished surface.

Reality-Shifting Properties: Unknown Form of Containment

ID#: ERW-CAT2-[REDACTED] / "The Hand of Gaia"
Status: Intact/Observed
Designation: Category 2 Weaponized
Physical Description: The actual Enigmata has not been directly observed, as it resides within a crescent moon-shaped container (4.8" x 2.4") made of what appears to be ancient filigreed cypress wood. The Enigmata itself is said to be the ancient hand bones of an unknown person or persons inside the wooden container, sealed with some sort of sap. It is not known at this time whether opening the container would neutralize the Enigmata's power.

Reality-Shifting Properties: Construct Conjuration

ID#: ERA-[REDACTED] / "The Scorched Banpo Ding"
Status: Intact/In Repository
Designation: Arcane
Physical Description: A small grayish-brown ceramic ding (a cauldron-like vessel with two handles sitting atop three legs utilized in ancient Chinese cultures) painted with faded red and white faces. The inside of the cauldron is blackened with soot and scorch marks. Able to hold 4.4 quarts of liquid.

Reality-Shifting Properties: Minor Mental Influence

ID#: ERC-[REDACTED] / "Heset's Compass"
Status: Intact/Out In Field
Designation: Curio
Physical Description: A circular, filigreed brass container (6" circumference), topped with glass. A chipped cuspid tooth (human) resides within and can rotate in place by some unknown mechanism.

Reality-Shifting Properties: Sentient Navigation

————

Entities: (2)

——

ID#: EER-IP-[REDACTED] / "The Watchers"
Status: (2) Deceased/In Possession; (1) Alive/At Large
Designation: Ravager - Code Ipos
Bonded: ERA-[REDACTED] / "The Wheel of Kurkoth"
Physical Description: The Entities known as the Watchers appear to have black skin, yellow eyes, and claws on both hands and feet. Other than these observations, not much is known about the physical appearance of these creatures, as they have so far only been seen wearing the flesh of other animals, with a predilection for human skin. When attempts were made to recover the Watchers' corpses in Cinter, WA, only the "skin-suits" remained behind, the Entities themselves having either been destroyed by or drawn into the Relic known as the Wheel of Kurkoth.

Reality-Shifting Properties: Skin Stealing; Mass Adaptation

ID#: EEE-IP-[REDACTED] / "The Overshadow"
Status: [REDACTED]
Designation: Evoked - Code Ipos
Physical Description: [REDACTED]
Reality-Shifting Properties: [REDACTED]

ACKNOWLEDGMENTS

Erin, my beautiful, patient, and hard-working wife never receives enough thanks. She supports me in every way, and I would not have any sort of writing career without her. Thanks to her I am able to bring my stories, my world, to readers. My family deserves thanks as well for their unceasing support and encouragement. They buy and read all my stories. Even my 99-year-old grandma who is not a fan of horror reads everything I write.

Thanks as always to friend and fellow writer Megan M. Davies-Ostrom. We always try to support each other as much as we can, celebrating each other's wins and supporting one another when the publishing industry decides to smack us down.

Much appreciation to Alex Woodroe and Hideki Nishino for their bountiful assistance in matters of language and culture. Important parts of this book wouldn't have been possible without them.

Many thanks to Michelle, Dave, and Kat for not only their enthusiastic support in both my writing but also as a member of our new town and community. You'll never know how much Erin and I appreciate you opening your home, stores, lives, and hearts to us.

And thanks to Willow and Fable for keeping me company as I write, even if you bark like maniacs sometimes or wrestle on top of me if I sit on the couch to work.

ABOUT THE AUTHOR

S. Alessandro Martinez is a Bram Stoker Award® -nominated author of Mexican and Spanish descent who writes horror and fantasy from middle grade to adult. He lives in a haunted manor and loves playing video/board games, practicing necromancy, watching bat videos, collecting skulls, visiting cemeteries, and generally lurking in the dark.

ALSO BY S. ALESSANDRO MARTINEZ

Abomination (2025) – Raven Tale Publishing

Root Fingers (2025) – Winding Road Stories

Helminth (2021) – Crossroad Press

FRIENDS OF FALSTAFF

Thank You to All our Falstaff Books Patrons, who get extra digital content each month! To be featured here and see what other great rewards we offer, go to www.patreon.com/falstaffbooks.

PATRONS

Dino Hicks
John Hooks
John Kilgallon
Larissa Lichty
Travis & Casey Schilling
Staci-Leigh Santore
Sheryl R. Hayes
Scott Norris
Samuel Montgomery-Blinn
Junkle
Vickie DeSantos
Quincy J. Allen
Allison Charlesworth

Thank You for Supporting Independent Publishing!

We believe that you should be able
to read your books, your way.
That's why this Falstaff Books
print edition includes a digital copy
at no additional cost!

Just scan the QR code with your device,
follow the directions on Prolific Works,
and enjoy!
You can also join our newsletter when prompted,
and never miss an awesome Falstaff Release!